NEW SHORT FICTION FROM CUBA

# New Short Fiction from Cuba

*Edited by*

**JACQUELINE LOSS AND ESTHER WHITFIELD**

*Northwestern University Press*
*Evanston, Illinois*

Northwestern University Press
www.nupress.northwestern.edu

Copyright © 2007 by Northwestern University Press.
Published 2007. All rights reserved.

Printed in the United States of America

10  9  8  7  6  5  4  3  2  1

ISBN-13: 978-0-8101-2406-6
ISBN-10: 0-8101-2406-8

Library of Congress Cataloging-in-Publication Data

New short fiction from Cuba / edited by Jacqueline Loss and Esther
    Whitfield.
        p. cm.
    ISBN-13: 978-0-8101-2406-6 (pbk. : alk. paper)
    ISBN-10: 0-8101-2406-8 (pbk. : alk. paper)
    1. Short stories, Cuban—Translations into English. 2. Cuban
fiction—21st century—Translations into English. I. Loss, Jacqueline.
II. Whitfield, Esther Katheryn.
PQ7386.5.E54N49 2007
863'.0108972910905—dc22

                                                            2007012855

# Contents

# Acknowledgments

"Landscape of Clay" ("Paisaje de arcilla") was published as a single volume by Letras Cubanas in Havana in 1997.

"A Maniac in the Bathroom" ("Un loco dentro del baño") was published in Ena Lucía Portela's 1999 collection *Una extraña entre las piedras* (Letras Cubanas, Havana).

"You Know My Name" was written in 1998 and published with this same title in the journal *La gaceta de Cuba*.

"Finca Vigía" was published with this same title in Alberto Guerra Naranjo's 2000 collection *Blasfemia del escriba* (Letras Cubanas, Havana).

"Puerta de Alcalá" was first published in the collection *La Puerta de Alcalá y otras cacerías* by Ediciones Ollalá in Madrid in 1998.

"Journey to China" ("Viaje a China") was published in the journal *Diásporas* in 1999.

"You Don't Have to Reach Heaven" was published in a slightly modified version as "¿Te acuerdas de Cirilo Villaverde?" in Francisco García González's 2003 collection *¿Qué quieren las mujeres?*

"Aunt Enma" ("Tía Enma") was published in Aida Bahr's 1998 collection *Espejismos* (Ediciones Unión, Havana).

"The Horizon" ("El horizonte") was published in Abilio Estévez's 1998 collection *El horizonte y otros regresos* (Tusquets Editores, Barcelona).

"The Girl Who Doesn't Smoke on Saturdays" ("La muchacha que no fuma los sábados") was published in Anna Lidia Vega Serova's 2001 collection *Limpiando ventanas y espejos* (Ediciones Unión, Havana).

"The House, Serrat, Cinema, and . . . Do Narrators Still Dream About Prose Poets?" and "Gerona" have not been previously published.

ᔕᔕᔕᔕᔕᔕ

This publication is made possible with public funds from the New York State Council on the Arts, a state agency, through a grant to PEN American Center. *New Short Fiction from Cuba* has benefited from the support of many dear friends and colleagues over several years. We are indebted to Esther Allen and Susan Harris for their persistence, as well as to all of the translators and authors, for their patience and belief in the publication of this book. We would like to thank those who, in 2004, successfully defended the right to publish translations such as these in the United States. We appreciate the editorial expertise of Susan Betz, Rachel Delaney, and Serena Brommel at Northwestern University Press.

# Introduction

JACQUELINE LOSS AND ESTHER WHITFIELD

These stories, all written during a period that saw the disintegration of the Soviet bloc, severe economic hardship, and the onslaught of tourists to its previously less accessible shores, take diverging tacks toward life in Cuba. The Cuban Revolution's strict policies for the promotion of a socially engaged culture have sometimes obscured a rich cultural history that extends back far before 1959. Like writers around the world, Cuban writers in this volume invoke their nation's past as they inscribe its paradoxical present and grasp, tentatively, at its future. The collection is rooted in Cuba's particular diversity: rather than constructing a unity based on writing styles, the authors' generations, historical events, or economic and sociopolitical factors, *New Short Fiction from Cuba* is resolutely eclectic in its themes, language, and form.

Cuba is a small country of only eleven million people, and its size can be deceiving in terms of comprehending its cultural landscape. The intellectual community is close-knit—"communal," in many senses of the word—and a network of government-sponsored institutions encourages a sense of cohesion. As a consequence, island writers are quite aware of what others in their profession are doing; this has sometimes made outside critics— prepared to find the uniformity associated with socialist states— too quick to group authors according to generations or schools to which they presumably subscribe. Just as in other larger nations, individuals continue to explore their own imaginations, without necessarily heeding prescribed categories. Cuba is the setting for fervent debates on literature and culture, and with so many ideas

ix

circulating in a confined space, these debates can be even more intense than they are in larger arenas.

Although Cuba is still one of the few places in the world that resists capitalism and globalization, the forces of neoliberalism influence the process by which Cuban culture makes its entrance into the rest of the world. The disparate themes and styles of these stories to some degree reflect the changes in society since the mid-1990s—a period whose dire economic conditions, in part, have contributed to a newfound tolerance toward foreign investment and moderate capitalism, as well as a cautious acceptance of difference and critique. The stories in *New Short Fiction from Cuba* leave us with echoes of this evolution and reveal elaborate connections between personal, intimate spaces and public ones.

While the Cuban Revolution is but one among many markers of literary production, there are undoubtedly links between the enclosed and private spaces that writers explore here and the socialist government's shaping of society. Literature is not divorced from the world around it, and the diversity of themes here attests to a transforming cultural scene where so-called micropolitics—intertextuality, transgressions, critique of bureaucracy, sexuality, and sensuality—are at least as important as politics. This detail is important since, for a long time, due to both the Left's and the Right's desire to project their own versions of closure on the island and the state's control of information, it was difficult to construe an accurate picture of the island's production. The U.S. government's embargo on trade with Cuba has only served to distort this picture. Furthermore, recent U.S. Treasury Department rulings have questioned the legality of publishing translations of not only Cuban writers but also writers originating from other nations considered to be inimical to the government of the United States. As in the case of many others, these rulings jeopardized the completion of this anthology.

An anthology by nature tends to frame, to contain literature; it sets its own parameters, and, despite its editors' best intentions, it can impose an apparently uniform reading on the most varied texts. It is our hope that by emphasizing the diversity of our selection and shying away from conclusive pronouncements on its contents, the individual richness of each story will break through the anthology's artificial limits. It is with this context of difference, creativity, and change at the forefront of our minds that we signal the tenuous threads running through some of the stories; threads that, far from suggesting homogeneity, in themselves call into question the notion of conformity.

Reading these stories—looking through them, observing their characters—the very act of our watching Cuba becomes a theme. The voyeur is a persistent, shadowy figure in almost all the stories. The figure is both official and very private: there is something about watching and being watched that seems to filter from the institutional to the intimate, and the process has both sinister and erotic resonances. Ena Lucía Portela's "A Maniac in the Bathroom," a tale with a tinge of the gothic, is exceptional in its initial positioning of a female narrator as voyeur in possession of an elaborate plot, allowing her a mysteriously secretive gaze. She is not, however, the only observer. The gazes in this story multiply, becoming increasingly layered, sensual, and uncanny. Likewise, Aida Bahr's "Aunt Enma" involves more than one character in the position of observer: a young girl observes her own body, with that of her aunt close in mind, and an adolescent masculine gaze further complicates the scene.

Francisco García González's "You Don't Have to Reach Heaven" is circumscribed by gazes that have private and public connotations. As the atmosphere subtly suggests that the individual is being watched by a greater force, he imagines sexual acts with a woman whom he observes, obsessively, on a bus. While gazes are similarly an essential aspect of C. A. Aguilera's "Journey to China," they are even more obviously directed to the public and communal sphere. Private lives are a function of public good and are on display to the viewer for almost scientific perusal; China, it seems, is laid bare. But what, in this context, is China? One would assume the narrator of this travelogue to be in control of the objective gaze, but he is, in fact, under continual surveillance: the ironies of a fictional Cuban traveler cataloging a showcase Communist China cannot escape us. Vigilance is a way of life for the students of the military academy in Alejandro Aguilar's "Landscape of Clay," too, and in "You Know My Name," Eduardo del Llano's comic critique of bureaucracy, whole teams of national and international observers come out of the woodwork to pass judgment on an individual and his name. The narrator of Alberto Guerra Naranjo's "Finca Vigía," also a writer, is similarly engaged in a process of finding an authorial voice with respect to his masters—all the time observing, from a fly-on-the-wall position, Ernest Hemingway's every move.

It is difficult to read these stories without considering briefly the Cuban Revolution's relation to vigilance. The Committees for the Defense of the Revolution (CDRs), the Neighborhood Watch–like committees throughout the country whose job it is to ensure that in each neighborhood individuals are making their contribution to the revolution, are but one component of this elaborate system of vigilance. These days CDRs are much less powerful than they were in the revolution's early years. The fact that a number of these stories address homosexual themes and totalitarian structures points to a somewhat more flexible understanding of societal critique and order. Moreover, in today's climate of Cuban "chic" abroad, when much of the world has its eyes fixed on Cuba, poised and ready to consume, voyeurism comes from outside as well as from within. The act of reading has long involved peeping into other people's thoughts, lives, and ideas; but these days, Cuba seems to be under observation from all angles, held in the spellbound gaze of those mesmerized by the nostalgic images from the movie *The Buena Vista Social Club,* hungry for the peculiar mix of socialism and tropical glamour they see in tourist brochures, and curious to know what will happen next in the ongoing saga of Fidel Castro versus the United States. The reader, editor, and indeed much of the general public have in a sense become Cuba-watchers, voyeurs of the fate of the island and its people.

Listening to these stories, we hear proper names echoing over and over again. There is a persistent preoccupation with naming, and it is tempting to hear it as a cry for personal identity, an attempt to set apart the individual—the author, the character, the reader—from the undistinguished masses. Naming is a way of bringing something, or someone, into being, and in a place where the public sphere encircles the private, the act of naming and creating becomes an act of self-preservation. "You Know My Name" performs this act loudly and ironically: the public good—here in the shape of a sinister World Writers' Congress—demands that the hero, himself a writer, relinquish his name; when he refuses, he is forced to relinquish instead his social existence. The allegory is clear as well as comical; and in recasting the public body as the professional overseer, it raises the same questions about the role of the writer in a highly socialized society that other stories here suggest. In one of his most frequently quoted speeches, the 1961 "Address to Intellectuals," Fidel Castro cast writers and intellectuals as workers for the revolution, as an integral part of a public whole that excluded no one (unless, as it was to emerge, they chose to "exclude" themselves): "Everything within the Revolution, nothing outside the Revolution," he proclaimed. Eduardo del Llano's story is a stylized exploration of the "inside" and "outside" options: to be an inside writer is to be a worker, with a skill cultivated by the revolution, while to be an "outside" writer is a dark fate, as the character Nicanor O'Donnell in "You Know My Name" begins to discover. The "inside" option is one all Cubans in the post-1959 world have grown up knowing about, wherever they choose or have chosen to position themselves: it comprises a network of training workshops and prizes for aspiring writers of all ages, which on the one hand provides a rigorous education in the art of creative writing but which on the other hand runs the risk—as is the case with organized creative enterprises the world over—of laying down the law, as it were, and stifling originality. The "inside" and "outside" construction is nevertheless too simple to describe writers, their locations, and their affiliations. It is complicated particularly by the movements and migrations of both people and texts: when this anthology was begun, for example, all its authors resided in Cuba, and, while such is no longer the case, their distancing from the country is not necessarily permanent. The Internet is one of the many factors that have transformed how Cuban writers are viewed and in turn how their aesthetic and political intonations are read. While Cubans' readings and readers were once dictated by the import and export of books, spectators around the world can now easily download their work and circulate it on a previously unfeasible scale.

Satire of "the system"—in "You Know My Name" and again in "Journey to China"—is another gesture not to be taken at face value. It has many dimensions, and the writers in this collection work and rework it in various and changing directions. Bureaucracy is the key source of tedium, and the olive green–clad government official is a ubiquitous figure, but in "You Know My Name" this bureaucracy has a Kafkaesque quality to it. It is restrictive and in a sense repressive, but at the same time so manifestly ridiculous yet so blind to its own absurdity, that its telling can take place on an almost jocular level. "Puerta de Alcalá," by Leonardo Padura Fuentes, plays up the inefficiencies and idiosyncrasies of bureaucracy as a way, perhaps, of resisting its more pernicious effects. Its hero, a journalist emerging from a small-scale disgrace, sees his own private/public dilemma lifted to an international level. His story begins in Angola, at the height of

Cuba's foreign crusades, and takes him to Madrid, where he meets a childhood friend who has emigrated to the United States. Between these two private lives, he comes to realize, the forces of transnational politics have intervened irrevocably; and, try as they might to recuperate the friendship of a former era, they are relegated to opposite sides of the socialist-capitalist divide. Politics, in the most general sense of the term, are lurking in the background here as elsewhere; the interest lies in whether, and how, they will rear their head. In Padura Fuentes's story, they do so through art: through the figure of Diego Velásquez and a later female art critic whose own emotional investment in the master's work inspires in the journalist a Borgesian obsession of his own.

The name of Diego Velásquez is one among many from the Western literary and cultural canon that appear in *New Short Fiction from Cuba*. Writers' preoccupation with naming is not confined to fictional characters naming themselves, although the naming of both great and obscure figures from different contexts is in some ways also an affirmation of identity. Naming intellectual figures—what we might more crassly call name-dropping— creates a web of intertexts into which the individual writer can insert himself or herself with some sense of continuity and importance. Intertextuality reflects a thirst for dialogue with a world broader than one's own—a significant consideration in a country whose communication with the outside has been limited for more than forty years, although it would be too easy to read into this a particularly "Cuban" situation, for is not the literary endeavor in itself, everywhere, an attempt to seek out new horizons? Name-dropping at the same time points to a concern with erudition, with knowing the great minds of our time and incorporating them into an eclectic body of learning; a concern that has characterized Cuban letters since before the country's independence from Spain in 1898 and has become particularly important to younger writers and readers of the revolutionary decades. The scarcity of foreign books in Cuba bred a peculiar respect for those that did find their way to readers' hands, and the prevalence of names in this anthology's stories is without doubt a reflection of the writers' avidity as readers. Canonical names make their appearance under various circumstances. "Finca Vigía" is a series of interrupted conversations between Ernest Hemingway and a young Cuban writer who visits his home upon winning the annual Hemingway memorial prize for fiction (which Guerra Naranjo's story itself won in 1998). The story implicitly explores Hemingway's status as a cultural icon in Cuba, where his erstwhile haunts—the Floridita and Bodeguita del Medio bars in Old Havana—have become magnets for foreign tourists. The young Cuban writer's relationship to the American great invokes further relationships: between Cuba and the United States and between culture and tourism, although these relationships are muted by the preeminent literary relationship, between the apprentice and the master, so that through the figure of the master the younger writer learns to find himself. A darker relationship to a past master is invoked in "You Don't Have to Reach Heaven": the name here, though, is Cirilo Villaverde, author of Cuba's canonical nineteenth-century novel *Cecilia Valdés,* a novel that, as Reinaldo Arenas's 1987 *La loma del angel* illustrates, lends itself to rereadings. García González's story is no tentative, awestruck attempt at conversation between an apprentice and his hero; rather, Villaverde's life and work seep into the structure of the narration, such that its protagonists cannot always tell whether they are in their own era or that of Villaverde. Nor can they trust their school-inculcated respect for Villaverde, for the figure they meet is a caricature of lechery and self-satisfaction, in the presence of whom the characters' own incipient sexuality pales. This iconoclastic treatment of Villaverde and, more mutedly, of Hemingway lends to the literary canon a complexity that many of this anthology's writers—for example, Ena Lucía Portela, with her network of cross-references to classical thinkers; Eduardo del Llano, in his grand finale of European novelists—have chosen to pursue. In Ernesto René Rodríguez's "The House, Serrat, Cinema, and . . . Do Narrators Still Dream About Prose Poets?" whereas citation comprises the essence of the narrator's world, it also marks the sphere of the uncanny. The narrator's surprise encounter with his refined and almost otherworldly musical preference—Joan Manuel Serrat—in the most everyday of spaces is the point of departure for the text's dislodging of refrains from their routine significance and for an essayistic reflection on the nature of poiesis.

Threading some of these stories together, too, is the fragility and latent power of sexuality. Manhood and womanhood are pushed far beyond the social roles that the Cuban Revolution's ideology once sought to inculcate, and both gender and sexual relations are seen to be tenuous and unstable. "Landscape of Clay," set in a military academy for teenage boys, unmasks the uncertainty behind the "new man" whom Ché Guevara sought to create in Cuba, the man whose conscience was rooted in sociality and, quite categorically, in heterosexual relations. The incarceration of homosexuals and AIDS patients is one of the darkest episodes in Cuba's recent history, and it speaks to the prevailing regime's obsession with the fit, fighting heterosexual man. The army, the bastion of male bravado, shows its cracks in Aguilar's fragmented narrative; "machismo" is less an essence than a shield, a short-lived refuge from the anguish and lovelessness of growing up in the military. "Landscape of Clay" touches on the nature of relations between adolescent boys cramped together in subhuman quarters: on the brutality and on the rare moments of tenderness. Female sexuality is a strong force in this anthology, in stories written by both men and women. The heroine of García González's "You Don't Have to Reach Heaven" is as caught up in desire as is her male observer, but in Ena Lucía Portela's "A Maniac in the Bathroom," the role of observer falls to the lone woman. As she watches her imagined lover stroking, comforting, and playing with a younger boy, she is herself aroused; the fact that the boy is mentally disturbed further complicates this feminine desire. Slow violence against the innocent excites her; this is the story of beautiful pain, of the subtleties and exquisiteness of perversion when it is perceived not as perversion but as normality. Portela's woman lacks the maternal and even the social instincts that society—particularly revolutionary society—might expect of her; she wields for herself a strange, erotic power in the vicarious experience of male pleasure. Aida Bahr's "Aunt Enma" is another story of feminine arousal through control over men and through violation of social taboos. The taboo here is incest: a young aunt watches as her adolescent nephew caresses the image of her body in a mirror. In a sense, this woman, like the observer in "A Maniac in the Bathroom," is passive: she does not move, and she merely watches as the men perform before her. This, though, is a dramatic rewriting of female passivity, for in doing nothing, the woman controls everything. The woman's body is in both stories a site for the redistribution of social power, and that social power cannot be expected to emerge unscathed. The female body wields a different form of power in Anna Lidia Vega Serova's "The Girl Who Doesn't Smoke on Saturdays," as a woman who believes herself to be disfigured refuses to leave her home for fear of ridicule but nevertheless exerts a consuming sexuality from within its four walls. Her fraught relationship to the idea of monstrosity is taken a step further in Soleida Ríos's "Gerona," in which the domestic space is invaded by bureaucracy that gives a bitter, if not violent, taste to intimacy.

Most of these stories were written in the mid-1990s and appear here for the first time translated into English. Many of the authors, however, are well known in the Spanish-speaking world. Leonardo Padura Fuentes's detective stories have a loyal readership in Spain as well as in Cuba, and Abilio Estévez's dramatic and fictional work has been highly acclaimed. Each of the authors has published widely in Cuba, and, following the post-Soviet collapse of Cuba's publishing industry and foreign publishers' subsequent interest in Cuban literature, most are represented in at least one Spanish or Latin American collection. This shift in the economy and geography of publishing has had a profound effect on who and what is published in Spanish, and some writers have suffered in a world where demands can be as commercial as they are artistic. The Cuban cultural institutions, though, still have their say over artistic content and can more strongly support the distribution of some books over others.

By broadening the range of Cuban short fiction available in English, this selection aspires to change monolithic perceptions of a nation in the current climate where restrictions on travel to Cuba by U.S. citizens are countered by an ever-more-avid desire to know. While the revolution and its consequences are certainly manifest in several of these stories, in this collection one witnesses evolutions as well. It is of utmost importance, both ethically and aesthetically, to recognize such evolutions at this moment. Focusing on them means paying attention to differences and particularities of national spaces but not allowing them to subsume those individual spaces of the imagination. This collection, we hope, will serve as an introduction to a literature in a state of flux; one whose towering political history and place in the imaginary of its foreign observers have in no way eclipsed the daring and creativity of its writers.

NEW SHORT FICTION FROM CUBA

ALEJANDRO AGUILAR

# Landscape of Clay

## THE BEGINNING

Gradually they are herded together on the sports field—the smell of bruised grass, mixed with the new smell of olive green gabardine. They are kept standing at attention beyond the limits of their strength. Finally they fall, one by one or in groups, casualties of the effects of the vaccinations in their backs, exhaustion from the drawn-out processing when they arrived, and this punishment by the sun. Too much weight for their eleven years, which is the average age of the thirty elements in the platoon, the hundred and twenty elements in the company, the five hundred elements in the battalion—the new boys of 1969.

## THE SCHOOL

The runway of a former military airport is now a kilometer-long strip of blazing hot gravel that runs between the gigantic barracks and the mess hall. Another five hundred meters diagonally across the landscape lie the classrooms. Out on the periphery, the sports field and the parade ground. Beyond that, and all around, the vast woods of pine and casuarina, the high-tension line with its eternal menacing whine, and the fences that stand between the pride of being in the school and the ordinariness of being some guy in the street, a hippie bum, a little faggot with tight pants or long hair.

## ELEMENT 621

He cannot seem to get rid of his little-boy sadness—or, from underneath his fingernails, the black shoe polish. His relief valve is fighting. There is always a good reason handy. And when there's not, he invites some friend of his to trade a few punches with him, as though they were really getting it on. If he can find another boy who needs to let off a little steam, they go out behind the showers. There, where nobody will step in, they immerse themselves in the ritual until they both drop, exhausted. Then they return to the classrooms all smiles, their arms around each other despite the bruises and black eyes, like the buddies that they are.

## OFFICERS

The principal (the "director") is a captain who gives the impression of an easygoing sort of guy. He also has an intelligent face, which is the perfect cover for his rigid mind. The battalion commander, a hero of the war of liberation and many other combats, managed to make lieutenant only because he lacked every possible degree of culture. Nothing saves him from being called a "limping caravel" as he drags his skin-and-bones self around on a leg rendered useless by a bullet. The battalion political officer is the perfect caricature of a Neanderthal, incapable of pronouncing his own name without making a mistake, incapable of treating a subordinate with respect or addressing a superior with dignity. His occupation: stuffing the refrigerator in his office with the food he steals from the students' mess and then wrapping it with twine, knotted so he'll be able to detect any tampering. The company commander is a sad sack who fought in all the wars without being promoted past corporal until the day he came to the school and formalities required that he be given a sergeant's stripes. The platoon leader, another sergeant, black to the soles of his feet and the palms of his hands—even his gums black—has emerged from some cane field to become, within a month, an infantry instructor, a position he obtained because he knows how to read and write.

## THE ELEMENTS

They are "elements." The boys who will be made men so they can defend *la Patria*. Their parents' pride. A few more years and they'll be officers in the various services, men of courage and chests full of medals. They bear the entire weight of this pyramid and the full brunt of its harsh rigors. Some come to resemble the machinery that depersonalizes them. Most simply bear up, waiting for the moment they can have their revenge. Others can't take it, and they choose suicide, or their bodies can't take what their spirits refuse to accept and they crumple on the parade ground or fall casualties to accidents in the field. One fakes madness and eats mud out of the mud puddles or sings at the top of his lungs as the sun comes up. That one there hits an officer so they'll expel him, and he lands in the stockade. Those over there make as much trouble as they can think of, so they won't get their passes and for months on end won't see the city, which they hope will make their parents, moved to pity, come take them out of the school. It is a mute struggle that goes on for three, four years. The most seasoned warriors are barely sixteen years old.

7

## THE TEACHERS

Most of them feel themselves not so much the students' teachers as their allies against the strict code of military discipline. The female teachers are also the greatest—in fact, only—temptation in this closed, secluded, and solitary place. There are no female students, so every female smell, seductive image, or sweet word possible in this place comes from those girls who cannot be more than twenty, twenty-two—the very peak of ripeness. And the boys are calibrated to catch the slightest vibration of those fallen angels. One sensitive student can't resist; he holds the hand of the girl-teacher who speaks to him with calculated sensuality, brings up inflammatory topics so distant from the classroom subject yet so appropriate to the tense and lustful atmosphere that fills the room. That other boy lacks the self-confidence needed for that, so he contents himself with dropping a little mirror on the floor so he can look up under the charitably short skirt. Other boys peek over the shower walls, hoping to discover a breast unfettered and offered up to the air, the light, their gazes. One of the oldest boys, a daring lad, tries to seduce a biology teacher with dark skin and blue eyes, and she allows herself to be seduced. When the story reaches the ears of those same officers who hound the girls with their brute lecherousness, the two are expelled from paradise for immoral behavior. Seduction aside, all the teachers are good friends. They get the boys alcohol from the infirmary or bring them cigarettes from town. One night they cover for several students who escape to attend a pop concert. But the officers get wind of it and give orders that in the future, teachers are to wear olive drab and are not allowed free passage in and out. And so they break the last link to the noisy, rowdy life that goes on outside the fences, beyond the woods.

## THE LANDSCAPE

Enormous expanses of red powder and gravel, with little pools of water. All the harshness, all the severity of the weather in these few acres. Then, the cement floors polished with burlap and kerosene, the walkways lined with rocks painted over and over again with white lime. The latrines, two footprints in a mound of dirt, with a horrible hole between them. Little concrete partitions that barely shield the sides, while along the front pass mockers and voyeurs. The showers, a huge room with a line of showerheads along each side. And everywhere humidity, infection, immodesty verging on indecency. Cleaning the barracks that holds a hundred and twenty people is four elements' daily detail. Make the bed so tight a coin will roll across it, or else a hundred push-ups. Track down and destroy the dust in every corner of that desert. Keep your overalls spotless, the overalls worn the whole week long—for sports, for military exercises, for working in the barracks, in the classrooms, in the mess hall. The zinc roofs, white-hot griddles in that implacable flat plain. The blue sky, sometimes menacing or openly enraged, always a handy chalkboard that they can secretly draw their favorite dreams on. And the clouds of soft, fine mineral powder—blurring, blinding, stinging, prodding.

Nature and its sounds. The wind that never stops hissing in the tops of the pine trees and the casuarinas, as it catches on the corrugations of the roofs and especially in the thick high-voltage lines that pinch off the farthest corner of the school. The sound of the wind causing a mute dread at every hour of the day and night. And panic at sunrise. Once in a while, there is the rumbling sound of lightning or the drone of a plane from the military airport nearby flying low over the school grounds, seeming to mock the slowness and tedium of that place below. Or the bell, with its periodic clanging marking out time. The clamoring, echoing world of the school. The sounds of the school, and of absolutely nothing else.

## PATRIOTIC ACT

On rare occasions, routine is broken by an assembly for the whole school or practice for some upcoming parade. One winter night, the parade ground is filled with all fifteen hundred elements, formed up in ranks and in strict silence. Into the cold, teeming air pours a voice from the loudspeakers, giving the play-by-play of the final game of the baseball world championship. The national team against the enemy. It is a patriotic act to listen to the game. At the last minute, our team wins with an explosive home run. But not everyone joins in the celebration. Many boys have been half asleep for a good while—standing there, not daring to request permission to return to the barracks. No officer would have given permission for such a thing anyway. No allowance can be made for ideological weakness.

## ELEMENT 533

He would be a wonderful student if he behaved normally. He has average intelligence, but his parents insist that he be the best in everything. He makes up for his shortcomings by constantly buttering up the officers and putting down his classmates. At the end of his four years, his record is one of the best. But on his record there are also reports of puerile attempts on his life and beatings received from the fifteen hundred enemies he has so scrupulously cultivated.

## READING NIGHT

Group by group, they march into the classrooms, which are still like ovens shimmering with the heat accumulated throughout the day. They march in single file and come to a halt, each boy alongside his own desk. When the order is given, they sit. Their pupils slowly adjust to the yellowish light of the three bulbs that pretend to illuminate the entire school. Soon, two boys come in with a big box of books, which they distribute randomly around the room. *The Volokolansk Highway, A True Man,* or volume 2 of *Les Misérables.* No one protests, no one says a word, no one tries to choose the book he wants. No one stops reading, or pretending to read. The book begun today will be broken off the next night by another. *History Will Absolve Me, The Three Musketeers,* or *The Battle of Stalingrad.* The title is unimportant. This book, too, will have to be put aside when the sergeant suddenly orders everyone to stand at attention and march out of the classroom. The ritual is continued every reading night, once or twice a week. A good soldier has to be well educated.

## ELEMENT 583

His parents sent him to the school to put a little "life," a little "spirit" in him and to make him strong. In his absentmindedness, his daydreaming, his quietness, they've seen a trace of weakness, and they have sent him here to make a man of him, in the military life. He is thirteen years old and speaks perfect English. All he's interested in is books. He skips formations to go out and lie in the grass somewhere and read. He's not interested in science, hygiene, or sports. He is neither graceful nor funny, and his only friends are two or three other lunatics who attend the school in the same absentminded way that he does. He is unmoved by push-ups, by corporal punishment—by punishment of any kind. *Don't worry, even if they stand me up before a firing squad and shoot me, they'll never make a soldier out of me,* he says, turning his eyes and mind back to his book.

## THE FIELD

Guinea grass chokes the fields of lemon and orange trees. The rain turns them into swampland. The legion of little olive green figures sinks into the loblolly of grass and mud. Across the sea of vegetation, pickaxes and mattocks look like the arcs of a huge school of flying fish. The blades fall furiously, cutting down the plants, amputating their roots. One, a hundred, a thousand times, the same act—in the sun, the rain, the mud, and with the insects, the hunger, and under the omnipresent eyes of the sergeants, always ready to shout, insult, give demerits, deliver a beating . . .

## SHAVED HEADS

The ongoing wrestling match between adolescence and the young manhood growing stronger every day can be seen in the boys' features. Sometimes in the eyes and ears, sometimes in the fuzz that soon will be a beard, a mustache. The big hands, the disproportionate extremities. And in all this sprouting, burgeoning growth, the shaved head—a terrible mockery that hounds the boys and brings them to bay with dismaying regularity.

The platoon marches into the lobbylike room of the Quonset hut fitted out as a barbershop. There are three men brought in from town—strangers, to avoid any possibility of special pleading. Coldly, implacably, their machines mow down the hair—that last trace of rebelliousness, as the officers see it. The sergeant major, the platoon leader, or the lieutenant, depending on how the "crusade against ideological diversionism" is going, calls out the victims by their number. *Elements 603, 604, and 605—in the chairs!* The operation is uniform and impersonal. They are three numbered creatures who take their seats in unison before the barbers, whose hair is clipped to the scalp in unison by the barbers, and who rise in unison from the barber chairs, looking as they are intended to look—like Uniform Man. Nothing personal, nothing distinctive. Just obey. Orders are followed, not discussed. Followed, not debated. Followed, not argued over. But this time, the machinery skips a beat. In the long count, four elements are missing. Someone asks permission to report that they are hospitalized. The sergeant hesitates, then notes it down. Everyone knows it's not true, but this time not even the worst snitches dare denounce them. The breach of discipline is too serious. The four boys hide in the surrounding woods and do not return until the whole company's hair has been cut. They, and those who secretly carry them food and water, have held out and gained three more weeks of proud life.

## ELEMENT 851

In these four years, all the humor generated by humankind is worn away. But his wit disappears neither out on the parade ground, nor in the cane field, nor even in the periodic fights when he takes more than he hands out. A rip in his uniform gets him a demerit and a warning to sew it up on the spot. Here comes Element 851 with a sock sewn to his shoulder, like the epaulet of some distinguished generalissimo. He manages to avoid punishment and bad grades by making people laugh. Years later, his laughter is cut off in a helicopter downed by enemy fire in a distant war.

## ONE . . . TWO . . . THREE . . . FOUR . . . AND ONE . . .

The shoe leather smacks the pavement and the footsteps echo like the discharge of artillery off the walls of the colonial houses. The radiant faces, the eyes fixed forward, savoring the pride of their martial spirit, just as they've been taught. People say even the army doesn't do it as well as they do. Their skin vibrates with each step. The onlookers marvel—the girls, picking out the most gorgeous ones; the relatives, trying to find their boy in that multiple-exposure picture in motion. They see the tip of the iceberg. They have no idea of the thirteen daily formations, the kilometer-long marches to the mess hall—*left, right, left, right* . . . The leaders compete by showing the pedigree of their trained animals. Orders called out, the cadence more and more exacting: "ONE . . . TWO . . . THREE . . . FOUR . . . and ONE . . . TWO . . ." and the sweat running down their backs until the thick fabric of their dirty uniforms absorbs it as voraciously as the boys when they fall upon the mess, chewing their hatred of the lieutenant, fanning their feet and heads against the terrible heat and the exhaustion.

## SUNDAYS

Relatives, friends, and girlfriends arrive. The large naves of the barracks empty, and around the pine trees at the entrance, groups sprawl into happiness with all the abandon of a picnic. This is the moment of sweet lies and vain pride. The "I love you"s and the "behave yourself"s. Every single boy is the smartest and the hardest working, the bravest, the strongest, the . . . Behind it, though, the tedium, the unbearable days of marches and orders, of shouts and iron discipline, of impositions and abuse. The school is the pride of the country at this point.

## ELEMENT 783

He arrives at the school looking for adventure. He craves danger. He wants to be a fighter pilot and he has to be in top condition. Only about five out of five hundred pass the aptitude tests. For him, it's an obsession that keeps him out on the sports field every free minute, going up against every piece of equipment out there. Gradually, he transforms himself into a muscle machine feared by the younger boys. One day he hits a freshman. Another day, he loses control and hits a teacher. His dream of becoming a pilot evaporates when he is expelled from the school. His strength finds a channel later when he volunteers for the police force, where he earns a reputation for violence, especially when he hits the streets in civilian platoons to forcibly cut the long hair off those lazy bums with their ideological deviations.

## FIRE

Five bells to "hit the floor!" two for the formation, three to begin classes, one for recess, and many, one after another, like now, to sound the alarm. Hundreds of boys rush out of the classrooms and barracks. The woods have caught fire from the heat and the summer wind. There are no firefighters, no firefighting equipment anywhere around. The boys themselves plunge into the flames, wielding branches to put out the liveliest fires they can. Someone cries out "Fire break!" and as the struggle continues, they try to make a line of burned grass to deprive the fire of fuel. It is almost a game, this break in the routine. A little farther back, the sergeants scream out orders. The fire retreats and now it's almost out. They return to the classrooms with tales of courage. This time, only six brave elements suffered slight burns. Tomorrow, their names will be announced at the morning formation and their circle of friends will expand . . .

## NO PASS

After twelve long days of brute routine, the day of their pass comes. Forty-eight hours to be at home, savor life on the outside, where the guys live that don't do nothin' which is why we have to make all these sacrifices ourselves, us real men that go out and fight just so these shits can strut around at home . . . where the girlfriends are, clean clothes, family, bright colors, parties, yeah parties, and real life. But . . . Element 622—Atten-*chun*! You have thirty demerits for missing formation, bed not made properly, insubordination, and not returning a superior's salute. *Pass suspended!* Saturday morning all the boys jump out of bed, rush to breakfast, and take the trucks to town. But before that, the jokes at the expense of the ones who are staying behind, the ones in the dirty fatigues standing in perfect formation so they can watch the others leave. That'll teach 'em. Then, off to work building laboratory Quonsets and more marching to the mess hall, to taste the ashes of retribution.

All Saturday goes by, drearily, and then Sunday. Late Sunday afternoon, the boys who left on pass are trucked back in, loaded down with the cool air of town, clean clothes, and the caresses of the prettiest girlfriend in the world.

## FAGGOTS

Noise, shouting, thumping, and banging in the middle of the night. The alarm hasn't sounded. What's happening? Behind the showers, two boys surrounded by a writhing, furious mob that is pushing them, cursing. In the middle, a pale blond boy with lynx eyes and a bewildered mulatto boy slapping at the air just in front of the other boy's face. More panic than real action. "Faggots!!" the other boys are yelling, trying to make them fight. It's hopeless. Somebody steps forward and with one punch floors the blond, who tries to escape on all fours, his nose dripping blood. Now they turn on the mulatto, who tries to get away, too. A hail of rocks, bottles, bars of soap. The boys from other companies join the hunt. At one point the officers appear and order silence, but the mob has a mind of its own now. Somebody cries, "Get 'em out of here if you want them to live! Faggots have to be killed!" And "If they come back, we'll kill 'em!" call out other voices in the darkness. Two sergeants catch the fugitives and keep them in custody the rest of the night. At daybreak a corporal goes to the barracks for their belongings. The blond boy's father, a midlevel political leader, protests. The mulatto is the son of a talented but now very old and powerless musician. Their protests are useless. In the school that is the pride of the country, there's no room for faggots.

## ELEMENT 602

He is the wiggle-worm. Hyperactive, intelligent, and a weakling. His honor forever being defended by his friends, who step in to save him from every adversary he comes up against. He repays them with unctuous adulation—to ensure that he'll be defended when "next time" occurs. The vicious cycle is broken in the second year, by which time he's almost learned to take care of himself. But his friends cannot protect him from the mortal blows of leukemia.

## TENSIONS

Out of the dark, someone is hissing obscenities at the company commander, an illiterate, bullying lieutenant. The blubbergut curses, pulls out his pistol, takes off the safety. He stands in the middle of the barracks, in the passageway between the bunks on each side of the long room. His right hand waves the weapon menacingly while his left hand grasps a boot brimming with shit. The livid face, the clenched teeth swearing to kill the joker that did this.

Sergeant "Hitler" mercilessly beats an element who answers back to one of his constant insults. Under a sun that inflames spirits, before the frightened eyes of the entire company, the man hits the boy over and over again, beating him as though each blow were the trigger for another even harder one. The boy falls (or drops), seeking pardon. The sergeant pulls himself together and decides to make the company march. He calls out the orders but no one moves. The hundred and twenty boys have gone deaf.

The contained fury has petrified them, like magma. The little man shoves, curses, insults them, but the mass has turned sharp-edged flint, defiant. He sinks helplessly into hysteria and disappears into the barracks. In the middle of the night, a storm of fists and sticks devastates what's left of the bully. Just before daybreak, he wades out into the underbrush beyond the fences. A few minutes later, a shot is heard, multiplied by echoes. The boys who go out to investigate with the other officers find Sergeant Hitler lying in the weeds, bleeding. The farce of suicide by self-inflicted flesh wound to the blubber in his gut succeeds in nothing more than having him demoted and expelled from the corps for conduct unbecoming. No one questions the student's beating.

## ELEMENT 695

He is intelligence under a guise of false and scathing madness, the scourge of officers who throw their hands up in dismay when he explains that he was absent from class because Garcilaso de la Vega came to visit him, was late to morning formation because he was chasing some protons that sneak into the dormitory every morning, can't work any harder because of an inflamed hypotenuse.

## LESSON IN PROPRIETY

Deterioration is everywhere. Everywhere, decay—frayed and threadbare uniforms, nails coming up through the bottoms of the boots, the linens in the little infirmary yellowing and mended, roofs leaking from the rock holes in them. But at today's 6:00 A.M. formation, the boys are informed that there is going to be an inspection by the general staff. A high-ranking officer with a name so exotic that the lieutenant who's now the company commander can't pronounce it will be coming. Headquarters must see that this is a model school. The next few days will be hard. A lot of things will have to be done so that the visitors will find the truth they want to see. New boots appear, and uniforms warehoused for so long. The mess in the mess hall improves notably. The rocks that border the walkways are whitewashed again. The elements receive orders to decorate the classrooms and create masterpieces of primitive art in the flower beds in front of each barracks. The tatters that have been hanging up there in agony on the flagpole for so long are replaced by a new flag. The requisite ceremony to burn the old one is not carried out; there is no time before the inspection. Up on the stage that overlooks the parade field there appears a banner with an inscription in red letters:

THE FUNDAMENTAL CLAY TO MOLD OUR DREAMS IS YOUTH.

—Ernesto Ché Guevara

The day set for the inspection begins with great nervousness on the part of the officers. The students, on the other hand, swing between smart obedience to the supervisory looks of their commanders and who-gives-a-shit slacking when they turn away.

## ELEMENT 603

He never tires of telling wonderful stories of the coast and of his family, whose men earn their living by making charcoal. He talks about his uncle, who can walk barefoot over the sharp limestone rocks they call "dog's teeth" with a sack of charcoal slung over his back. One day he tried to imitate him and his feet got all bloody. His uncle picked him up, sack and all, and just kept walking over the razor-sharp rocks, which seemed to turn soft under his firm, sure strength. The nephew smiles timidly when the other boys laugh at him as he tells his tales in that half-magical, half-archaic dialect of the swamps. And reflects that there's no use bothering with these poor city people who have none of the wisdom taught by the good earth.

## THE EDUCATION OF THE NEW MAN

"Element 853 requesting permission to answer the question!" Permission granted! He stands up and comes to attention. "Permission to stand at ease!" Permission granted! He plants his feet slightly apart and crosses his hands behind his back. His body remains rigid. His eyes look straight ahead, not even at the teacher who's asked the question. This is the way it's been for four years. Once the answer is given, "Element 853 requests permission to take his seat!" Permission granted! The teacher assesses what they've learned. From the back of the room, or on the sly, through a window, the sergeant looks on. At the slightest transgression of the regulations, he will loom up and demand that the element be reported. That is the way he will mold the New Man that his superiors have charged him with molding.

## ELEMENT 701

Perhaps the noblest of them all, the only one able to adapt to military discipline as the simplest of routines, to keep his boots and uniform clean, even to study, to get the highest grades and to arouse not envy but admiration, to be a friend to all, officers included, and never once be reported. He is the son that every parent would like to have, so they could send him off to a military school and later show him off to their friends as the crowning jewel of their pride.

## FREEDOM AROUND THE CORNER

They run out of the classrooms after the last exam. It is the end of their fourth year at the school. For many, the school is just the beginning, for they will be entering a military institute of higher education that they'll leave in five years with officer's bars. Then they will have the authority to give orders that their subordinates will obey. For others, today is the beginning of the end. Freedom! The failure of the parental dream despite the pressures, yet the achievement of their own dream—to be a civilian again. To be a normal boy who dresses the way he wants to, sees his girlfriend, runs around with his friends every day. A boy who can walk down the streets of the town, see cars of all different models and colors, clothes that aren't all alike, people of all kinds. The marches, the commands that blast your eardrums, your brain, your patience—over and done with! Likewise standing guard at night with a wooden rifle to give you the courage to go up against the stray dogs and cows that sometimes wander over to the barracks. No more demerits, reports, passes denied, no more the girlfriend replaced with furtive masturbation. No more military simulations with blanks, the heavy mortar bases slung over your fourteen-year-old back. No more fires in the woods that you have to put out just because somebody says so and never letting the other guys see that you're as scared of the flames as everybody else. No more field maneuvers and hard, rough work because that's what seasoned veterans are for. And no more officers.

**THE END**

The last night brings the uncontainable catharsis. There are fights aimed at settling last scores, stupid jokes, shouting and yelling. By three in the morning, the situation is out of hand. From one barracks to another, boys are throwing rocks or sometimes jars full of "crud," which is organic matter—any kind of organic matter they've gotten their hands on in the last couple of weeks—buried for days so that tonight it will have reached its maximum stink and sliminess. The explosions are gratifying and disgusting. A boy is hit by a paving stone, and at this point the officers decide to step in. It's three in the morning, and the drizzle and cold is itself a punishment for the members of the company ordered into formation by the battalion commander in person, who dresses them down harshly, calling upon all his years of pedagogical experience. In an interminable speech, he uses words like "disgraceable," "hemosexuals," and "queers." But everyone knows that this is the last speech—not just of the day but of their entire lives. Worn down by the cold and sleepiness, the disgraceable boys sleep quietly through the rest of the night, at least until daybreak. There's a graduation ceremony at ten, but many boys don't wait that long. They are free, and there is nothing to make them feel they have to go through that last act. They walk off in groups, leaving behind their personal effects, the ceremony, the school, and four years of their lives. They go with their hearts and eyes open, young Turks ready to "take" the city. To take back the time they've spent in this damn laboratory. The guinea pigs that escape this time number about seventy, of the five hundred that are graduating. A minority, that is, unimportant when you consider the percentages . . .

**ELEMENT 610**

He's everyone's pet. A likable, affectionate sort of goose who can never seem to get it through his head that he's in a center for military instruction. He never manages to come to attention. His body sways, totters, his fingers twitch nervously, his head bobbles, trying to find the point of balance between his shoulders. He's an olive drab live wire blissfully unaware of mental and physical order. Like a stray dog who's wandered in from the country. But today is the last day, and he stands at perfect attention, makes a face at the lieutenant, and walks off toward the main gate. After four years of being molded by "military discipline," he is among the first of the boys to desert.

## THE END OF THE END

More than the summer vacation, when they would get to know the town and their friends again, they have been looking forward to this day in September when school starts. This is the first time these first-year boys, entering high school, have been in a classroom with girls and without military regulations. A mind-blowing experience awaits them. They are as nervous as the day of their first love. They hunger for friendship. You can see that the minute they start up the stairs at the institute. The first period has barely begun when somebody knocks at the door. The teacher opens it, and two officers come in, carrying a red file folder. The boys are dumbfounded. The guinea pigs tremble. An officer reads off their names, one by one. They are to appear the next day with their belongings, ready for induction. By special order of the high command, they are being sent to a punishment center to cut sugarcane for an indefinite period of time. Six months later, they are transferred to the rear guard of the army to serve out the rest of their three years of obligatory military service. The dream of freedom is over almost before it's begun.

## ELEMENT 622

Every afternoon he sneaks off and lies in the tall weeds and reads, column by column, page by page, the section on arts and letters in his little one-volume Larousse dictionary-encyclopedia. His treasure and his escape. He writes and illustrates naive novels about long-haired men who live their own lives, regardless of what the world thinks, regardless of the demands the world makes on them. "Peace and love." His friends ask him for help in writing love letters and carving bars of soap, "putting some-thing" on the flyleaves of books for Mother's Day. After "the end" is written at the school, he becomes a kind of tropical hippie, and brigades of civilians set upon him in the middle of the street. That was the period he studied art and drama. Twenty years later, immersed in the daily grind of creation, short stories and poems, he is assaulted by these memories. And so he writes . . .

*Translated by Andrew Hurley*

ENA LUCÍA PORTELA

# A Maniac
# in the Bathroom

Chantal was still hiding behind the pillar when the woman dashed past her, looking like a panic-stricken fugitive from hell.

Chantal had spent over four hours in the darkness, watching Danilo's every move: his footsteps, his inflections, his cigarettes. The angular shadow, of average height, that Danilo cast on the walls. There were moments when that shadow became distorted into a vaguely expressionistic form, like a leaning tower, a trapezoid-shaped window, or the set of an old German film. From time to time, Chantal would recklessly inch closer, hoping to make out at least a trace of his words. The words of a shadow. At this very moment, for example, what could Danilo possibly be whispering to the freak at the door?

In this surreptitious manner, as if playing a game of cat and mouse, carnivorous plant and insect, secret agent in the corridors of Langley or the labyrinth of London, Chantal had moved from the back of a dusty classroom, whose floor was covered with bits of crumbled ceiling (because there is an isomorphic relationship between what's above and what's below, according to Danilo, who had his esoteric moments), where a pile of dilapidated furniture was jammed together to form a strategically located hiding place, to the most dimly lit corner of the library two floors below, just as deserted as the classroom and the rest of the school at this hour. She had remained for a long time in that secluded little spot, from which she was able to observe, in relative comfort (Chantal loved to crouch), Danilo's vague silhouette, immersed as a Scholastic in the syllabified reading of massive, moldering tomes that seemed to be turning to dust between his slender fingers.

Chantal found the profile of a young man letting his greedy eyes fall on unimaginable deliriums irresistible. (One day it was Restif's *Monsieur Nicolás,* the next the Marquis de Sade's *Juliette, the Fortunes of Vice;* Danilo also discovered an album with sepia prints of *fêtes galantes* that seemed to indicate a possible interest in certain men and a certain era, then suddenly his interest turned to a collection of epic poems, written in Sumerian or some other ancient language, and Chantal didn't know what to think anymore.) It was as if a magnetic force that attracted particles with opposite charges were compelling her to watch in spite of herself, to leave aside her virtual scruples in the name of dogged pursuit.

Danilo's gaze wandered interminably, dreamily, as if rearranging the world, from the letters on the page to another possibly lettered space. He frowned and allowed a languid "Ahh!" to escape from his lips. He scribbled notes in the air. He lit a cigarette, exempt, it seemed, from the prohibition on smoking in that sanctuary where paper and, consequently, fear of ecpyrosis reigned. The rising smoke took the form of a slender blue figure, with eyes. Danilo brushed his fingers across his brow as if to push back an unruly curl or some overly practical, overly constructive and ordinary idea. She trembled at this and, crouching there, thought that nothing could be more exciting than to secretly spy on the digressions of a young bookworm who thought himself safe from interlopers. Nothing so delicious as violating with impunity the ineffable solitude of the reader.

The librarian appeared silently from another corner carrying an armload of books—four enormous tomes of a critical-etymological dictionary full of all kinds of crazy stuff: an atlas from the time when the earth was flat and the sun revolved around it, a complete volume of Didot's *Scholia Graeca* on Aristophanes, and other rarities that he was determined to preserve despite the fact that these days hardly anyone was interested in the singular pleasures they might afford. They were undoubtedly priceless and the coveted prey of collectors of archaic tomes and other specimens of learned fauna. Simply by carrying them in one's arms as if they were very small, sickly children, "rock-a-bye *Scholia,* on the treetop, when the wind blows, the cradle will rock," one acquired the air of a medieval superscholar.

With such monastic rigidity that even his shiny bald pate resembled a tonsure, the librarian looked out of the corner of his eye at Danilo, engrossed in the shadows, and muttered something like "Keep it up, my dear Faust, keep it up, and you'll ruin your fucking eyesight." Then he disappeared back into his corner, all the while hugging his babies, and Chantal imagined him wandering like some ghost of the Dark Ages through the stacks, where, a few days ago, someone had made off with the school's only fan, an unfortunate incident that almost cost the freak at the door his job. She assumed the librarian wasn't particularly fond of Danilo, since the young man with the curly ponytail and the vice of reading more than anyone else always obliged him to stay until closing time. Even that "my dear Faust" was as ironic as it was affectionate, and for her the only acceptable love was romantic and unconditional, a love without jokes or parodies, operatic and eternal, like her own.

In the haze, Chantal imagined the librarian with the twisted grimace of a cadaver laid out for burial: an ashen, spectral complexion, sunken eyes, and a hard, straight line for a mouth. A skull. By the light of day his ugliness was unremarkable, not the least bit diabolical; he could walk down the street without frightening a soul, maybe even with a pretty woman on his arm. But not that evening, when he approached Danilo to expel him from his domain. "All right, my illustrious young man, let's see if we can finish up here; there are other things to do in this life," he said, and then he grew fangs, a pair of horns, and his hands took on the appearance of claws. It sounds strange, but he seemed to mean something else.

While the abusive reader lingered, Chantal felt her heart pounding (she also loved tachycardia) in the very vortex of her espionage; she would have to make her escape *after* Danilo and *before* the librarian, without being seen, of course, by either one. It was the moment of greatest peril, suspenseful as a thriller. The mere possibility of being locked up in that shadowy, suffocating place all night horrified her. It smelled of mildew and cockroach slime, as if she were underground, inside a thousand-year-old sarcophagus or an Inquisitional dungeon complete with pit and pendulum. What a ghastly experience, she thought, and she got goose bumps, broke out in a cold sweat, and thought she was going to shit her pants. When it came right down to it, any anxiety, any torment, the bite, in short, of any pincered vermin (the librarian could accuse her of stealing the fan, and she, though knowing full well who the real culprit was, wouldn't denounce him because she was no rat), was preferable to being discovered by Danilo with her hands on the goods. Or rather, with her eyes on the goods.

How would he react? Maybe he'd ask, "What kind of imbroglio is this?" or "What do you want with me, girl?" He might try to seduce her—Chantal had the face of a depraved virgin, a fatuous butterfly, the type who could be exorcised only by a brutal and savage penetration. He might try to hit her. He might do both; what a brute! And what if he decided to gouge out her eyes, like Apollinaire's outrageous protagonist after every deflowering? He would sink his fingernails into the depths of that gelatinous substance and, deaf to howls of pain, mash everything up inside. It was another form of penetration, the definitive annihilation of the last bastions of virginity. A true voyeur, she feared for her eyes: so indiscreet, so bold, so guilty. Her nightmares were full of empty, bloody sockets, nauseating flaps of hanging skin, always about to crack open and smear ichor and other putrescent matter all over everything.

And if he decided to show his dark side, his Gilles de Rais? Yes, that other monster so beloved by his vassals, Joan of Arc's alter ego. Every man has a *Gilles* inside him, you just have to uncover it. You push the right button and the Beast is unleashed, thought Chantal, who, as we can see, sometimes got her inspiration by reading the same books as Danilo. The nearly deserted school and the night presented quite favorable circumstances, of course, for the slaughter of innocents. She shrank back into her corner as if she could transform herself into a spider and dissolve among the library's other creatures, like one who clings to anonymity with all her strength. She undid her blouse, and her small breasts thrust their erect nipples into an ever-thickening darkness. Danilo was now gathering up his books, and Chantal felt a thrill of fear mixed with desire. What would have been the point of furtive pursuit without that annihilating yet simultaneously invigorating panic of being discovered?

But what if Danilo were prone to exaggeration, to getting carried away by misunderstanding, attacks of political paranoia, an indeterminate fear of Santeria, or any of the countless clichés that begin with a shrill "I'm being followed"? It would be better to avoid an encounter. They had barely exchanged hellos, without the usual kiss on the cheek or in the air (he'd say, "Hey, what's up?" and she never even had time to reply that nothing was up) in their very distant daytime coexistence. And so, Chantal could not imagine (with any shred of verisimilitude at all, that is) how the most quiet and aloof boy in the class, the one whose head was always buried in a book, the mysterious one, would react if he were to suddenly find himself in the extraordinary situation of being besieged in his retreat by an anxious, half-naked little beast. One thing was certain—all the magic of her strange pursuit would have ended right then and there.

Danilo returned the books to the librarian, picked up a rather ragged-looking backpack, and left. He must have had more books and something to eat in there, since when he wasn't talking in whispers to the freak at the door, who seemed to be his only confidant—they often shared a sandwich and a last cigarette—he could be seen reading cross-legged on a bench in the vestibule until late at night. The librarian, who, in Chantal's opinion, looked like a vampire or some other somber denizen from beyond the grave, exited back into his corner to shelve the books and dust them off. She took advantage of the moment to leap up and bolt out of there as fast as possible, without even bothering to button up her blouse.

The hallway was all darkness and silence, with a slight draft coming from somewhere—enough to blow out the candle that, for the sake of atmosphere, she should have been carrying. Footsteps, faint echoes, and traces of expressionist distortion. The breeze grazed her taut skin but, rather than cooling it, made it prickle even more. In the distance, Danilo's silhouette.

Chantal, somewhat unnerved, would have time to hide behind the pillar before the librarian left. Although, come to think of it, she had *never* actually seen him leave. Not the library, or even the school. At least not by the front entrance, a glass door with a few stairs where some of her classmates would sit during the day to look out at the street and the trees, gossip, and escape, while they were at it, from Semiotics or History of Philosophy. (In those days everybody wanted to escape from something.) Perhaps there was another door, Chantal said to herself, another less-conspicuous door behind the stacks in the other room. The librarian would lock up from within like a wizard his castle and then . . . But that was unimportant. The late-night adventures of that hideous prig were only of interest to Chantal insofar as they were connected to Danilo's world—Danilo, so desirable, so calm, so unknown. As soon as he was gone, the library, with all the knowledge it held, all the unrepentant murmur of the voices of the past, and all its mythology, seemed insipid and boring. She ran to catch up with the living object of her fervent curiosity, who had already made himself comfortable, as usual, in the vestibule.

Why wasn't Danilo leaving? He must like it there. Maybe his house, in Juanelo, Lawton, or La Lisa, was full of noisy people who spent their time drinking cheap rum and playing dominoes, "It's my turn and I've got the bones, I'm putting down double sixes and an ace . . . ," listening to salsa, "Let Roberto touch you, let him put his hands on you . . . ," some band playing, "Watch out, they're on to you; get down, they're after you," at full blast on the tremendous sound system with the tremendous amplifiers; or else they were arguing at the top of their lungs about the ball-game, "You don't know what the fuck you're talking about, man! The bunt was exactly the right move with a runner on third and such a tight game, come on! Even with the cleanup hitter on deck . . . ," or telling him not to read so much because he was obviously going to lose his marbles and books give you cooties, or simply because the electricity was out.

But in the dusk of the empty school where a few dim lights still burned, peace seemed to reign. As if it were the temple of oneiric flight in a hospital zone.

With the air of a remote odalisque, a victim of distant turmoil, the freak fanned himself with a *penca* leaf and stroked the edge of the bench. He and Danilo shared a bottle of some indefinable liquid—cold coffee, an herbal concoction, or cough medicine, no alcohol. Though he dressed poorly and his shoes were falling apart, Danilo was a good-looking guy, with a trace of Arab or Indian in him, whereas the freak was a freak in the broadest sense of the word. Yet there flowed between them a harmonic current that linked them like beads on a necklace. There was an inexpressible bond between them, and neither had ever been known to raise his voice to the other.

From her hiding place behind the pillar, Chantal often contemplated those tender, almost domestic scenes that were like antique tapestries imbued with ocher and burnt sienna, dusty rose and old gold. Later, exhausted but unsatisfied, she would jump out onto the street from one of the hall windows, which always locked again from the inside thanks to a curious mechanism that the intrepid voyeur never managed to figure out. But that was of no importance either; doors, pillars, corners, and locks served her as a means, not an end. A kind of neo-Gothic decor with haunted parlors, secret tunnels, subterranean passageways, and hidden staircases, somewhat reminiscent of Horace Walpole or Guy de Chantepleure and created in large part by the boundless imagination that enveloped her adventure in suspense. Anyone who chanced to be passing by at night, on seeing her spring out into the moonlight in such an unconventional manner and fall into the dirty courtyard, overgrown with weeds and full of rotting garbage, might have thought of a restless, or perhaps even mischievous, apparition, but nothing dangerous. A sylph, a little copper bell, an errant soul from the forest of Broceliande. Besides, there were few nocturnal passersby around the school, since it was rumored that the zone, so abundant in trees and so lacking in public lighting, was creepy and violent, crawling with muggers and maniacs.

Drenched in sweat, Chantal finally managed to position herself like a sentry behind a pillar so broad it was more than able to protect her body from the eyes and intentions of others. She took off her blouse once and for all, drying herself off with it as much as possible, since the blouse too was soaking wet. She looked around for her bag, where she kept a black pullover, more appropriate for nocturnal intrigues because of its mimetic disposition. But she noticed with annoyance that, as usual, she had left the bag in the library and wouldn't have enough time to retrieve it. She'd have to wait until early the next morning, after yet another vertiginous night, but for now she was stuck there, because if a half-naked sentinel, an urbanized version of a siren or a harpy, was a highly suspicious character, a wrung-out and dirty sentinel was beyond the pale. No one would approach her, amid tears and sighs, to ask, "Hey, you, watchman, what of the night?"

Danilo, meanwhile, with the sublime gesture of one who appeals to the gods, was offering the freak something that from a distance looked like a banana. This and other more or less similar actions (he was also adoringly caressing the freak's face, kissing his hands, and sticking one of his fingers into his mouth to suck on more eagerly than a lollipop) converted the boy into Chantal's hero again, the undisputed protagonist of this story, the craziest of all our crazies. The freak, a diffident deity, paid no attention to Danilo's slobbering and sniffed a little before grabbing hold of him with a scrawny paw. There was something bewitching about that scene, and Chantal forgot about her recent annoyances and focused all her attention on the outrageous pair.

His condition must be the result of a congenital defect, she thought, trying to make sense of the freak. Down syndrome combined with other infirmities, perhaps an accident at birth or a syphilitic mother. Maybe he was the product of an incestuous romance, of forbidden pharaonic inbreeding. Whatever it was, someone had to be guilty of that anomaly who bore a strange resemblance to the winged, androgynous, and always mistreated little angels of the AIDS hospice, invoked by some militant gay artists and AIDS patients to throw the age-old hypocrisy and indifference of the Catholic Church in its face. That frail transparency (Danilo's fingers left faint marks on his skin) crowned with orange fuzz like a Muppet, that membranous neck with the texture of a cabbage leaf or some other unearthly thing, that sorry imitation of a voice, made of litanies and laments, and shriller than a girl's, that flaccid, prematurely aging chimpanzee's face, and a body covered with reddish brown warts aroused in Chantal, as in everyone else, a feeling somewhere between pity and revulsion. It was better not to stare; one ran the risk of becoming wrapped up in the petals of an unwholesome guilt. Chantal had begun to notice him, to discover him and wonder, only because of his surprising affinity with Danilo.

The freak was a good person, without a doubt: he parked cars, washed them and changed their tires, kept an eye on bicycles and anything else left in his care (the fan had been an indiscretion, a petty crime hatched with his friend), went out for cigarettes and aspirin, brought Evanol for the girls, helped people with their overnight bags, ran errands, threw out the devilish little puppy that sneaked into the principal's office every day, scared off the owl that had set up housekeeping on the third floor, of all places, and went out prowling every night (there wasn't a single mouse in the building, and even the bats had deserted the premises—the owl didn't have it easy), made coffee, a fine cup of coffee in his beat-up coffeepot, rang the bell punctually at the joyful hour of the stampede, let people laugh at him without getting mad (everyone felt beautiful in his presence, even the librarian), and always seemed to know the exact location of every person in the building, information he gave out with a smile and the pleasant blinking of his almond-shaped eyes. He was, in short, the errand boy, the porter, the fire extinguisher, the shoulder to cry on, and even the school buffoon. Outlandish as he was, it never occurred to anyone to hurt him. This was, after all, a school of the humanities, which ought to serve some useful purpose, right? But Danilo was the only one who thought to talk to him— as an equal, I mean—to embrace him as if he belonged to the same species and to kiss him on the mouth, to Chantal's eternal envy. He complied when the freak, pretending to be a unicorn, rested his head in his lap, and asked him, please, for a French lullaby—the big snob—or a fairy tale by Perrault in which the nymph Melusina and company appeared in all their splendor.

This always occurred late at night, without witnesses to Danilo's, for lack of a better word, originality. Or so he thought. The freak lived in a part of town that was just as marginal as everything else about him, and the neighborhood kids would shout awful things at him and chase him with sticks and stones, amid fury and laughter, in a vestige of blood sacrifice, the ancient ritual of the *pharmakós,* the ritual slaughter of the scapegoat who would save the mob from all misfortune. Once he got distracted and went the wrong way. It was a bad move; he found himself trapped in an alley and almost didn't live to tell the tale. He turned up later all disheveled, with a black eye, deep scratches, cuts and bruises, and even a couple of broken bones. Yes, we know, lord of the flies. Usually some neighbor lady, playing the role of a ferocious, grandmotherly matron, would come out to defend him, hollering curses and brandishing, like an avenging scimitar, a lethal scrub brush with the power to disperse the raucous brood in a few seconds.

Someone so accustomed to persecution, thought Chantal, who had managed to piece together the story from the random fragments she heard night after night behind the pillar, ought to be quite capable of defending her, were she discovered, from Danilo's *Gilles* side or the sadistic potential that might be lurking within him. The freak was better able than anyone, she thought, to placate his friend and make him understand that being stalked by a degenerate virgin, similar to the picaresque images carved in stone that flourish on the facades of certain medieval structures, a shy and cowardly young girl who was removing her clothing one piece at a time (Chantal had also slipped off her skirt and wrapped it around her head like a turban, and the fresh thing wasn't wearing panties) in a kind of striptease for her own benefit, never daring to leave the shadows and strike, wasn't exactly the worst thing that could happen to a guy, no matter how misanthropic he was.

Chantal thanked him in advance and in her imagination she

37

also curtsied, bowing before the freak to cling to his knees, wrap him in a purple cloak, call him Your Majesty and, if necessary, kiss his feet. If he was Danilo's household god, she was prepared to abandon all her traditional beliefs about beauty, that fraudulent faith, and adhere to even the most abject manifestations of the true religion. Chantal, despite her name, didn't speak French and had long ago forgotten the tales of Mother Goose, but she wasn't lacking in other means of expressing her gratitude. At that very moment, for example, she felt more warm and moist than she had all night and she wasn't exactly sweating. As the freak peeled the banana and put the peel in his shirt pocket, she placed the palms of her hands on her breasts; their touch was electrifying. Her hands slid gently down her concave belly to her hips and once there they closed again as if trapping and at the same time revealing something of great value . . . with the sublime gesture of one who appeals to the gods.

And it was at this moment that the plot thickened, with the inopportune (or too opportune, which, strictly speaking, adds up to the same thing) arrival of a character from the street: the ordinary-looking woman of indeterminate age who rushed in and asked for permission to use the bathroom. Since the freak was occupied in the parsimonious swallowing of the banana, it was Danilo who pointed her in the right direction, follow the arrow. The ladies' room was located on the bottom floor, right in the middle of the hallway that connected the library with the vestibule, the same dark, silent, and slightly drafty hallway where Chantal executed her little sprints and pirouettes each night.

It all happened in a flash, in the blink of an eye. The woman went into the bathroom, saw something that made her hair stand on end, and flew back to the lobby as if she'd been blown out. Chantal, who at this stage of the game was wearing only her sandals and her improvised Phrygian cap, had the disastrous impression that the woman had caught a glimpse of her and that she was prepared to make the scandal of the century. But, what *else* could she have seen? Because the truth is she seemed awfully frightened, too frightened, and poor Chantal, naked or clothed, had never in her life upset anyone to such an extent. "It must have been the King of Shit," she thought, trying to calm herself down, because the woman had transmitted her terror and Chantal's legs were already beginning to tremble. Despite her adventurous nature, Chantal was more skittish than a cat, her nerves always on edge. "Yes, that's who it was, the King of Shit. A kind of viscous jester who lives in the sewers, in the world of detritus and pestilence, and navigates the bowels of the entire city, popping up in the toilets every now and then to grab someone's butt for kicks. He must have even stuck a finger up the poor thing's ass."

The woman landed in front of Danilo and the freak, who was choking from fright on the last piece of banana. She fixed her eyes on them with a glassy stare.

"Listen to me, there's a guy masturbating in the ladies' room!" she screamed. "And he's stark naked!"

"Stark naked?" said Danilo, pounding the freak on the back. "Stark naked, you say?"

"Yessir, naked as a jaybird in front of the mirror and rubbing his thing with both hands."

"So it must be really big," Danilo wanted to say but for personal reasons chose to keep the comment to himself.

"Did you see him?" asked the freak, still hoarse.

"Of course I saw him! He's skinny, bony, half bald, and he looks like a priest," explained the woman, waving her hands about. After a brief pause she added, "But it can't be a priest, because priests don't do that sort of thing in front of people."

"No, they don't," murmured Danilo.

"What about *him,* ma'am? Did he see you?" the freak asked again, once again in possession of his usual soprano register.

"Of course he did! He saw me in the mirror. And you know

what that disgusting pervert did?" Danilo and the freak shook their heads emphatically. "He winked at me! The impudent creep!"

"It's not such a big deal," thought Danilo. "You'd think nobody ever winked at this lady before." But once again, he was careful not to express his thoughts.

"All right, then, this man in the bathroom," the freak endeavored to reason, "is he crazy?"

"Of course he is!" exclaimed the woman.

"Well then, what do you expect?" The freak opened his arms as if giving up in a pose of very Christian resignation.

"What are you saying?"

"I'm saying that if the man who winked at you in the bathroom is crazy, there's nothing we can do about it. Try to be understanding. We don't know any psychiatrists. Perhaps you could recommend one?"

The woman opened her eyes wide as saucers. This wasn't happening. That response, so totally unexpected, simply could not be. They were pulling her leg, yes, that must be it, they were playing an incredibly tasteless joke on her. It was illogical, implausible for them to take it so calmly, so philosophically. There was a maniac in the bathroom, an insinuating paraphiliac, and the only thing that occurred to her interlocutor was to pronounce the *p* of "psychiatrist"! A sound that suggested the archaic or the etymological, and was certainly philo-Hellenic. But neither was it very plausible, in a strictly realist sense, for an ordinary-looking woman of indeterminate age to think in these terms. Besides which, she was unfamiliar with the theater of Ionesco, Beckett, and our own Virgilio, so she had no grounds for comparison. She felt so dumbfounded that she had no idea how to respond to the situation.

Suddenly, as if going back to the beginning, restoring the order that had existed in her life before the resounding irruption of the absurd, she noticed the freak. She took a good long look at him, as if finally seeing him as the spectacle he was trying not to be. From his orange fuzz to his skinny legs, to the banana peel sticking out of his shirt pocket instead of a handkerchief. She became aware of his warts and his preposterous voice, the boy who accompanied him and treated the freak like a normal person and not a monstrosity, the bottle on the bench, the place, the time. She remembered, quite clearly now, the fleeting appearance of a naked girl (the girl had very white skin, which made her seem even more naked) with a totally schizophrenic turban behind the pillar. Yes, in a place where so much depravity coincided (and it was just her luck to be the one to go in there!) it wasn't the least bit strange that there be a maniac in the bathroom, a buck naked, masturbating pseudopriest.

She no longer felt the urge to pee but she still stood there, not knowing what to do, anxious and afraid that the entire pack of demons would pounce on her and eat her alive (most likely they were cannibals too and capable of committing all kinds of other atrocities) when, at exactly that moment, as if to drive home the point with a magnificent and really dramatic coup de grâce, the owl from the third floor left its roost, took flight as it did every night, and, in the manner of a brave and triumphant beast, fell upon the woman in a kind of forced landing.

It fastened its talons on her disheveled hair and set to pecking at her head, which in no way resembled that of Pallas Athena. They rolled around on the floor joined in the hellish embrace of a single beast. A hybrid and spectacular tumble à la Laocoon. The woman shrieked, turning around and around and trying to decapitate herself as if possessed by some demonic spirit that was trying to speak through her mouth and give her a terrible migraine. The owl, a sensible varmint, almost never attacked people, but it went berserk whenever anyone or anything crossed its path, and the woman, unfortunately, had been standing right in front of the main entrance, which the owl liked to fly in and out of when making its rounds.

The freak had to make a strenuous effort to pull the bird off that suffering head—"Let go, you demented bird, let go, you son of a bitch!"—which lost a few hairs and even drops of blood in the conflict, while Danilo, in the meantime, held the woman down, first on one side and then the other, in an attempt to control her jerks and spasms, her state of complete hysteria. It seemed that at any moment she might roll back her eyes and start foaming at the mouth, get thee behind me, Satan. But since it's three strikes and you're out, Danilo couldn't hold his tongue any longer, and as he held her clammy body (the woman had peed on herself thanks to the stimulating contact with the owl's talons), he whispered in her ear, "Don't worry, *madame,* the man in the bathroom isn't crazy. I assure you. He's only an unhinged lover, a *renifleur,* you know, one who delights in the smell of ladies' rooms. If he winked at you, it was out of courtesy, a small tribute to convince you that his intentions were not predatory. To gain your confidence, do you understand? Moreover, he is a cultured, elegant, civilized man . . . he's our librarian."

These words had the opposite effect from what he had expected, as usually happens when innocence is confused with irony and all the signals are crossed as in an ode to chaos. When the freak finally managed to separate the two entangled creatures and put the bewildered owl, minus a few feathers and still furious, to the left, and the woman, in an indescribable state of panic, misery, and indignation, to the right, she shouted something like *Noli me tangere!* and, her hair having turned white in a matter of minutes, fled at top speed from that den of iniquity and was lost in the night. Given the habitual violence practiced in those streets under the cover of darkness by some other less-sophisticated maniacs, we can only hope that *madame* arrived safe and sound at her destination.

Alone again, or so they thought, Danilo and the freak, still panting and soiled from hair, feathers, blood, urine, sweat, and dirt, exchanged questioning glances. It was no more than a rhetorical gesture, because the agreement seemed to have been made long ago. The freak walked to the front door and locked it from inside, perhaps to prevent the return of sanity and the owl, recently expelled with a kick. They looked at each other again, and then, very slowly, as if enveloped in an oblique smile, holding hands, and with the majestic aura of tragic specters (Chantal, still petrified, could see them only as specters, beings from the beyond with unfinished stories), they headed for the bathroom, where, as he had so many times before, their other accomplice awaited them.

Transfixed, Chantal walked after them.

*Translated by Cindy Schuster*

෬෬෬෬෬෬෬෬෬෬෬෬෬

**EDUARDO DEL LLANO**

෬෬෬෬෬෬෬෬෬෬෬෬

# You Know My Name

In February, during the Book Fair, my first novel was published. It merited two reviews, one in the May–June issue of *El Caimán Barbudo* and the other in *La Gaceta* of July–August. The first was wary; the second frankly cryptic. I will cite one typical excerpt.

> *Nosotros los impotentes* is, then, genesis and epiphany. The discursive *continuum* flows without stumbling, meandering from the initial spell to a sudden surprise, and at the end of the eternal adventure of reading, to the fruitful revelation of the essential numina; through the length and breadth of the text, Nicanor O'Donnell avails himself not of the precarious ingredients of the adornment *ad usum,* but of a rich foundational marrow, tasty lure for unprejudiced hermeneutics. It is a matter of a promise and a rupture, a narrative exercise of beautiful semantic flights that invite complicity with the emerging estrus, and with the hope of its next arrival . . .

To the extent that I could understand it, the critic was speaking favorably of my novel. Since it was the first book of an unknown author, it looked promising. Full of enthusiasm, I dedicated a volume of stories to the publisher and sent it along with a request to join the Writers' Union. There things remained until October, when I received a summons. A slip of paper slithered under my door, urging me to appear the following morning at a certain section of the Ministry of Culture.

At ten o'clock in the morning I gave my name to a secretary with impossible breasts and prepared to put in a couple of hours in the waiting room. That's not the way it went: thirty seconds later the girl opened a door and said the compañeros were waiting for me. The compañeros were two individuals who came toward me simultaneously both with hands outstretched. So as not to slight either one, I held out both hands at the same time.

"Nicanor O'Donnell," said one of the men, savoring the syllables in a strange manner, "the author of *Nosotros los impotentes* . . . A pleasure. I am Segura. He is Rodríguez."

They served me coffee. While I was drinking it, they were looking at me so fixedly that I began to feel uncomfortable.

"Is there some problem?"

"No . . . Why do you ask?"

"I've never been called in for anything good."

I said it in a joking way, but they didn't laugh. Rodríguez put a blackish document on the table within my reach. I glanced at it. It was a photocopy of my birth certificate.

"Nicanor O'Donnell, no second name, born in October 1962, son of X and Y. Look it over. Is it correct?"

"Certainly it is correct. But I don't understand . . . Is this some procedure in order to join the Writers' Union?"

"In a certain way," Segura replied. "Listen, have you ever thought about changing your name? Or using a pseudonym? There are some very attractive ones. The history of literature is full of authors who sign with a false name. Mark Twain, Rubén Darío, George Sand."

"George Sand was a dyke who slept with Chopin," I explained, "and look, if you can't give me an explanation . . ."

Rodríguez nodded and took a copy of my novel from his briefcase and placed it on top of the photocopy and then various other documents that made a much larger stack. I looked at the new group and felt a chill. There were newspaper articles, novels, movie scripts in various languages . . . all signed by Nicanor O'Donnell.

"I didn't write these," I stammered.

"Yes, we know," Rodríguez said. "These texts have been signed with pseudonyms by authors whose numbers would surprise you. And the nom de plume chosen in every case—Nicanor O'Donnell . . . What conclusion can you draw from that fact?"

"That they should find themselves another pseudonym," I hazarded loyally.

"No. Rather, you will have to come up with another name."

Taking note of my stupefaction, Segura took the initiative.

"Some years ago . . . well, the date is not important, a World Congress of your colleagues decided that all those filthy works of a particular type that must be written by someone, meaning scripts for soap operas and grade B movies, local news items for newspapers, publicity tracts, notices of accidents, and so on, well, they decided it was bad enough that an author of some standing would have to waste time writing such garbage but on top of that would have to sign them. They chose to establish a universal shield, a cover for such tasks: an improbable name, a first and last name together in a combination that never ever should have occurred in the history of mankind. I suppose you can guess what it was."

"Of course. It's very comforting to know that one ought not to exist."

"Oh, you can exist, except you should give yourself some other name. In fact, the congress approved 'Nicanor O'Donnell' as the universal pseudonym to protect the true authors of monstrosities. And so it was registered with the Pen Club of London, the appointed *depository* of the rights. That's how the world began to be filled by works by Nicanor O'Donnell."

"I've never seen any until this moment."

"The truth is that here we neither publish nor exhibit many of these products," said Segura, not without pride. "We watch to make sure that our public does not become contaminated. For every bad book available to the national consumer, ten worse ones are rejected. For every infamous movie, we reject fifty out of hand. And those, almost all, will carry your name. I know because I have video."

"And why have you waited until now? Didn't you notice when I offered my novel for publication?"

"There was no Cuban delegate in the congress," Rodríguez admitted, "and we only learned about the whole business a short time ago. In any case, the officials of the publisher that brought out your book have already been penalized."

"Even so, I don't see what the problem is."

"Your novel is good, that's the problem. As for us personally, we like it a lot. And it has sold very well. Some tourist who bought it must have alerted them, because yesterday we received a complaint and an ultimatum. You cannot have new books of high quality signed by Nicanor O'Donnell, or a demand will be filed against the Writers' Union. A demand for damages asking several millions that the Writers' Union cannot pay."

"Obviously it doesn't have to go that far," said Segura. "You change your name or take a pseudonym for your next book and that's it."

"And if I don't want to?"

Segura looked at Rodríguez and smiled.

What is so momentous about an individual name? Keeping in mind that it is a matter of convention, a row of sounds lacking any correspondence with the named subject, why do we cling to it as we would to a ledge in an abyss? Does it make any difference to a person if they're called one way or another?

I think so. Oscar Wilde explained the importance of being called Ernest, but only to devalue less euphonious names. Well, I've known guys named Eleuterio, Cipranio, or Idelgrades who would ridicule any suggestion of replacing any of those abominable phonemes.

Examples of the aforementioned determinism? They are ready at hand. A proud progenitor bestows on his offspring his proper name, or that of a great person to emulate. After the Second World War and until today, German fathers have avoided calling their sons Adolf. Or they chose it on purpose, without being fascists at heart. And it is a scientifically proven fact that two-thirds of gays are named Roberto.

We do not use a name: we *are* a name. It's not by chance that in the armed forces, where the individual is supposedly annulled or nearly so and only the mass counts, people are known merely by their surnames. Major Bolaños, Sergeant Estrada, Private Monero (or General Grant, Marshall Zhukov, foot soldier Cambronne). And even so, history remembers the illustrious ones. Not even the most rigorous army manages to divest a man of his syllabic *I,* although it snatches some beloved portions away from him.

And the pseudonyms in general are not chosen so much to hide the name as to have two. The author always enjoys beforehand the instant of anagnorisis.

I am Nicanor O'Donnell. That's how my family and lovers *see* me. With that name in blue letters, like insignia on a ship's mast, I visualized the cover of my first book even before I'd begun to write it. Blue, I repeat. Words have color, as do months and days. And, of course, names. How could I resign myself to being green or purple, I, a blue Nicanor?

When I came out of the office, the secretary bestowed a smile on me.

"Your book is very good," she said, in such a way that her breasts now seemed to be possible.

I had asked Rodríguez and Segura for three days to think it over. Actually, I didn't need to think over anything, but it was prudent to concede them a fair chance at my cowardice. The two compañeros had even prepared a list of alternative names and let it be known that by taking any one of them, my entrance into the membership of the Writers' Union would be a matter of hours. Otherwise . . .

The real lengths of the otherwise case I was not yet able to foresee. I crossed the plaza and presented myself at the ministry.

"Hi," the secretary said. "My name is Ana."

"I'm Nicanor," I said firmly. "Tell them that Nicanor would like to see them."

She looked at me a bit skeptically, but with sympathy.

"The compañero who was here the other day is asking for you," she called to them and they immediately asked me to come in. As she went past me, she blew me a kiss and sighed with her probable breasts.

In the office, in addition to Rodríguez and Segura, there was a bald, nondescript-looking guy. Segura took charge of the introductions.

"This was Nicanor," he said, and I understood instantly that they hadn't believed seriously that I would need three days, "and compañero . . . ah, you there."

"Piñero," said the bald guy. "I am the attorney for the ministry. I've been given the task of speeding up the paperwork."

I sat down and ran over in my mind the statement I'd prepared. They served me rum. I took a drink and suddenly realized I'd forgotten the beginning.

"So you've already thought it over," said Rodríguez. "When my kid was about to be born, my wife and I were going nuts trying to decide on a name and it wasn't easy. We ended by calling him Ernesto."

"Nicanor," I said.

"No, Ernesto."

"I mean to say that I will continue to call myself Nicanor O'Donnell. There is no change worth it."

There was a silence. The attorney cleared his throat. Segura cracked his knuckles.

"Have we heard correctly?" asked Rodríguez.

I nodded vigorously and started to scratch my testicles in open defiance.

"Well, I think not," Segura said. "You have no idea what can happen to you if you refuse. He'll explain it . . . you there . . ."

"Piñero," said the bald guy. "Look, in the first place you wouldn't be able to publish anything again in this country. Or in any other. Perhaps you might manage to interest some sensationalist foreign press or a fly-by-night publisher, but as soon as the claims against you start falling on your head, they'd no longer be interested, I can assure you. And neither would we allow you to use your name in any official proceedings, which means that your ration card and your Identity Card will no longer be valid, and will remain invalid as long as you persist in calling yourself Nicanor. No company will hire you; if a friend sends you money, you will not receive it. You will be Nicanor only for your conscience. Every one of the aforementioned restrictions will be revoked only when you come to your senses."

Three big triumphal smiles surrounded me, while I asked myself if something like this would ever have occurred at the old Berkeley campus.

"Suppose," I said, "that the damnable congress had chosen Lezama or Carpentier as a pseudonym. Would you have forced them to do the same?"

"Yes," said Segura.

"No," said Rodríguez. "They had a name. Isn't that right . . . you there?"

"Piñero," said Piñero.

As I left I touched Ana's breasts.

The first weeks were very difficult.

Well, the worst was not to be left without money. In my circle of friends, and I suspect that even going further afield than that, to defy a stupid prohibition—and all prohibitions are, as the French students saw very clearly way back in '68—had become an attractive pastime. I was not illegal within myself, only if I undertook any sort of social activity. So I gave up social activity. Burned my ration book and Identity Card and shut myself up at home to write. I wasn't sure why I was writing. Sympathetic acquaintances brought me food and paper, read my stories, and urged me to resist.

The worst was also not that they cut off the light, water, and telephone. A century ago people didn't have such conveniences. I cooked with wood, got water from neighbors, used their phones. Anyway, my neighborhood had always suffered numerous cutoffs of all those things.

The worst was not by any means that I'd become a punishable vagrant in the eyes of the police. The chief of the area, Lorenzo Columbié, was a fanatic admirer of my novel and chose to turn a blind eye.

The worst was when they withdrew my novel from bookstores. The Pen Club had issued a warning only against my next works, but the officials had gone to the extreme and also withdrew *Nosotros los impotentes*. Quite a few copies had already been sold, but that didn't console me; it was hard to see that the institutional culture had forgotten me. In the long run the result of this policy was that my novel became an *underground* myth, and one copy came to be worth fifty dollars or a thousand pesos on the black market. That was definitely a relief as well as vengeance.

Two or three days a week Ana came to my house and made me depository of her breasts. According to her, also of her heart, but the usufruct of that organ did not matter so much to me. Not because of machismo, or not mainly, but because the unwritten law of the relationship was that no one where she worked must know of our connection. She protected herself, so the love she confessed to me was partial, while the breasts were not. One could say anything about her breasts except that.

The second month the attacks began.

One day they threw a brick against the door. Then another and another. I used them to build a protective wall in front of the house.

Another time while I was walking alone through the neighborhood a group of strangers started screaming that I was the villain of a soap opera and pounced on me as if to lynch me. I escaped by running away. However, I could swear that I'd seen at least two of the provocateurs a long time ago in literary workshops.

A new attack happened one morning when suddenly water went gushing through all the pipes. I collected several gallons and boiled it with wood. Not well enough, I guess. I caught amoebic dysentery.

"As long as you're alive, you're a potential menace," Ana said to me one afternoon. We didn't make love at night because of the heat and the darkness. "How can you live this way?"

"I don't know," I said in all sincerity.

"Do something. To change your name, no, I agree. Write a bad book and sign it."

"I can't write a bad book only because someone suggests it. It requires a certain talent, or the entire world would be full of Corín Tellados."

"And it isn't?"

"There are epigones, but she was a genius. On the other hand, even though I could write such a book, all the publishers are so prejudiced against me they'd always find something of value in it. They'd do it so as not to compromise themselves, but there would be some truth in it. The quality of literary writing is relative, you know? Someone should invent a bad-smelling ink for texts that are bad. Impartial. That way we'd know."

Ana caressed me gently. Next morning she left me.

People often visit me: admirers, misfits for whom I am a living idol, curiosity seekers, and provocateurs. I've learned to fence with all of them. They help me pass the time, not to miss Ana.

Last night I had a special visit.

They knocked at the door. I was writing by the light of a torch. For some reason, the knocks sounded strange. Resigned, I went to open the door.

There were Milan Kundera, Tom Sharpe, Steven Spielberg, Nanni Moretti, and Ray Bradbury.

"Take any seat," I gestured in my dyslexic English. "I'll light another torch."

"We're here incognito," said Spielberg, "and what's curious is that we're all in agreement. We all wanted to see you."

Kundera had brought peach tea. We drank it in silence.

"How are you?"

"Getting by," I answered stupidly. "I often have doubts, crises. Rodríguez and Segura send me messages to see if I've changed my mind. I've finished my second book. I think it's good. Here it is."

I held out the only copy, with a huge *Nicanor O'Donnell* tattooed on the first page. Tom Sharpe started to read it.

"You're not going to give in," cautioned Bradbury. "You are our only hope, for Mars."

"I thought that you, well, the big guys . . . needed my name to sign bad things."

"Oh, a name as a cover would be fine. It doesn't have to be yours. You know, once creativity becomes institutionalized, it slips from our hands. Including ours. The next congress will be held in the upcoming year. We'll see what we can do. Until then we're caught up with attorneys and bureaucrats."

"Resist," said Moretti.

We kept on drinking tea. Talked about our next projects.

"You never know if a work is going to be good or bad," said

Spielberg. "It's easy when you're dealing with garbage. But sometimes you put your heart into a film, and the critics blast it and the public takes to another. To repeat: I am Spielberg."

They said good-bye at four in the morning.

"The book is quite good," Sharpe said as he handed me the original. "There are certain weak stories . . . But you can see it's by the same guy who wrote *Nosotros los impotentes*. Good title, for sure."

"Don't give in," Moretti repeated.

Ten minutes ago Segura called me at the neighbor's. I told him, as I had before, that I had not changed my mind. Back at the house, an attack consisting of the ten volumes of Lezama's complete works came crashing down beside me. I didn't even bother to see where they fell from. What for? With all the threats, I am still Nicanor O'Donnell.

The one and only.

*Translated by Cola Franzen*

ALBERTO GUERRA NARANJO

# Finca Vigía

*This time you'll sail through,* said Hemingway. There he stood in moccasins on the old antelope hide, in front of his Royal. He noted down the day's word count with a pencil and finished work for the day. Wiped the sweat off his hands onto his shorts, straightened the pages, and lingered in the sunbeams filtering through the side windows. The stag's head on the wall, the collection of Nazi daggers, the rifles and fishing rods all shone brightly in these rays. He walked to the front window, leaned on the sash, and looked outside. The trees were still nice and shady, though the nearest ones kept pushing up the cement and the tiles with their roots. He looked at the garden tables, those dusty garden tables, then stopped to watch, unperturbed, a young man and two women carrying packages. They came in, left the parcels in the frame guesthouse, and went out again. From the back of the truck, another young man, black, shirtless, and sweaty, passed down the boxes. The ceramics were left till the end, and one of the women asked him to take care not to break them. Bored by the spectacle, Hemingway said, *Very strange people have slept in that little frame house, but none so strange as Sartre and his better half, Simone.* Then he returned to his Royal, took up the pages, handling them as if they were the best thing he'd written in ages, and straightened them again. He looked at the stag, at all the objects and dead animals hanging on the walls, and smiled. The whiskey bottle and glass on the shelf were empty. *I'll drink gin, then,* he said and took two steps toward the little table where a bunch of bottles awaited him. He took a few seconds to make the drink, leaning over, all smiles, like a white-bearded child in enormous Bermuda shorts. *I'm not working so well,* he said. *I impose this damned discipline on myself, but I'd better stop, keep the well from running dry. Never empty the well of your writing.* He enjoyed the first drink, knocking it back in one gulp, then went back to the table and made another. As often as he could, he wiped the sweat off his hands onto his shorts, looked at the Royal, and turned his eyes away to look outside. On his fourth gin he burped like a pig, yawned, and sat down beside the attendant.

She was one of those mulattoes, the ones you can watch for hours; bored, she crossed her legs and was contagiously trapped in a yawn of her own. *Nothing like an after-work drink,* said Hemingway. From where he sat, the attendant revealed a bit of thigh, and old Ernest slyly signaled me to take a look. *She's not bad, is she? But these attendants never put up with me for long, they last a few months and then take off.* Hemingway stood up, farted loudly, laughing his head off, and the girl looked at me as if I were the disgusting culprit. I was at a loss; I just smiled at the maestro's witticism and watched her plug her nose, then turn her back on me. The writer took a few steps toward the door and pointed at an older woman wearing a uniform like the young mulatto's. *The resigned ones are like that,* he said, still smiling, *they've been here fifteen, twenty years and spend them counting the days until they can retire.* Then he looked back at the gin bottle, rubbed his hands on his shorts again, and said, *If it weren't for such moments and the sunbeams, I don't know what I'd do. Did you see how they shone on the stag?*

But the fat guy kept me from answering. Holding his Nikon and baring his yellow teeth, he attempted a focus on the angle of the shelves, determined to get the Royal in the picture. He was almost squashing me against the wall. I wanted to push him in, see him trip over the rope and tumble through the air. Probably the camera would smash to pieces and he'd leave a couple of yellow teeth on the floor of Finca Vigía as souvenirs. Hemingway motioned me to let him take his photograph and take himself elsewhere. Has the old man ever changed, I thought, for much less than that Lisandro Otero, though he prefers to deny it, was thumped in the middle of the Floridita in the fifties. When the fat guy was about to shoot, the attendant stood between him and the object of his attentions.

"Excuse me, sir," she asked, "have you paid the photograph fee?"

"We've got to pay for that too?" he retorted.

"Yes," she said and went to sit down again.

The fat guy's wife, another tactless camera carrier, who'd not heard the conversation, raised her arm and I could see the long, dripping hairs in her armpit. I felt sick; no one could enjoy the sight of those hairs, much less after smelling her rancid husband, excited behind the camera. I was annoyed, as well, that thanks to him I'd not answered a question from a writer like Hemingway. As if situations like that were commonplace.

"You know, Henry," the fat lady waxed ecstatic, "he wore the same size shoe as you, love. Come and see."

But the fat man barely looked, he just wiped his sweat on a soaking handkerchief.

"You know, Marta, you have to pay to take a photo," he said. She looked incredulously at the attendant, who nodded slightly.

"Well, I'll put it away then," she said, "but take a look, Henry, his feet were the same size as yours, love."

"You know, I'd like to climb that tower," said the fat man, changing tack after walking a few steps toward the stairs. The indulgent Marta enjoyed each and every one of those steps, sighed, and asked me:

"Don't you think he's just like him?"

"There is some resemblance," I said.

"They're even the same size."

"And they're from the same place," I concluded.

I looked to the attendant for an ally. I wanted to mock the fat lady, Cuban style, but the girl looked the other way.

"Are you game to climb the tower with us?" she asked very quietly. "It's really expensive, up there we can take photos and they won't notice."

"You two go, I'd rather stay here," I said.

"Wait for us, then."

I'd never had so much to do with tourists before. They'd been hassling me since early this morning, and I was completely fed up. The constant "You know, Marta"s and "You know, Henry"s had me ready to explode. When I saw them on the stairs, I felt relieved, I was free of them for a while and comforted. I stayed by myself to talk to the maestro, hungry and nervous, the tiredness of Havana's streets in my feet. I was going to answer him, tell him I had seen those rays, which lit up the stag so well, but suddenly another couple of tourists interrupted us. I got out of the way as best I could, my tummy rumbled, and the attendant looked at me again. She must have thought me the most disgusting pig in the world, and didn't her simple gesture let me know it. I should have bought one of those cheap ketchup breads I saw in Old Havana but hadn't; I'd thought my obese little friends would invite me to lunch. There I was, hungry and nervous, confronting the maestro, a victim of heaving tourists and hateful glances from a gorgeous attendant. I wanted to get a couple of guys out of my way so as not to lose my place by the window, but too late, their sweaty bodies were already blocking me, and Hemingway signaled me to let them in.

*This time you'll sail through,* he repeated as I made myself some space by one of the little side windows. We felt secluded in that corner, there wasn't much to snoop at (just the collections of boots, watches, and bits of costume jewelry) compared to the antelope, tiger, and leopard heads hanging on the walls or the skins carpeting the floors of the other rooms. Not to mention the torrent of letters spread over the bed in an eternal mess just as they'd been left, which outstripped this part of the house. The group of tourists scurried through the outer hallways like mice in search of space. They dipped their heads in, sweaty, careless, implacable, wanting something to rub off at any price. I could see their strange, trancelike gestures in various crannies of the old house; they climbed the stairs to the tower, walked laboriously toward the pool, focused their cameras on the slightest hint that might bring them closer to Hemingway's ghost, evasive of them but friendly and cordial to me. *This time you'll sail through,* he'd said. Words I knew by heart. I'd been hearing them for five years running, on the same day, from the same person's mouth. It was like some sort of formality I found disconcerting. Sailing through didn't depend on him or on me but on the sails, the weather, angst, fate, a jury, vices, clichés. Despite the wave of tourism, he pronounced them as usual that time. Then he looked at the attendant (the mulatto still lost in her yawning), over at his Royal, at the little table with the bottles, at my anxious eyes, folded his arms, and asked:

"What've you got now, boy?" That was the interrogation behind the formality. I had to look away, let my eyes wander over the dusty tables of the little terrace.

"Nothing important, maestro, another one of my weird stories."

Hemingway smiled, uncrossed his arms, leaned on the window ledge, as if he were a bearded girl being serenaded, and declared as only a classic could:

"Everything is important to a writer, never forget that."

"It's about what will happen at the award ceremony," I told him, "as if it were already going on."

"If it's a good story, you can always explain it."

"A writer's been wanting to win this competition for years. I describe the day the prize is announced, that's all."

"It's you. So what's so weird?"

"It's how I tell it, maestro, describing it in detail."

"It's good to be interested in the how: one must write in order to write perfectly, boring old Sartre used to say. But is that it?"

"I include my conversation with you."

"And my gin drinking for lack of whiskey?"

"Yes."

"My farts and burps in front of the attendants?"

"Yes."

"Remember, pal, myths can be forgiven little things like that. They might accuse you of iconoclasm if you don't manage to convince them. That's what they did to me. I wrote *The Torrents of Spring* and they refused to publish it, only good old Scott would dare. I mocked Sherwood, he wrote a novel so terribly bad, silly, and affected that I could not keep from criticizing it in a parody. Do you mock me, by any chance?"

"No way, maestro."

"OK then. It's fine to mock the baddies, but not the goodies. Let's hope you convince that damn jury. How old are you now, boy?"

"Twenty-five."

"I was twenty-five once and lived on dreams too."

"But those were other times, maestro."

"Don't be so sure, maybe there weren't competitions like this one, but you had to live on what magazines paid you for a little story."

"That's not so easy here."

"And you think it was in my day? Not everyone who wrote when I was twenty-five published their stuff."

"It's not the same, maestro, this competition in particular has never published the winner."

"Now, that is serious. To get published is a writer's most precious aspiration. I thought it was an important competition."

"It's named after you, that makes it important."

"Thanks."

"But it's not, because they don't publish the winners."

"And which damn competitions do publish, boy?"

"*La Gaceta de Cuba, Revolución y Cultura,* for example."

"They're magazines?"

"Yeah."

"And why the hell don't you send something to those magazines?"

"I do, but I never win, maestro."

"Who are the ones who win?"

"Guys like Alberto Guerra, a black guy with writerly pretensions and terrible stories. Or like Juan Marcos Serrano, so narcissistic he seems mad, all beads and bangles, if you saw him you'd be wary of calling him a writer. Or like Raimundo Miyares, a punk who thinks he's God because he won the Casa de las Américas. And others I'd rather not mention."

"I don't know these guys, boy, but never show your bitterness so easily. It's good to hold back your bitterness and just crush them with your writing, not for any other reason. It's always difficult to make a start, wherever you are, remember that."

"But you were in Paris."

"True. Paris was a feast. We were very poor and very happy."

"You, Scott, Gertrude."

"Poor Scott, his shortsightedness killed him, his naïveté of his twenties and a damned woman called Zelda. Scott was really good."

"And Faulkner? How were things with Faulkner?"

"We're talking about good guys here, boy, not gone-to-seed alcoholics."

"Sorry, maestro, but Faulkner was in there too."

"That's another illusion, an envious Southerner could never be."

"The influence of his style transformed Latin American writing."

"Don't bullshit me. If you're here to bullshit, you better get lost."

"And you've influenced them too."

"Well, that's better. Tell me about it."

"Almost all the current ones start by reading you."

"And do they study my iceberg technique?"

"And they go on about the bullshit detector."

"I'm glad."

"But they try too hard to imitate you."

"Over-the-top imitations are always bad, boy."

"Yeah, always."

"That's right, never go over the top."

"No, never."

"Good."

Hemingway stopped to think, as if ruminating over our every word. He scratched his head, looked at the attendant, at the group of passing tourists, and looked up at the top of the tower. He seemed out of sorts; something in the conversation hadn't agreed with him. No writer, famous in his own lifetime, could be pleased to have his name associated, years later, with a competition that doesn't publish its winners. And I should never have criticized the guys who imitate his style, at least not in front of him. But I couldn't help it. Too many writers in this country wasted their good ideas trying to achieve Hemingwayesque economy in a land of total baroque. Lots of stories, influenced by the iceberg technique, ended up in a fuzzy mess from so much hiding their two-thirds underwater. I've witnessed Hemingway's ghost burying the talent of numerous fans of *The Killers* in literary workshops. At the same time, among the so-called vanguard writers, that logic (hardly operational for us if taken literally) had been doing its damage for more than thirty years. From Finca Vigía, the maestro cast a very big shadow indeed, dangerous and too close.

"Anything else in your story, boy?"

"I describe my anxiety, with a telegram in my pocket. Those in receipt of telegrams have probably won prizes. They arrive early and sit at one of the little tables to wait."

"And have you got a telegram in your damned pocket now?"

"Yup."

"Great. I told you this time you'd sail through. Literary prizes don't make you a good writer, but the money comes in handy. And recognition from a few power-wielding numskulls. That's how it was with us."

"That's good advice, maestro."

"When I finished *The Sun Also Rises,* I knew it was good, it was just a matter of placing it. You need to know where to place your damned work even if you don't win competitions. Don't surrender."

"Clear as day, maestro. I'll never surrender."

"That's the way to think. A man can be destroyed but not defeated. Have you heard that, boy?"

"It's the freedom fighters' motto."

"And writers'."

"Writers' too, maestro."

"I was your age when old Gertrude told me the story 'Up in Michigan' was *inaccrochable,* you can imagine my face in that little Paris flat. One should write with lots of confidence and very carefully too. But that's enough lecturing, you must already know what I said about the iceberg and the bullshit detector. Carry on, carry on."

"I also talk about a fat couple who came with me."

"Yes, I've seen them."

"She keeps insisting her little husband and you look alike."

"You think that damned fat guy looks anything like me, boy?"

"He doesn't think so, but it's fashion, she's just following fashion."

"At least he's got more sense than that fat woman."

"I think he hates you because of her."

"Much better, pal, much better. You want to tell me where you got them from?"

"I met them this morning, he's a writer and gives classes in cordon bleu cookery. A friend sent me a package of paper, I went to pick it up, and while I was there they invited me to go out with them."

"Did you notice they didn't want to pay?"

"You still don't miss a trick, maestro."

"And still writing five hundred words a day, boy."

"They made me visit the places you favored."

"The Bodeguita?"

"And the Floridita."

"Do you want to tell me all about it, boy? From the beginning, full speed and from the beginning."

I felt like declining, telling it could prove as tiresome as the walk itself. But the maestro's expectant face won out. I figured I had an hour to go before the awards ceremony and yielded to temptation. I heard the voice of the fat lady from the reception desk in the Hotel Vedado. I hung up the phone and sat down in the lobby. The caretaker and a few receptionists glared at me as if I were a poor wretch. No one scorns a poor wretch more than a poor wretch in uniform, I remembered reading somewhere. I had arranged to meet them, the fat couple, early in the morning, then we'd walk the old part of the city, and in the afternoon we'd arrive at Finca Vigía. We'd only spoken on the phone. She was from Jalisco and he was from Michigan. That's what they told me on the way down Zanja heading for the cathedral.

"That's a long way, boy, don't you think you should've taken a taxi or two?" said Hemingway.

"We'd rather walk," said the fat man, she nodded in agreement looking like an Indian in a quandary, and I simply pointed out the street. We walked all the way down Zanja at my pace. A good pace. The two of them, fat, sweaty, and reluctant, silently cursing my pace, until there we were on the Obispo boulevard. The woman couldn't take it anymore and asked to rest on the park wall.

"You know, Henry," she said, "my feet look like hams."

Henry didn't answer, nor did he make any attempt to examine the pair of hams. He was captivated by the sign on the restaurant across the street.

"Flo . . . ri . . . di . . . ta," he said, scratching his head, "like to drink *mojito* like Hemingway."

"Aren't they a pair?" the fat lady asked. "They even have the same tastes."

"Goddamned fat woman," said Hemingway. Didn't she have anyone else to compare him to?

"The *mojito*'s in the Bodeguita," I told him.

"And here what's it to be?" asked the fat guy.

"Daiquiri."

"What do you say, Marta?" said Henry, and she didn't have to be asked twice. We went in. Once again I thought a doorman looked at me as if I were a poor wretch. Sure my little friends weren't going to buy anything, I wanted at least to enjoy the air-conditioning and recover from the hike. We sat down.

"The drink Hemingway invented has to be good," said the fat guy.

"He was a genius, Henry, he even invented drinks," she said.

"Damned idiots," said Hemingway. "Didn't you tell them it wasn't me who invented that drink?"

"He didn't invent the daiquiri, he just modified it a little," I said.

"There lies his brilliance," smiled Henry, "geniuses invent not, they modify."

"And who was the inventor?" asked Marta.

"Did you tell them Jennings S. Cox, a North American, a fraction less of an idiot than her goddamned fatso husband?" said Hemingway.

"No, I don't know who it was," I said.

"In his spare time, this poor engineer, dying of heat, experimented with cocktails in an Eastern mine," the maestro explained, "until one night he came up with the perfect combination: lime juice, rum, sugar, and shaved ice. He named it daiquiri in honor of the beach, learn that, boy."

"And how did Hemingway drink it?" she asked.

"Did you tell the fat idiot double and no sugar?" said Hemingway.

"Double, no sugar," I said. Then I went to the bathroom; when I came back the fatties were waiting for me at the door. I always knew they wouldn't buy anything.

"That drink's very expensive," said Marta.

"Hemingway was a millionaire, but we're not," he said.

"And didn't you punch the fat slob in the face for me?" asked Hemingway.

"It's not worth it," I said.

"Well, of course it's not worth it," said Marta, leaning her enormous body on her adored Henry, "the prices here are ridiculous."

"And what did they expect, those two?" said Hemingway. "Daiquiris are expensive because I made them famous."

"When you're famous, Henry, you'll have to invent a drink, too," the fat lady said.

"We'll name it Marta in your honor," said Henry, and she stopped to kiss him in the middle of Obispo. We were walking slowly, them looking around, me hand in pocket fondling my telegram. The fat lady, with a woman's universal curiosity, made us stop at shopwindows, in doorways with exhibitions of Cuban handicrafts, and anywhere some street vendor was displaying wares. She'd finger things, ask the prices, calculate, then leave them by their cursing, disappointed owner. The fat guy, for that matter, giving himself airs of a great writer, invited me to go into the little private bookshops with him, remarked on the cheapness of the Cuban editions, found famous authors and texts from his country, was surprised at my literary knowledge, speculated, conjured up the great novel he would write, but didn't buy anything either. I'd never been as annoyed walking around Obispo as I was that morning. In everyone's eyes I was a hustler in the company of two big fat scores. From thinking so much about lobster, shrimp, fried plantains, rice, and black beans, I was hungry. I saw a cart selling ketchup bread, but probably my friends would also be overcome by hunger and decide to eat something.

"This is the Ambos Mundos," I said.

"You're not helping me out, boy," said Hemingway.

"Is it a hotel?" she asked.

"Correct," I said.

"Which room did Hemingway live in?"

"Don't tell them, boy, do me a favor," said the maestro.

"One on the fifth floor that has no room number," I said, "but not for long. He bought Finca Vigía and stayed twenty years."

"You know a lot about Hemingway," said the fat lady.

"He's my maestro."

"Thanks, boy," said Hemingway.

"I don't admire him so much as a writer," said Henry. "I hate his novels. They're ridiculous and badly written. I prefer his hunting expeditions in Africa to his literature."

"Moron," said Hemingway, "he's just repeating what other hacks have written. Never do that, boy, always think for yourself."

"Don't take any notice, he admires him," said the fat lady.

"He knows quite a bit about Hemingway himself, and looks so much like him. Doesn't he look like him?"

"Of course, maestro, I should always think for myself."

"Stop telling me about those fatties," he said.

"Fine."

"I was never a cheapskate gringo, of that you can be sure. And that fat guy, he sure is."

"He hates you to fend off his hatred for her," I said. "He may be fat, but it can't be easy acting up to your wife's whimsy."

"True, it must be terrible being compared to me when he's so fat and writes so badly. Because he's got to be a bad writer, eh, boy?"

"I haven't read a word by him."

"OK, then, go on."

"Then we got to the sea."

"Were they down at the bay?"

"Yeah."

"How'd they do in the midday sun?"

"Brutal, maestro, but they didn't want to move."

"Did they look at the boats, the Morro, the Cabaña, the statue of Jesus on the opposite shore, and interrogate you?"

"Yeah, but how'd you know?"

"And the fat woman went off a little ways and started praying, while he called you over?"

"That's right, maestro, that's right."

"Shame the water's so dirty," said the fat man. "You like the sea?"

"Of course, I love it, that fat guy expected you to say, but heard something else," said Hemingway.

"I can't stand the sea," I said.

"Strange you don't like the sea," Henry smiled spitefully. "Take the sea away from Hemingway . . ."

"And in the Pilar, damned fat-ass, I caught the best marlin and tunas ever seen."

"They say he detected submarines during the war, but I don't believe it," said Henry.

"Not 'they say,' idiot, I did, and I've got witnesses to prove it."

"And that Gregorio, his skipper, inspired *The Old Man and the Sea*."

"Gregorio and lots of other Gregorios," said Hemingway. "Literary characters are never based on just one person but taken from here and there. But tell me, why the heck do you detest the sea?"

"Because I lost a brother."

"I'm sorry," said the fat man.

"That's really tough, boy," said Hemingway. "I've lost friends to the sea, too."

"It was when tons of rafters were leaving," I said, "in '94, he drowned or they drowned him, we never found out."

"Good reason to hate," said the fat man, pointing at the dirty water. "I don't like it either."

"We better go," I said.

"And you left with a huge lump in your throat," said Hemingway. Then he looked at the little terrace. There were nervous, chatty faces around the dusty tables; a lot of people were starting to mill around the house. I saw a few friends, people taking part for the first time, and others, who looked like jury members.

"Who's that guy with the beard and glasses?" Hemingway asked. I picked out a pale face in the crowd, average height, stooping, arms that had never wielded a farm implement, greeting the literature expert.

"Must be on the jury," I said.

"And her?"

"She's the expert, her name's Angela, she virtually runs the whole show."

"Angela, pretty name," he said. "I saw her a while ago carrying packages with two black guys."

"They're gifts for the winners."

"They unloaded some sandwiches and sweets too."

"I could use a few of those sandwiches right now," I said.

"Are the gifts any good?"

"More or less, maestro. The ones who win the marine award get coral or a stuffed marlin and an invitation to dine at a first-class restaurant of their choice."

"That award's not for you, then, boy, you hate the sea."

"True, I hate the sea."

"And what other gifts do they give out in this damned competition?"

"A thousand pesos to the grand prize winner and those meals I mentioned."

"But they don't publish the winning stories?"

"No, they don't publish the winners."

"Then it's shit," he said.

"Better than nothing, maestro, I'm up for a couple of nights at the Marina Hemingway even if I don't get published. I'd take my girlfriend and we'd really let loose. Get blasted in your honor."

"Is the Marina Hemingway a nice place?"

"Ask the girls trying to get a ride on Fifth Avenue."

"Tell me, pal, who are those girls?"

"I'd better not let you in on that story, maestro."

"Look, once you insinuate something, you've got to go on and tell it, otherwise, you're finished."

"But it's better to keep quiet about those girls."

"As you wish, but keep my advice in mind."

"I will."

"I don't see why the walk with the fatties was such a disaster."

"Put yourself in my shoes, they didn't even buy me a soft drink on the whole walk. It's not worth laboring the point anyway, I'm getting nervous, they'll be announcing the prizes soon."

"Are you saying you're going to terminate the fatties midstream?"

"You asked after them, I didn't want to talk about them."

"You know the risk you're running?"

"I can imagine, maestro, but I just can't."

"Make an effort, you've got a telegram in your pocket and you could win."

"I'll leave it there. Us talking and them up there."

"Have it your way."

"Thanks, maestro."

"They must be on the jury too," he said and pointed at a slender woman, early forties, garish lipstick, helloing effusively, a woman in the know about the workings of the competition. Beside her a young man, small, chubby, smiling, bestowing his bureaucratic blessing on all and sundry.

"I don't know them but they must be on the jury," I said.

"She looks the honest type despite the way she wears her lipstick."

"Yeah, she's got the look of a good person."

"The young man's trying too hard."

"Why do you say that, maestro?"

"I don't trust people so eager to greet everyone."

"At least he's young, it's no bad thing for young people to be part of a jury," I said.

"Let's hope he's a good writer; if he is, it doesn't really matter if he's a good person or not."

"Why?"

"Because no writer is, boy, none. We're too individualistic even to make the attempt. We get along with one set of people and hate another with the same intensity."

"You know more about such things. I'll bear it in mind."

"If you win, it's better not to know the jury. You won't be resented."

"I've got a telegram in my pocket and I don't know them."

"When they gave me the Nobel Prize I didn't know the jury."

"Back in fifty-four, maestro."

"In fifty-four, boy."

"It's rained a lot since."

"I remember after a banquet, right here, I said: As you all know, there are many Cubas. But just like Gaul, it can be divided into three parts: the hungry, the survivors, and the overeaters."

"You and your friends belonged to the last group, maestro."

"And you, to the first."

"You'll be late for the awards ceremony," said Marta, tapping me on the back. The fatties looked at me contentedly and pointed to the little frame house. I felt a cramp in my stomach, my heart speeded up, there was hardly anyone left outside.

"We got a lot of photos," said Henry. "This Marta sure is smart, real smart."

"And you, my love, will be as famous as Hemingway," said she.

"Hope God's listening," he said, "but let's get going."

They walked. I stayed behind; my feet barely obeyed me. I looked at the attendant, the Royal, the stag, the maestro, for the last time, and said:

"Happy birthday, wish me luck."

"I already did, boy, this time you'll sail through, but remember competitions don't matter. Write even if you don't win, you'll win."

He watched me go down the stairs behind the fatties, turn down the walk, and go into the guesthouse. He looked at the attendant, who still had half her thigh uncovered and was getting ready to close. She had her purse and a little mirror propped up on her lap; she brushed her hair, fixed her makeup, and, every once in a while, yawned. Hemingway thought: *a real looker.* He walked over to the drinks' table, poured himself a gin, and stood in front of his Royal. *Of course I can try,* he said, *there's water in the old well yet.* He set down the half-finished drink on the shelf, wiped his hands on his shorts, picked up the pencil, and wrote that, in the company of a fat couple a young man of twenty-five, a telegram in his pocket, made his way through the crowd. They couldn't get very far but they could make out what was happening at the front without too much trouble. Before an anxious public, eager to know the results of another chancy competition, the characters representing the various institutions were already holding the ceramics, paintings, stuffed marlins, and diplomas that would be going to some of the chosen with telegrams in their pockets. Meanwhile, the three members of the jury were arguing over who'd read the statement and Angela, the expert, inaugurated the proceedings. She said the competition was sponsored by prestigious institutions this year: the Cuban Publishers' Association, the Writers' Union, and the local Party, that more than two hundred works, most of them excellently executed and lavishly literary, from every corner of the land, had given the jury a demanding and worthwhile task. She gestured toward the corner where the whispering about the presentation was coming from and asked for a big hand. They felt lifted by so much applause from so many nervous people and showed it with big smiles. Hemingway was exhausted; never in his literature had he described such strange ceremonies. With great difficulty he managed to press the awards script into the woman's hands because the young bureaucrat, in a fit of egocentric loss of self-control, was about to grab it from her. But the maestro persevered and, by force of writing, left the chubby young man in disarray. She smiled her lipstick smile and there was a profound silence. For the umpteenth time the competitors wanted their names to come out of that mouth. Some shut their eyes, not to look. Others imagined the bliss of a thousand-peso check or sitting at a table groaning under longed-for platters. The woman's lips broke into another big smile and then said, "Awards presentation, Finca Vigía, on the twenty-first of July of the current year, the jury comprised of . . ." The boy squeezed the telegram, his tummy rumbled again, the fatties watched expectantly. The woman, sure everyone was eyeing her face, her lips, modulated her voice to pronounce a name, a simple name, the name of the new winner. *But that's enough for today,* said the maestro, motioning toward the attendant, *I'll just have another look at those thighs, before she leaves.*

*Translated by Peter Bush and Anne McLean*

**LEONARDO PADURA FUENTES**

# Puerta de Alcalá

*That was something wanting to
happen, Marcus Aurelius*

—Written over the doorway of
Seymour and Buddy Glass's bedroom
in J. D. Salinger's *Franny and Zooey*

He had always heard that to name disasters was sure to make them happen. And now, once again, the *Jornal de Angola* was announcing an imminent South African invasion. Every week the same announcement was repeated with absolute certainty along with irrefutable evidence, logistical facts, and government statements. Nevertheless, despite the fact that over the last twenty-three months the Boers had crossed the Namibian frontier several times with an occasional menacing plane and what were indisputably tanks, the predicted invasion had never actually materialized. Still, reading the news always gave him the same cold shiver. It was a dark, tangible fear that started in his guts, made him weak at the knees, and caused him to send up a prayer to who- or whatever might be listening to please let the imminent event wait until after February when he himself would be far away from it all and his two-year mission in Angola would have moved irreversibly into the distant past.

The trouble was that his fear tended to have certain more immediate effects. He had barely read the headline and some of the first paragraph when he had to abandon his bed and rush to the bathroom clutching the newspaper under his arm while he unbuttoned his trousers. After so many months, he already knew the causes and effects of that uncontrollable emotion he had acquired in Angola, and in a way that seemed ambiguous even to himself, he came close to relishing his fear, certain in the knowledge that it was not exactly cowardice.

That was why, seated on the toilet, he devoted himself to neatly tearing out that section of the front page that he blamed for triggering his anxieties. He was bent on taking the most scatological and symbolic revenge he knew: he would wipe his ass on the news item. While he was waiting for his unconditioned reflex to come to an end, he turned the piece of paper over and spotted a small ad with a headline in font no bigger than 10-point announcing THE COMPLETE VELÁZQUEZ. The announcement went on to say that between the twenty-third of January and the thirtieth of March, the Prado would be hosting the so-called exhibition of the century, bringing together, for the first time since they were painted, seventy-nine of the Seville artist's greatest works brought from around the world to join the great Spanish museum's permanent collection.

As he wiped himself carefully with the sports page, he turned his thoughts to another of his favorite obsessions. The world's a pile of shit, he told himself. Here am I shitting myself in Angola while people in Madrid are getting ready to see a once-in-a-lifetime exhibition of Diego Velázquez. He hadn't stopped thinking that the world was a pile of shit for one single moment since he had left Cuba two years before. He thought it twice a week when he wrote those interminable, heartrending letters to his wife in which he voiced his despair; he thought it in the evenings when he leaned out of his bedroom window to study life in the *museque* occupied by several families in a warehouse abandoned by the Portuguese in 1976. He watched how the men, squatting on their haunches and chewing some herb, in their turn watched the withered women boiling the yucca and fish for *funche* on a wood fire while they offered the breast to tiny, slow, shriveled children who would perhaps never even know the word "happiness" existed. He thought it, too, when he walked the streets of Luanda, avoiding the piles of garbage on every corner, turning his face away from the endless maimed victims of a real and interminable war. He asked himself why the hell people were condemned to live like this whereas he, precisely he himself, wandered without hunger or hopes through that sick, alien city that would not give itself up nor let itself be understood and whose final destiny was unimaginable.

From then on, every morning meant an *X* on one of the three calendars stuck up over his bed, the last of which came to an abrupt stop: they were just into January 1990, and now he had only eight numbers left to cross off.

"How did you manage to fix it, compadre, rum, marijuana, and what else? Because this note sure as hell isn't regulation." The editor of the newspaper seemed so sure of this that he shook his head as well and smiled. Most things usually seemed to make him laugh, though in this case, Mauricio told himself, he was right in a way, but he still persisted.

"Look, Alcides, you know I'm not stupid. There's loads of people here flying back via Berlin or Madrid and if you make the effort, I'll be able to go via Madrid too."

"And what am I supposed to say, that you want to look at some pictures in Spain? If I say that, Mauricio, the very least that will happen is that they'll pack me off home for being an asshole."

Outside, a breeze came up suddenly and the editor had to throw his arms out to stop all the papers flying off his desk. It looked as though it was going to rain in Luanda for the second time that summer, and Mauricio hoped it would be a devastating downpour.

"Why? Because they're going to think I plan to stay in Spain, that's why, isn't it? That's a pile of crap, Alcides! You can sweat it out for two years in Angola, blinded by chlorine, your guts totally fucked up by tinned meat, and there'll still always be some bastard who thinks you're planning to try and stay! Well, that's charming!"

The editor stopped arranging papers and lit a cigarette. He stopped laughing and passed a hand over his face as if trying with a gesture to wipe out all the tiredness and worry lines of the last months. In Cuba he'd been no more than subeditor of a provincial newspaper, but he was also a reliable bureaucrat, so they entrusted him with the job of editing the weekly paper for the troops in Angola, and he did his job very conscientiously. Anyway, he was an affable and even an intelligent man.

"Look, Mauricio," he said, unsmiling at last, "I think I know you. I think you get to know people better here in bloody Africa, but don't expect other people to think like me. You've got a blot on your files and everyone here knows that, down to the crazy guy who wanders naked round Kinanxixi Square. And if you did try to stay in Spain, you wouldn't be the first. Plus which there's the problem of the flights . . ."

"So they're not going to let that one drop, are they? The screwed-up thing is that other people have no problems at all. At least those who do stay out of the country don't have any!"

The editor reluctantly smiled again and threw his cigarette out the window.

"Don't blackmail me, bastard . . . so it's a Velázquez exhibition, is it . . . OK, I'll see what I can do, but remember, if you do anything stupid, it's my balls they'll have."

"That'd be a good enough excuse," said Mauricio. Life wasn't always a pile of shit.

At least for Velázquez, life hadn't been a pile of shit. Emma Micheletti tried to show this fact in her booklet about the painter that Mauricio had found in one of Luanda's three bookshops during the first months of his mission, when he still visited museums and bookshops. The stained, dusty little tome *Velázquez* sat on a shelf at the end of the shop alongside other incongruous titles: Plato's *Republic* in German, selected works of Erasmus in Italian, and some leaflets on soccer in Portuguese. Although the book was sold as new, it had had a previous owner: María Fernanda. She had not only signed and dated the book (9/7/74) but she had underlined various sentences and paragraphs that seemed to have interested her for various reasons . . . or possibly for one and the same reason.

Perhaps because of his inability to look beyond the anecdotal or because of his total lack of artistic skill, Mauricio had never been particularly knowledgeable about painting. But ever since he had discovered María Fernanda's underlinings, that particular volume, number twenty-six in the Diamonds of Art series, published in Barcelona by Toray in 1973, had become full of enchanting mystery to him. The fact that that particular book should have been for sale was the first mystery, and the person of María Fernanda herself was the second, most intriguing one. At first he decided that she must have been one of those Portuguese who fled Angola in 1975 and '76, leaving behind businesses, houses, and even dogs and books. However, when he began to trawl through her clues and obsessions, he knew her better and he decided that perhaps María Fernanda had been an uncontrollable romantic who had never found love.

Two particular underlinings in the book led him to this conclusion: at the top of page 5, the original owner had drawn two parallel lines in blue ballpoint in each margin of this passage:

> In 1624 he settled with his family in Madrid in Calle de la Concepción. His relationship with the king would end only with the painter's death and if, at times, this patronage restricted his freedom, on the other hand it enabled him to lead a quiet life, free from financial worries. Nor did the sovereign overburden him with obligations or conditions.

Three pages further on, at the beginning of the section entitled "The Work," the woman he presumed to have been unlucky in love had underlined the whole first paragraph, in red this time, and at the end she had added a sad exclamation mark. "Velázquez's life," wrote Emma Micheletti, either to María Fernanda's pleasure or angst,

> was decidedly happy, and an observation of some aspects of his life leads one to draw a clear parallel with that of Rubens who, as we have seen, befriended him. Both were born in June and the fact of having been born in this luminous summer month seems to have augured both of them a comfortable and happy life and a sure, precocious, and glorious artistic talent. Both were in the service of understanding and generous monarchs whom they served with fidelity and love. Both died at a vigorous age, at a little over sixty when they had already achieved the peak of their artistic lives and when really they had little to add to their style and perfected technique. They were, perhaps, different when it came to their spirit, their emotional and expressive force, their characters. Rubens was passionately vital, impulsive, and extroverted; Velázquez was calm, reflective, and a careful observer.

Only a sensitive soul, in love and with certain suicidal tendencies, worries so much about happiness and security, Mauricio told himself. He was definitively convinced of this when he found the strangest of all the clues left by María Fernanda in that book she must have loved so much. There was a barely visible colon at the bottom of illustrations numbered 63 and 64 in the catalog of Velázquez's works that took up the second half of the book. Mauricio discovered the colon because he too was drawn to those two paintings, less well known than *The Drunkards, Las Meninas, Venus at Her Mirror,* or *Joseph's Tunic,* but unique and magnetic in their theme and conception. The reference to the works read:

> 63. VIEW OF THE VILLA MEDICI GARDENS canvas, 48 ×
> 42 cm, Madrid, Prado. The painting is known as
> *Evening.* Together with its pair, known as *Midday,* it
> was probably painted in 1650. Both paintings are truly
> unusual in the Master's Oeuvre. They are first men-
> tioned in the Alcazar inventory of 1666 and have been
> in the Prado since 1819.

Ever since then, Mauricio dreamed about María Fernanda and of visiting the Prado to see that dazzling diptych in which Velázquez moved away from enclosed spaces, kings, popes, princes, and fools and casually announced, two centuries ahead of time, the advent of Corot, Van Gogh, Renoir, Monet, and the whole of nineteenth-century impressionism. This was especially true of the painting known as *Evening.* The leaves of trees that Mauricio guessed must be cypresses, though he'd never seen a cy-press in his life, cast their shadows on the arches of a Renaissance gallery. The warm light, diffuse and yet resolved, blurred the outline of the two figures poised in conversation in the fore-ground and of the caped man in the background, his back turned to the viewer, admiring the landscape of pines and willows re-ceding into the distance. That magnificent evening in the Medici gardens gave one a lust for life. One could feel the sheer joy the artist must have felt as, freely and without constraints from any king, no matter how generous and understanding, he let his best brushstrokes flow: the brushstrokes of a peaceful man.

After a while, Mauricio had absolutely no doubt: Diego Rodríguez de Silva y Velázquez had been truly happy for at least one afternoon in his lifetime, and María Fernanda was an ethe-real and enchanting woman going about the world with that book that drove her mad with envy because she herself had not known happiness even for half a day. María Fernanda had understood that happiness is a privilege too elusive for all but kings; perhaps she had vanished into the jungle in search of her own kingdom of solitude.

Alcides told him, "Go on, buy a bottle of rum, you owe it to me." And of course he smiled. Mauricio just stared at him, serious, incredulous, and hopeful.

"Don't fuck with me, Alcides."

"You're leaving for Madrid on the third. You arrive at four in the afternoon and fly on to Havana at ten the next morning. That should give you enough time, shouldn't it?"

Mauricio went to his room and got the seven thousand kwanzas. It was well worth the bottle of rum the editor was demanding, and he went down to the fourth floor. Ortelio, the store manager, always looked after him and his friends. That was his motto. For his friends, a bottle of three-year-old Havana Club cost seven thousand kwanzas, and he had a few other tasty items on offer, like cartons of cigarettes, for example.

Sitting together on the balcony of the apartment, they opened the liter bottle, and Mauricio couldn't resist a toast.

"To Velázquez."

"To me, for fuck's sake," said Alcides as he clinked glasses with his junior, "because if it wasn't for me, Velázquez could go fuck himself."

And they drank. They drank several shots and talked about the heat, about how long Alcides had left to go and about what Mauricio would do when he got to Havana: screw his wife ten times in a row, spend a week on the beach, eat a pizza on the Rampa. How he was never going to jerk off again in his life because his cock had got so it had four ready-made finger grips like a bicycle's handlebars. But most of all how he was just going to walk through the streets at night without anyone telling him he couldn't and without invisible enemies waiting for him in the dark.

"And what job will you do on the newspaper?"

Mauricio finished his fifth drink before answering.

"I don't know. I hope after this two-year stretch they'll get off my back and let me write about culture again."

Alcides threw his cigarette butt into the street.

"They came down hard on you, didn't they?"

"Like a ton of bricks. First they set me to rewriting provincial reports, then they sent me out here to prove myself."

"They put me in charge of you. They told me to watch you and everything."

"Now you tell me, asshole!"

Alcides lit another cigarette and drank some more rum.

"What do you expect? Would I spill my guts to you without knowing who the hell you are? Don't be stupid, Mauricio."

Mauricio smiled and watched the sun disappearing behind the Hotel Trópico.

"But I'm glad to have gotten to know you well. You're the best journalist I've ever worked with."

"Thanks for the compliment, boss."

"I hope things work out well for you, and I hope you don't try to stay in Spain. Not for my sake, but because of those who fucked you over. Don't give them the satisfaction."

"It looks like I'm going to spend my whole life proving myself, like a *Challenger* spacecraft."

"Give me some more rum. Looks like it's going to rain again."

"Do you realize, I'm going to see the exhibition of the century, compadre. At last I'm going to see *View of the Garden of the Villa Medici.*"

Alcides smiled again and took another sip of rum.

"You'll end up mad or gay. I'll put money on it."

But this time he wasn't smiling. He looked into Mauricio's eyes and said, "Do you think we'll see each other again in Cuba?"

The rum and the news of his flight to Madrid had produced a certain euphoria in Mauricio, and he thought of making a joke but held back.

"Do *you* think we'll still be friends when we come out of this?"

"I'd like to think so." Alcides sighed and looked sad. Alcohol usually threw up his closely guarded nostalgia. "Because I think I'm going to miss you. I've been staring you in the face every day for fifteen months."

"I hope we'll stay friends. No fucking war should leave you without the most important things at the end."

"I'll come and visit you one day and then I'll bring the rum. I'd really like that."

Mauricio looked out at the street darkening with ever-lowering clouds and regretted the mistrust he'd felt for this man for so many months. Possibly in Cuba Alcides would never have been his friend. They might never even have spoken to each other. But here, in the middle of so much homesickness, fear, and loneliness, there was a chance for everything to be quite different. Yes, he'd like to see him again with his three pens in his guayabera, his unbearable smile, and his manner of a man with a mission and too many responsibilities.

"I'll be waiting for that rum," he said at last.

"I almost want to hug you," said Alcides.

"You'll end up mad or gay too," said Mauricio, and he tried to imitate his editor's perpetual smile.

He still couldn't believe it. The chain of events placing him in Madrid on that third of February 1990 seemed too complex to be even a possibility, far less a reality. He thought how much he would have liked to have told it all to María Fernanda, from his problems at the paper to the discovery of her book. He would ask her to take him to the Prado so they could see the Sevillean's seventy-nine pictures together. Then, he could be sure at last that the owner of the book was precisely the woman who had been looking for him all her life, never dreaming that he lived in a dusty, quarrelsome neighborhood of Havana, a place he never could have imagined feeling so homesick for until two years ago.

When he was very young and used to read biographies of famous men, Mauricio enjoyed spotting the strange twists of fate that make up people's lives: a casual meeting, an unexpected decision, a fortuitous act. Why was there nothing like that in his own life? He thought of himself as a mistake, and his whole existence seemed to him to be a series of errors and frustrations that had led him to lose all dreams and ambitions. Since he wasn't an art lover and had never in his life seen a reproduction of Velázquez, why had he come across just the book and not the woman who had left her revealing marks on it? Lately he had begun to imagine what María Fernanda might look like. At first she had been just essence, voice, and mystery, but now she appeared to him as a pale, gentle woman with large moist eyes who smiled at him through a mirror as he came toward her. That was how he found her in illustration 67 of the book, naked and reclining. But she would never see him come toward her. For the time being he would have to make do with Velázquez's *Venus*.

"Can you tell me how long the Prado museum is open until, please?"

The immigration official looked at the passport photo and raised his head.

"I'm afraid, sir . . ." he answered and shrugged, confused and uncertain.

"It doesn't matter," said Mauricio and collected his papers. He went through to the baggage hall and couldn't help being stunned by the shining cleanliness of the airport. Two years walking through streets cleaned only by the wind and the very sporadic showers of Luanda and sharing a flat with three other men who took it in turns not to sweep were enough for him to be enchanted by a floor free of dust or cigarette butts.

He looked at his watch and sighed. Four twenty-five. Nobody around him looked the type to know what time the museum closed. He had guessed it would be open until nine and that he would be out of the airport by five, pass by the hotel to leave his luggage, and at the latest be at the Prado by six with enough time to get drunk on Velázquez.

He went to the bathroom and consulted his watch again while he urinated. Yes, I'm in Madrid, he told himself, at four thirty in the afternoon, and as he came out he realized he was in luck because his suitcase appeared on the moving luggage belt. He wiped the sweat from his hands and forbade himself to look at his watch again.

The bus left him at the Puerta del Sol. The man who had sat next to him from the Hotel Diana explained what he had to do: one of the streets leading onto the Puerta del Sol is Alcalá. Go down the whole of Alcalá, and when you reach the Bank of Spain you are already in the Paseo del Prado, turn right at the Cibeles fountain and there's the museum, macho, he said and confirmed the most important fact: it's open until nine.

He crossed the square and resisted all temptations: the cafés, the shops, the African layabouts-turned-street-sellers of sunglasses, earrings, and other black-market trinkets. Then he had a sudden attack of homesickness. Ever since his companion on the bus had talked to him about the Paseo del Prado, two bronze lions from the Prado Boulevard in Havana had installed themselves in his memory and reawakened his desire to be home at last with the wife, the dogs, and the books so necessary to his life.

The cold of Madrid was bearable. A digital display attached to a traffic light showed the temperature and time: 13 degrees Celsius and 5:39 P.M. Mauricio felt a desire to run. People all around him were walking hurriedly, talking incessantly, and smoking like condemned men. They went in and out of the bars, adjusting their leather or woolen coats; they looked at the shop displays and calculated whether the seasonal sales were good value; they ran to the mouth of the subway with a frenzy capable of pushing aside any human obstacle. Mauricio enjoyed the thought that none of those people could have the faintest idea of who he was or what he was doing here in Madrid with this desire to run and this feeling of euphoria that he hadn't known for a long time. His hands weren't sweating anymore, and he wanted to stop for a coffee but didn't allow himself the luxury. All he had in the world was sixteen dollars, and he'd drunk enough coffee in Angola.

The Paseo del Prado took him by surprise. There it was in front of him, unmistakable even without bronze lions, and he joined a group of people waiting for the traffic lights to change. Without giving himself time to look at the famous Cibeles, he crossed the street and turned right on the central corridor of the avenue full of dark bare trees, cypresses perhaps. Now he was less than two hundred meters from the museum and at last he began to believe that, yes, it was true. For a moment he remembered Alcides, and in his memory, Alcides was smiling. Then he began to run toward the peaceful evening in the Villa Medici.

When the museum guard told him that they were closed on Mondays and opened at nine on Tuesdays and that he was sorry he had come all the way from Angola, that's in the Congo, isn't it? that he should come back the next day and that there was nothing he could do, they were closed, sir, closed, Mauricio realized again that life was a pile of shit even in front of the doors of the Prado on a third of February just the width of a wall away from seventy-nine great works by the affable Diego Velázquez. Especially if it was a Monday.

His mother had died on a Monday, he remembered. It was Monday when UNITA attacked the convoy and his friend Marquitos the photographer was the only one killed in the skirmish. He had gotten married on a Monday too, and he told himself that he didn't even have consistency in bad luck.

The Cibeles fountain was throwing its jets of water onto the marble chariot, and Mauricio had to smile at one detail: a small notice announced that the red, yellow, and purple tulips planted around the monument were a gift from the mayor of Amsterdam to the town council of Madrid. He stopped at the beginning of that Paseo del Prado bereft of lions and felt empty and extenuated. He thought about going back to the hotel, burying his head under the covers, falling asleep, and forgetting about everything, but a street sign and a song made him change direction. The sign read: PUERTA DE ALCALÁ and an arrow pointed right. He started to sing the song he had grown to hate two years before when his brother copied the Ana Belén cassette and everyone in the house was condemned to hearing ten times a day at full volume: "*Mírala, mírala, mírala,* \ *La Puerta de Alcalá,* \ *mírala, mírala, mírala* . . ." Damn it, he would go and see it.

Looking at it, Mauricio could see that there had been enough Dutch tulips to decorate the Puerta de Alcalá, the monumental entrance to old Madrid commissioned from Sabatini by Charles III to be built in his own honor as illustrious and victorious king. Those five triumphal arches were blocked to pedestrians now by tubs of tulips, but for many years the best fighting bulls destined to die in the ring, along with kings and armies, beggars and water carriers, all had passed beneath them. Perhaps his ineffable María Fernanda had also admired the austere monument some time after relaxing in the Prado with Velázquez's delicate color and light and buying the little booklet in the museum shop, which destiny placed years later into the hands of an obscure, disgraced Cuban journalist. What would she have been thinking as she looked at it? Mauricio wanted to think the same thoughts as María Fernanda but ended up thinking about himself. Would he ever in his life have another opportunity to go to Madrid and finally cross the portals of the Prado? What was he going to do with his measly sixteen dollars? Should he set out to get drunk and offer his own monument to Bacchus? Should he spend it on a dinner in Madrid or should he buy his wife the bras she had asked him for? What would happen to him when he went back to the paper, redeemed and purified at last by his sacrificial time in Angola, reevaluated as exceptionally positive, hardworking, militarily and politically and ideologically correct by Alcides and endorsed by the Party nucleus and head of mission? As he was thinking and looking at the Puerta de Alcalá, Mauricio forgot about the song and even about Velázquez. He had just decided on the meal when he saw the man dressed in an elegant gray suit standing on the other side of Alcalá Street just at the point where his eyes rested below the arch and looking intently at the figures on top of the monument. Then the man lowered his eyes and his gaze followed Mauricio's exactly but in reverse order, over the tulips, through the arch, avoiding the traffic in the street until he caught sight of him too.

"It can't be!" said Mauricio and the man in the gray suit together, each on his own side of the Puerta de Alcalá.

There were just three months left until they graduated, Mauricio in philology and Frankie in architecture, when Frankie's girlfriend, Charo, called Mauricio and told him, "Frankie's left the country from Mariel. He went to the office they opened at the Four Wheels and told them he was gay and they let him go. He's left you two books."

The books were the two volumes of *The History of Modern Architecture,* by Leonardo Benévolo, which Mauricio had always wanted. Yet since they had belonged to him, he'd never read them.

They'd known each other since they both started tenth grade in a secondary school in the Víbora, and they were classmates until they graduated from high school. The five years of university separated them a bit. They only met up on the occasional evening to go to the stadium if the Industriales were playing well or on Saturdays sometimes to listen to Chicago or Creedence and share a few rums, but still Mauricio always thought of him as a good friend. Besides, they had other tastes in common—Marilyn Monroe (the exception) and brunettes (the rule), the novels of Raymond Chandler, blue jeans, sandals without socks, and the Hotel Colina bar with its mural of little drinking dogs. They both felt sorry for the stray street dogs, and they both felt a certain contempt for gays. And since Frankie was Catholic and Mauricio a blasphemous atheist, they never discussed religion. They preferred dreaming about what they would become in the future: a great architect and a famous writer, obviously.

Much later on, when he was the most sought-after young journalist on the paper and the editors were assigning him special features, Mauricio wrote a prizewinning article about Chinese immigration to Cuba and for the first time gained direct insight into the trauma of rootlessness. He thought then of his old classmate and companion in arms and remembered how they had talked about it one evening walking through Chinatown.

"Don't you feel sorry for them? Those Chinese just tear me apart, they're eaten up by loneliness and they haven't got anywhere to go back to anymore," Frankie had said on seeing an ancient, dirty, poor Chinese man remove the sleep from his eyes and then examine it at his fingertips through half-closed lashes.

So when Charo called him and told him what Frankie had done, "he told them he was gay," Mauricio couldn't believe it. They had never considered such an option and even though in the last two months they had only spoken over the phone because they were both immersed in their final theses, Mauricio didn't think anyone could come to such a final, irrevocable decision in such a short time. So he searched fruitlessly for some message in the pages of the architecture books, he talked to Charo, who swore she hadn't known either, and he spoke to Frankie's parents and only managed to make them cry. How could two such similar people as he and Frankie behave so differently, he asked himself? He never found a satisfactory answer, nor did he ever receive any letter attempting to explain. Something had come to an end.

They had circled the roundabout surrounding the Puerta de Alcalá and met with a smile. Frankie looked healthy and complacent: his gray suit was neat and sober, and the pullover under his jacket looked warm and protective. Mauricio couldn't help feeling both at a disadvantage and yet, somehow, more principled. His faded jeans were the symbol of his fidelity to cherished habit, and the nylon and padded cotton of his Soviet jacket cushioned the embrace of the man who appeared out of memory and the past. They looked at each other for some time without speaking until Frankie set the tone.

"Shit, you've gone gray, Mauricio!"

"It's all the quinine and the jerking off . . . I've just come back from two years in Angola," and he laughed.

Mauricio had sometimes imagined this meeting. He thought Frankie might come back to Havana for a few days to visit his parents and would call him. The difficult thing to imagine was how the conversation might go. Would Frankie justify himself? Would he be triumphant and offer him money to buy whatever he wanted? Or would he be as ruined and devastated as one of the Chinese men on Zanja Street?

"So what are you doing here if you've been in Angola?"

"You can't begin to imagine. How about you?"

"I came for an architectural conference and I'm leaving tomorrow morning."

"Things going well for you?"

"I guess so . . . And how are you?"

"Fucked up but happy," said Mauricio using the phrase Frankie's father always answered with.

"This is amazing. Who the hell would have thought it? And how's your family?"

Frankie seemed to be moved and avid with curiosity. He wanted to know everything. He was sorry about the Velázquez exhibition. "Shit, and I went to see it yesterday," he said as they walked with no apparent destination away from the Puerta de Alcalá.

"Look, Mauricio, what have you got to do now?" he asked when they reached the Cibeles, and Mauricio answered, "Wait till tomorrow comes and then fuck off."

"Right, well let me buy you a coffee. There's the Café Gijon, the one the writers go to. Have you written a book yet?"

"What a memory you've got!"

"You can say that again. Come on, there it is across the street."

"Isn't this going to get you into trouble talking here with me?"

Mauricio was studying the atmosphere of the old Madrid café, so suitable for literary gatherings, and had to look at Frankie.

"Perhaps, but don't you worry about it. I'm an internationalist and you're certainly one of the ones who fled, but the truth is I'm happy to see you. It's been ten years since you left me with a question on the tip of my tongue."

"Two coffees and two JBs," Frankie ordered "Do you want yours with ice? Both without ice, please, in brandy glasses."

"You're different."

"And you're just the same. More fucked up than happy. I'm pleased to see you too. I never managed to send you a letter though I must have written at least ten. Especially at the beginning."

"And what did you say in those letters?"

"Everything. I think I said everything: that I really cared about you, more than I did for my own sisters, and that I was always going to want to go to the stadium with you. Hey, man," he smiled, "compadre, I don't go to ball games anymore."

The waiter came back with their drinks and placed them on the marble table. Frankie took out a pack of Kaiser cigarettes and a gold lighter. He lit one and sipped his coffee.

"I'm living like God, as the Spaniards say. Living bloody well. I started off working in a bank and enrolled in night school and got my degree in three years. I got a good gig . . . it's years since I've used that word, 'gig' . . . I earn good money and I can come on vacation to Spain every summer. New Jersey is terrible in July and August."

"So now you're going to tell me that even though you've got a car, a house, cable TV, and a bank account, you're missing the most important things. Please don't give me that story, I know it by heart. Do you remember what Havana's like in July and August?"

Frankie smiled and finished his whiskey in one gulp.

"Cheers," said Mauricio as he raised his glass and finished it in one too.

"Two more," ordered Frankie and stubbed his cigarette out in the ashtray.

"Life's a pile of shit," said Mauricio, and for the first time for many days, he felt like laughing.

"I'll be in Havana again tomorrow night," he said as he drank the second glass of whiskey, "and instead of having seen Velázquez, I'll have seen you. Have you heard anything of Charo?"

"No, and I don't want you to tell me either. I have to protect myself, and I decided to cut myself off from everything."

"Including me."

"Don't joke, Mauricio. Listen, about three years ago when I was reading Proust I thought of you. Do you remember you were the only one in high school who'd read *Swann in Love*? And there's one bit, I think it's in *In the Shadow of Young Girls in Flower*, in which the bastard says something more or less like this, that people are more strongly united by consanguinity of spirit than by identical ways of thinking . . ."

"Proust had serious ideological problems. He was in deep shit . . ."

"Are you going to go on fooling around?"

"I've got to protect myself too, haven't I? Go on, order more whiskey. Nostalgia's going to become expensive for you."

"Two more, please, and bring us some green olives. The black ones taste like shit. Hey, Mauricio, have you really not written anything?"

Mauricio took his coat off to give himself some time. He threw an olive into his mouth and arranged his glass in front of him.

"Before I went to Angola, I still used to try now and again. I published three stories, but they're crap, they're not the sort of thing I want to write. They were too obvious. Now I might try and write something about a woman called María Fernanda who gets lost in the jungle and a journalist who falls in love with her and tries to work out what happened to her."

"What are you getting off your chest with this one, man?"

"Nothing, I just like María Fernanda. What about you? How many houses have you built?"

"None. I work for a firm that specializes in demolitions. What do you think of that? Demolition man," he said, and they both laughed. And Mauricio wondered if Proust wasn't right in the end. He could feel that the urbane man in the gray suit and the Italian shoes handmade of Argentinean leather was still his friend after all. But he told him:

"I don't know, I feel I don't know you. Did you know my mother died four years ago?"

The story needed to be very simple but with a touching simplicity. Really it would be the story of missed encounters throughout Europe and Africa between two people who were born to be together. The main character would be called María Fernanda, he couldn't imagine any other name, and he must be careful to avoid any Hemingwayesque influences.

Some elements of the story were already completely decided: the prose would have the colors of Velázquez, and María Fernanda would have the body of *Venus at Her Mirror,* that astonishing nude that started a whole Spanish school of daring, human, and tangible painting. This decision was in effect essentially cerebral rather than aesthetic. On one of the days when he was leafing and looking through María Fernanda's book on Velázquez, he lingered longer than usual on figure 66–67 (*Venus at Her Mirror,* canvas, 124 × 130 cm. National Gallery, London). The mythological goddess's ass was offered to the viewer right in the foreground and was the focal point of the painting. It gave Mauricio a sudden erection, the result of which was a copious and satisfying masturbation. Ever since then he thought that María Fernanda had to look like the Venus, and that if ever they met, she would be waiting for him, naked and reclining, looking at him through Velázquez's mirror.

However, he had most trouble with his male character. Mauricio knew he was going to write the story in the first person, even though he felt hampered by the closeness between author and narrator-protagonist implied by this perspective and especially by the autobiographical aspects the character would assume. Even though he himself had never launched into the world in search of a woman, his views, desires, and disappointments would permeate the character who would inevitably end up resembling him. And that wasn't right, when it came to a person who didn't even want to be like himself, he thought, who didn't want to be what he had been, who had never placed any value on risk taking and who still thinks that life, his life, is a pile of shit. How was he ever going to make a character like that unite with the romantic and existential vitality that María Fernanda would have?

In the end Mauricio knew he was never going to write the story no matter how much he wanted to. It was quite simply beyond him, but he enjoyed thinking about María Fernanda's adventures because it was the only tangible evidence, after so many months in Angola, that he wasn't permanently blocked. So he scrutinized *Venus at Her Mirror* again and admired Velázquez's courage and his sense of artistic freedom that no king could ever rob him of. Who were you, who are you really, María Fernanda? he asked himself, trying to snatch her from the shadows of the painted mirror and dreaming.

Mauricio accepted the invitation. Frankie knew an excellent Argentinean restaurant near the Castellana where, even though the wine wasn't outstanding, they served the best steaks in Madrid. "They bring the meat in from Buenos Aires," he said, remembering for sure that Mauricio could never resist a good steak. And it was more than just a good steak: Mauricio calculated that his must weigh around a pound and come accompanied by another pound of fries and half a bottle of red Rioja. He rounded off the feast with pancakes in syrup and a large piece of Alicante Turrón.

"That was a long-standing hunger, man," smiled Frankie as he lit his cigarette.

"I never eat in planes, it makes me feel sick. And I was already starving before we left."

"How are things over there?"

Mauricio felt like a cigarette. He had given up five years before and managed to survive the trauma of his first months in Angola without starting again. He remembered that it was he who had introduced Frankie to his first cigarette twenty years ago, and he himself was the one who had given up. He lit his cigarette and found it tasted excellent.

"Worse, I think. Things aren't going well," he said, with no desire to offer further explanations.

"And you've never thought of getting out?"

"I'm not going to leave the country. In spite of everything, I'm never going to leave. You know, three years ago they turned the guns on me and my time in Angola was part of the punishment. But I couldn't ever leave."

"That's what I thought, but I did leave and look, here I am. I was able to do it."

"Congratulations."

"Don't joke, Mauricio. You have no idea what I'm feeling right now. I haven't seen you for ten years and I don't know how long it'll be before I see my folks. Your mother died four years ago and I didn't even know about it. To be able to get out, I had to say I was gay and luckily another little pansy in the office said that yes, I was in the closet but that he'd seen me with 'the girls' in the Coppelia ice-cream parlor."

"Well, that was your choice, right?"

"Yes, that was my choice. What about you? How was Angola? I've read that it's hell there."

Mauricio thought of telling him that he hadn't had a bad time there, that it wasn't as terrible as they made out. But he remembered Alcides sitting behind his desk at the newspaper, finishing the letter to his wife: don't tell her I'm getting old or that my blood pressure's up, Alcides asked him as he sealed the envelope.

"The truth is, I was afraid all the time. But I endured and I'm happy to have survived in spite of the fear."

Frankie smiled and reached out across the table as though to seize the moment just by touching his friend's hand but stopped at the packet of cigarettes.

"Fellini says the character he hates most is Achilles because he was never afraid of anything. I remembered that because I remember the day you told me that *Amarcord* was the best movie in the world. Now I think it's *Amadeus*. Some things have to change in ten years."

Frankie looked around as though he were afraid someone might be listening to them. Mauricio knew he was about to say something important to him.

"Are you going to tell anyone we met?"

"Even if I hadn't met you I was going to go and see your parents. Of course I'll tell them. You haven't told me if you've got a woman?"

"Not anymore. It's not as easy as it is in Cuba. Sometimes I feel bloody lonely."

"Like a Chinese man on Zanja Street . . . I feel lonely too at times, don't worry. Angola wasn't easy. Honestly, I was afraid from the moment I got there: afraid to die before I returned, afraid that Graciela was putting horns on me, afraid of having writer's block forever. Everything has its price and everyone pays as best they can. I don't have a car or a color TV, and my wife needs bras and we don't have kids because there'd be nowhere for them to sleep except in our bed, but all that's my choice. Still, I often ask myself if all that's right, if our living like that is inevitable. Honestly, I don't know. The screwed-up thing is that life is a one-off project and if you make a mistake, you'll never have time to put it right."

"But you could change the project."

"No, I couldn't. Don't give me fairy tales. Tell me, are you so sure you didn't make a mistake?"

Frankie sipped his coffee and lit another cigarette.

"No. I think about it every day. And I know it's going to be very hard for me ever to be happy again."

"Oh, *happiness*? Did you see the two paintings in the Velázquez exhibition called *View of the Garden of the Villa Medici*?"

Frankie thought for a moment before answering.

"The ones that look like impressionists?"

"Those very ones. That is the most perfect example of happiness I know. I think if one day I could write something like that or feel as if I were really there myself, I think I could be happy."

"You're really going bonkers."

"Better said, I'm mad already. But I know what I'm saying. You can't go through your whole life demolishing buildings or thinking everything's a pile of shit. Once in a while you have to create something like that even if you're not a genius like Velázquez."

There was a sudden silence at the table. Frankie and Mauricio looked straight at each other. Mauricio saw a tear gathering in his old friend and companion's eye and lowered his gaze so as not to see him cry.

"Do you realize we might be seeing each other for the last time?" Frankie asked, and Mauricio nodded without looking at him.

"Just thank God we saw each other again at all. There were things I had no idea about and now . . ."

"You were always more sentimental than me, that's why you could never explain what you had done. But I'm happy to have seen you and to have eaten this wonderful steak. Go on, order more wine," said Mauricio and without thinking he took the last cigarette from the packet and calmly lit it. "Everyone has their own cross to bear, right? That's the truth of it. Did you notice the ass on Velázquez's Venus?"

Madrid was getting cold now. The street thermometer showed seven degrees and even though the meat and the wine cushioned the cold, Mauricio regretted not having drunk the eau-de-vie Frankie ordered with their last coffee. However, he enjoyed walking through this frozen, semideserted city at this hour. During his two years in Luanda, it was forbidden to walk the city after six in the evening, and to be able to wander the streets again at dawn gave him back one of his most treasured habits. He imagined himself wandering through Madrid with María Fernanda whom he had met in the Prado, standing bewitched by Velázquez's happiness and by the calm of the *View of the Garden of the Villa Medici.* He recognized her immediately and he said, You are María Fernanda and I've come to give your book back, and they both realized at last that they had been looking for each other for many years . . .

"I don't want to say good-bye," said Frankie and lingered on the pavement. "I know it's going to be irreversible. Why don't we just walk a bit along here . . ."

"It's already irreversible, *man,*" said Mauricio and smiled. Then he realized it was a poor joke and regretted it. "Let's go to the Puerta de Alcalá, go on, stop a cab."

They drove in silence. Some of the thermometers were showing five degrees and Mauricio wanted another cigarette. The taxi left them on the corner where they'd met and Frankie paid.

"Hey, compadre," said Mauricio, "give me your cigarettes."

Frankie smiled and passed him the pack of Kaiser from which only a couple were missing.

"Are you going to take up smoking again?"

"I think so. Here, take one."

They lit up and smiled.

"Mauricio, do you need money for anything? Your wife's bras? Anything?"

"No, I don't think the bras will cost more than sixteen dollars and I don't even think I'll have time to buy them."

"Take this money to buy yourself a bottle of whiskey at the airport."

"Don't, Frankie. There are some things, as you said, that are irreversible . . . Make me a present of your lighter."

Frankie hastily found the gold lighter in his pocket and gave it to his friend. Mauricio looked at it and said thanks, and he put it in the same pocket from which he took the book. He looked at the jacket a moment where, under the title and Emma Micheletti's name was a detail from *Las Hilanderas*. The drawing seemed to glow in the amber of the streetlights. Mauricio thumbed through the book and stopped at page 23, looked at Frankie, and read.

"'On his return to Rome, Velázquez visited the Villa Medici again and was intensely moved by the sweet poetry of the time and place. Everything he paints almost seems to be an echo of a distant moment in time, reencountered and experienced once again with a deeper, more mature sensibility.' . . . María Fernanda marked this passage. For some reason, God knows why, it had seemed important to her. It's good to think that we will visit the Medici gardens again one day. Take it, I'm giving it to you," and he held the book out to Frankie. "From me and from María Fernanda," he added and threw his cigarette butt onto the street.

"Thanks," said Frankie after rereading the passage marked in red ink.

"See you later, man," said Mauricio and began to walk away. He felt his throat burning, and he knew it was not from the cold nor the cigarettes but something much deeper and, yes, irreversible. He circled the Puerta de Alcalá and stood at the spot from which he had admired it earlier. There were the Dutch tulips, fresh and gallant, Charles III's triumphal chariot, and the perfect symmetrical arches leading in and out of Madrid. Looking through the central arch he saw, at the other end of the street, an elegant man dressed in gray with a book in his hand, etched against the cloud of golden light spilling from the streetlights. It was like an unreal vision, appearing from a distant moment in time, to be reencountered and experienced once again with a deeper, more mature sensibility. At last he began to cry.

*Translated by Claudia Lightfoot*

꙾꙾꙾꙾꙾꙾꙾꙾꙾꙾꙾꙾꙾꙾

**C. A. AGUILERA**

꙾꙾꙾꙾꙾꙾꙾꙾꙾꙾꙾꙾꙾

# Journey to China

In China the highways are made of mud. The mud is red, and when it solidifies it looks like a sculpture of smooth clay. On the outskirts of Beijing there is an area where the mud is gray. They call that place the "round enamel vessel."

The highways are long. They are not level and they are narrow.

There are two lanes: pedestrians walk on the left, with an invisible separation from the traffic that everyone senses. Long trucks manufactured in the republic pass on the right. If someone with a car (for example, a 1975 Oldsmobile) wishes to travel on those highways, the person is obliged to obtain federal permission a week ahead of time. If permission is not obtained, the person is fined and taken to the district police office. There, the person's driver's license is suspended for several months.

Chinese highways are very complex. There are lowland highways and mountain highways. The first three days after leaving Beijing we were on mountain highways. These highways make life difficult. Not just because of their constant vertical climb but because of the drizzle, the mist, and their seemingly endless dimension.

Obviously, for the Chinese everything on the highways is easier. In the West there is a proverb, according to Michaux, which says, "Only the Chinese can draw a line on the horizon." After ascending the Beijing/Beijing Outskirts highway for three days, I never tired of repeating this proverb.

Along mountain highways this trip is shorter. If we needed three days on mountain highways to leave Beijing, on lowland highways (sometimes more slanted and winding) we would need five. The only difference is that the lowland highways are paved.

A mountain highway leads to two or three lowland highways. One in general runs straight ahead, toward some town or museum; another runs backward, toward a plain or a piece of wall; another branches off from the first and gets lost in another direction.

According to the Great Mongol, the chauffeur granted by the republic's Ministry of Culture, those highways that stop after passing through some fortress merge again into the principal artery of the low, forming a serpent with large and small rings across the whole territory.

The main problem on the mountain highways is the mud. When it rains, the road becomes impossible. When it does not rain, given the fact that the earth is finer than any reserve known in the West, the highway becomes slippery and it becomes impossible for either people or cars to proceed.

One very sunny day we saw a string of ten trucks in a pile-up that slid constantly without being able to do anything but try to come to rest against something.

On mountain highways there are stones. Not little stones, but big ones. Stones the size of a house that a Westerner could climb only by scaling them.

In those places, to the delight of travelers, one finds the Chinese monkey men. These men with just their hands, and without bracing their feet, climb stones on the mountain. When they reach the top they jump as though the "exploit" could never be repeated again.

These stones add greater beauty to the landscape. They make it harsh, and when they are observed up close they smell like cow manure and lead. From a distance, these stones look like cardboard.

If in the West the landscape suggests greenery—stretches of grass with rivers, lagoons, mountains, and so on—in China it is not so. In China the landscape is mental. The stones become little brains that observe, and their eyes cannot rest a minute as they keep vigil.

Once, walking from Shexuon to Huangcheihuan, we saw how several people hit each other, trying to strangle each other, and one ran to a cliff on the edge of the mountain, opened his arms, and jumped. It is common knowledge that this type of suicide happens frequently in the republic; they call it "disjointed movement toward sleep."

On the mountain highways there are fried-food stands. These stands are attended by people who wear costumes typical of the region and who sing quietly while the diners stick their fingers in sweet-and-sour sauce and put them in their mouths.

The stands are small. They have enough space for two people and a medium-size flat metal grill with little rectangular pieces of coal. When the vendor serves, the woman squats next to a wooden stool and watches. Later she runs to offer *xixem* and sticks the color of mother-of-pearl. These sticks, they said before retiring, mean good luck, and they give them to all who visit.

These stands are easily recognized and are present throughout the republic.

At night they are illuminated by lights of different colors.

## THE GREAT MONGOL

The Great Mongol is small (approximately five feet, four inches) with slanted eyes; he is yellow and fat. His beige jacket and his manner of walking make him look like one of Ozu's little men. He is about fifty-two years old.

On mountain highways he steers around trucks very well, and he passes with caution. When he speaks about them he calls them the enemy (opening and closing his hand). On lowland highways he drives fast, speeding up or slowing down as required for us to take photographs.

Some nights when we stop in a hotel, the Great Mongol sings. He goes to the karaoke (called in Cantonese a "repetition box") and sings annoying songs: "New York, New York," in Frank Sinatra's style, or Chinese pop ballads. (Since neither Maki nor I understand, we prefer to look at the decor or go out to chat as we walk through the town.)*

Every entry of the Great Mongol into a repetition box can last two or three hours. Everyone sits around a table and talks quietly. If someone tells a joke, they smile with a single outburst of laughter, which explodes quickly and stops, in complete contrast to the West with its drawn-out laughter.

When someone decides to sing they stop talking. They look with wide-open eyes toward the stage and applaud. Afterward, they invite the singer to the table and make him drink "dragon cola" and chew "caterpillars from heaven." They ask him about

---

* For reasons of style, Maki speaks little or never in "Journey to China." I did not know how to depict her, nor how to elaborate situations in which she appears with other people. As a result, one should not think that our journey was always "a sea of peace and calm." Besides sharing good times and visiting places worthy of photographing, we had our disagreements also. Thus, if she appears little or not at all, it is for reasons of style, never for revenge. A journey, however mundane it might be, is also a work of fiction.

his family and introduce him to the rest of the diners with customary bowing. Later, everyone bids farewell.

Because the Great Mongol knows songs in English, the applause doubles and they continually insist that he keep singing.

If the applause is insufficient, the Great Mongol drives as though the mud highways were paved. He accelerates deliriously and brakes suddenly, he beats on the steering wheel, he stamps his foot . . .

If the applause has been sufficient, he drives in a good mood, at the speed necessary for us to handle a Polaroid camera, and he asks permission to turn on the radio.

On those days he is a great help. He talks little and chooses places that, according to him, are pure photography. When I argue, he answers: Westerners do not know how to frame a portrait. They are too slow.

## REPETITION BOXES

In China, in contrast to the West, the karaoke bars or repetition boxes (*huanxhipo*) are small. There are only four or five tables and a large television. The one who is singing stands in the middle and is applauded when finished. Nobody who is not Western laughs.

The people who work in the repetition boxes are young: girls from fifteen to twenty-five years old dressed in red-checked short skirts and white blouses. None wears chains or bracelets, just a tattoo on the upper right arm. To call them one must say "miss" and snap one's fingers. They all think for some reason that the client speaks English and they run immediately to practice speaking it. When they realize that the client is not American they smile.

In the repetition boxes alcoholic beverages are not sold. *Xixem* is sold, as in the fried-food stands, as well as tea from the country's different regions.

There is a tea called "dragon cola," another called "water from the Yangtze," and another called "spring stroll."

The "dragon cola" is drunk with oil. It is prepared with *buanxhi* (beet sugar) according to taste, and according to the instructions it is recommended for rheumatism. It is made with flowers from the region of Huangcheihuan.

The "water from the Yangtze" is drunk cold. It is garnet-colored and served in porcelain cups with transparent eyelets. If one lifts up these cups one will see how the eyelets change and take on the color of the light that illuminates them. This tea grows in Jiayum (central China).

The "spring stroll" is white. It is made by grinding sprouts of *guin,* a shrub that grows in Xonjhia, and it ferments with cinnamon, ginger, and flower petals. It is consumed throughout the republic and in some places they add ground peanuts, something that enhances the flavor. Because of its thick consistency (and the slowness with which one must drink it), they call it dialogue tea.

In the repetition boxes there are no decorations.

Their walls are covered with dark taffeta like that used by plumbers to bundle their tools, and the lights hang inside the finely crafted lanterns that are changed according to the season: red for winter, green for autumn, white for spring, blue for summer.

At the end of the year, these boxes are converted into little rice salons. The women adorn themselves with traditional costumes that vary according to ethnicity, and they serve little plates with half-prepared ingredients at each table. Afterward they form a line and perform a welcoming ritual for the new year.

That day going to bed early is "prohibited."


## LANTERNS

In the republic the lanterns are made of paper.

If in the West the lights are hidden behind different kinds of lamp shades, in China there is no variety. The craftsmen manufacture paper lanterns (from rice, onion, or tree fiber) and the only thing that changes is the decorative emblem or sketch.

For the Chinese, perfection does not mean inventing new things constantly but rather reaching the ultimate degree of subtlety in the repetition of the same thing. Thus, for millennia they have been practicing this art.

The lanterns can be square, round, or rectangular. They are folded when they are intended for the entrance hall of a house, or smooth when they are going to hang in a hotel parlor.

Some have landscapes: a bird on a branch, a stone, a bridge, a hunting scene. Others are decorated with inspirational messages.

The inside of these lanterns is very simple: a wooden framework of rectangular sticks, and special glue to bond the sticks. After two days outside in the fresh air, the frame is papered and sold.

Now this art has become vulgarized because of its success. For example, in a go-go in Jiayum we saw large paper lanterns (almost a yard long) with masochistic/erotic designs: a Chinaman with a whip beats another one while a woman passes her tongue over the wounds and another woman with a manipulable phallus sodomizes him.

But, in general, the lanterns are small and contain traditional messages: "luck in future life" or "a person who does not trust his family will never be able to trust himself."

Since the beginning of the 1960s these lanterns have been exported.

## LOWLAND HIGHWAYS

The lowland highways are vast. They cross the country from one province to another and facilitate journeys and the transport of merchandise. There is no town or city that does not depend on the highways. If a purchase is to be made, one goes out to one of the places constructed along the highways. If one is looking for entertainment, one does the same. The highways are pipelines of impulses. People drive along them at high speed and they only brake because of hunger or boredom. The only problem is that they lengthen journeys.

If a mountain highway reduces the distance from one place to another, a paved highway goes around the obstacle until it hooks up with another stretch of road and continues.

There is no lowland highway in the republic that sustains a straight line for fifty miles. There is always a rise or a drop, a deviation or a descent.

This has converted China into chaos, where the constant flux of cars and people resembles worms that wiggle through the rotted eyes of an animal.

On lowland highways time does not pass. Journeys are so long that alongside hotels, coffee shops, garages, road movies, and Buddhist temples, a proliferation of little green cabins has sprung up to relieve tension.

The traveler enters these cabins (there are approximately five together, one next to another) and with a solid ball breaks objects that shatter and produce a sound similar to crystal: glasses, cups, mirrors, framed portraits, and so on.

It is said that this sound is much more relaxing than one or two hours of sleep, and it seems to be true. After having traveled for five days on lowland highways and three on mountain highways, we laughed again and spoke of the possibilities offered by a foreign society for a photographer interested in "the political ritual of objects" and "areas of devastation on the outskirts of the city."

The lowland highways have very dangerous curves.

On one of them (Zhuixin-Luanpong) we observed some of the most talked-about collisions in the republic: two Fiat trucks hit head on, with eight fatalities, and the road was closed for six hours.

According to the authorities, the bodies of the passengers

were mutilated, and of the two children in the Fiats they found only one leg and pieces of a body.

In this region (south curve of Luanpong) the landscape is very arid. Great extensions of land reach into the distance, and there are burned trees and stench.

Other places are not like this. In other places one sees a town in the distance or peasants in rice paddies or mountains or remains of the great Chu wall. But in this area there are bloodstains, continuous wrecks, and bones.

The most beautiful landscape that we observe on the lowland highways is that of a coffee shop (half American style, half traditional restaurant) surrounded by cows and an extensive pasture with water troughs all around.

According to what they told us, the owner of the coffee shop is the owner of the cows, and each morning he puts them out to pasture behind his business until night, at which time he herds them into a hut.

In the republic animals are very closely controlled.

The owners of cows—in general owners of businesses—contract with the regional public authority (*huanzzo*) to avoid illegal traffic and indiscriminate slaughter of animals. This has converted the *huanzzo* into an efficient public agency, with authority to go out freely through the area to inspect all the towns. On the stretch of highway from Huangcheihuan to Juyonggtai alone they searched us ten times.

When a foreigner arrives in a town, the people usually try to sell him little carved figures of Buddha or representations in imitation ivory of the goddess Zhao Ta with her arms raised to spread rain across the fields.

To make these sales they place tables in the doors of their houses. Ocher awnings with messages in English invite the client to notice "the harmony possessed by the face of Buddha, of Zhao Ta, or of Mo Lao Zhu." If the customer makes a decision, he only has to reach out his arm and say "eh" with his mouth half closed, and immediately they will place the figurine in a little box, and bowing their heads they present the client with the box.

The most that a carving of Buddha can cost is seventy cents.

## OPIUM DENS

Opium dens are prohibited in the republic.

A decree issued in the late 1960s legally closed all the dens and made opium and the culture it had generated a "perversion." The law sent the east-west emperors to jail for twenty years and prohibited any public reference or mention of the matter.

If a Westerner wanted to visit the dens now he would have to make a "descent into hell." First, because of the scarcity of opium and the fear generated by the state's repression. Second, because of the control of the current *wangxhi* and the long journeys required to reach them.

In all of China there are no more than a dozen dens, hidden in old country houses or in abandoned fortresses in the outskirts. Nevertheless, they are always full and they are vacated only when the opium runs out or when the weather, for one reason or another, prevents travel to those places.

The first thing they serve in the dens are the pipes: they are long and bear a bronze plate with the name and year of production (Sun Over Jiayum, 1912).

Second, the opium.

Contrary to Western belief, there are various types of opium, although the dens in western China specialize in three types:

Gray opium (or bird's smile)

Bladder green opium (or dragon's breath)

Mud red opium (or stars behind the mountains)

Gray opium awakens the senses and calms physical pain. It induces sleep, well-being, relief . . . In its unrefined state it is soluble in water.

Bladder green opium produces hallucinations, excitation.

It is consumed for better sexual function, and besides being smoked, it is chewable.

Mud red opium is the intense opium. It makes the individual enter into a state of lucidity, and it is what students consume most frequently, in the form of cigarettes or mixed with tobacco before exams.

According to Wei, an employee of the Sun Over Jiayum, opium enters the bloodstream when three pipes are smoked and one can stop to observe "the waves that the bull makes in the great lake."

The faces of the people who frequent the dens are striking: drawn like the skin of a fruit and toothless, with grayish gums, slack-jawed, and pale complexion; with pipes in their mouths all the time, walking and talking alone, as though they had broken a complex code that is difficult to solve.

These persons are called *gutan,* which means "one who circles his own head."

Women also go to the dens, although something curious happens in their case: they are given free opium with the condition that later they rise to the podium to narrate what they "observe." Thus it was that when we were consuming the opium of excitation, a woman confirmed that she "saw" a horse circling a tree that, instead of fruit, bore mice. The image of a mouse (or a rat) hanging from a branch left me thinking and I began to imagine mice everywhere: mice like tow trucks, mice like hammers, mice like hatchets, and mice like mouths that bit and hung above me showing their teeth. One of them said, "I am above the concept of a mouse," and he tried to cut off my arm.

One of the peculiarities of the dens is their screens, which are rectangular and white. When the women stop speaking, pornographic films or amateur films of girls discussing their sexual experiences are shown. It seems that this type of "documentary" is the most popular. There are no scenes of violence, nor are there persons in any determined position, but just a girl, a close-up shot or normal frame shot, and she discusses how she had sex with this or that person. It is true that these stories are full of minute details.

When a movie is not projected, the atmosphere in the dens is peaceful, with light music that helps metabolize the opium in a fog where things—heads and pipes included—seem to float.

Months later, when we had settled again back in the West, we received a letter from the Great Mongol explaining, along with photos depicting arrests and the places that had been found, how some dens had been dismantled. In one of these photos there is a person whose arms are being held by one policeman while another kicks him in the head.

The newspapers called this operation "moving the furniture without disturbing the dust that covers it."

## CONTORTIONISM

In China contortionism is a tradition. It is taught from family to family, and it is practiced in improvised circuses or alongside highways. Sometimes it is a woman, sometimes a woman and a man, sometimes two men.

The woman that impressed us most was the one we later called the woman of Zhinku. She twisted herself very slowly, and in her movements there was something more than the technical pleasure of moving her feet from one side to another. She did it so calmly that you scarcely noticed, like a spring that is compressed under pressure.

One of her numbers took place on top of a cow. When she had assumed the strangest position, the cow circled the audience, allowing different views from several angles and with varying light. Then the cow would remain motionless except for the movement of its tail, which produced a muffled crack. The woman's rigidity and the sonorous wagging of the tail constituted yet another spectacle.

The most incredible thing about this contortionist is that

when she performed she did not move her eyes. Her concentration was such that she could remain for hours in that state without looking anywhere. When she finished, she untied her body from its knot and got up, slowly moving her arms with movements of her shoulders and elbows and straightening her legs gradually, until she was standing.

Once when we saw her on the Zhinku-Befendong stretch of highway, she said, "Contortionism is the art of talking with nobody hearing you."

## BOLL WEEVILS

The boll weevil is small and ocher-colored. Its colonies are organized into states, and it is one of the most feared populations in western China and south-central China.

It is known that a plague of boll weevils can devour entire fields of cotton in a few hours.

The interesting thing about this insect is that it not only destroys the plant, but it also loosens the soil and decreases its mineral content, something that does not happen with locusts or with other insects. When a colony settles in a field, as a result of the poisons and insecticides that are used to eliminate them, the land cracks (*funxawhi*) and becomes sandy; extremely fertile fields are converted into near desert.

Because the boll weevil is such a small animal (two centimeters at most), its populations are numerous and its activity is rapid. The male spends the day devouring cotton, biting leaves, and chewing stems; the female builds nests.

When an entire field of boll weevils is exterminated, the peasants gather them with sticks and pile them in four or five heaps the size of *suizhe* (toolsheds). Afterward, they soak the land and the heaps with oil and light them. There is no movement so beautiful as that of the females running across the ground to avoid being burned and that of the fire across the land frying them.

Only a few save themselves from this burning. The children trap them, cut them in half, and fry them on a flatiron; later they chew them for a snack.

The boll weevil can live up to four months under favorable conditions.

## WAR MUSEUMS

The war museums are like little puppet theaters. They have been put together with large black-and-white photographs accompanied by nameplates identifying the hero, his birthplace, and his dates of birth and death. These panels with images of dead men, without eyes, or tortured, are known in the region as the sons of the people.

Behind the museums are little cemeteries. There is a stone vault with glass windows and small boxes with dust inside. In front of the vault are stone benches for family and friends.

Because the museums are tense places, the republic's musicians, commissioned by the state, compose solemn pieces to help create an atmosphere and to give these places the pathos that they would not have otherwise.

Thus it was that when we visited Fonxhuá with a group of Lithuanians, we saw several women frightened by the "force" of the photos and the music that split their heads like a hammer.

Lola, a white crane,* added the comic touch. Lola is the symbol of the museum and the mascot of Comrade Chung, secretary of finance of the republic. Lola began pursuing the Lithuanians and pecking the panels where every day the visitors show reverence to the sons of the people. When we left, we saw how those faces with holes for eyes and bloodstains on their mouths seemed less like heroes and more like dolls perforated by horror.

---

* So called for the coloring acquired by its feathers and feet when it flies.

Because the idea behind the museums is to create a natural sensation, one of its strategies is to use samples: boots with mud and saliva, pieces of a watch with the remains of a skull, armor with bullet marks, stained chamber pots, and so on.

This has converted Fonxhuá into one of the most visited sites. There in a display case are the hands of General Wong, a guerrilla military genius. According to the pamphlet (*Treasures of Fonxhuá Museum*), this general was captured by an infantry group, and one of the tortures to which he was subjected consisted of cutting his hands little by little until he bled to death. Later his hands were given to the Maoist front and exhibited as an ideological relic "for the new generations to come." (From close-up, each hand can be seen to have an inventory number and an identification mark.)

Nevertheless, in spite of their association with death, the museums are excellent places to rest. They allow escape from tedium caused by days on the highway, and they have little stores that sell banners with slogans and parasols. There is only one drawback: it is forbidden to take photos.

## FREEWAYS

The freeways of western China are famous. They stretch out like earthworms on the outskirts of towns and connect these towns with corridors of movement in all directions.

The best thing about these freeways is that they do not become clogged with traffic. They have been designed with ramps on the sides and with shaded lookouts for observing the nearest cities.

Thus, Huangcheihuan can be seen in its relation to Lake Yantzu or to the bridges that cross the different bends of the rivers and that divide the city into two islands. One is to the south (the old city), with little antiquarian shops and a bohemian life without par in all the republic; the other is to the northeast (the new city), with the most robust economic sector and the most technocratic jails in all of China.

The curious thing about these freeways is that they cross the city very harmoniously, above the highest buildings or the trailer-style houses visible in almost all of the republic. And they do so without disturbing the architecture or the landscape, and without converting the city into a mass of flying iron and hardware.

One morning, walking through Huangcheihuan, we had the impression that we were the incarnation of characters in some documentary about the American Midwest.

One of the attractions of the freeways is their temples. They are painted green and have a narrow room with a cardboard Buddha a foot and a half tall. Because the journeys from one province to another can take days, the monks of the republic take these prefabricated temples along all the highways (hitched to a truck that they drive themselves) and they "open" them along certain stretches. It is not difficult to see a small line in front of the temple, one or two people praying, or a family in silence.

These trucks that tow temples with dwarflike Buddhas painted white have resulted in the phrase "highway Buddhism."

The difference between this Buddhism and that which is practiced in traditional temples rests in the manner in which the ritual drum (*ko'on*) is played: much softer and without intermissions, with several blows that are repeated without variation while the people are in a state of rest. This music continues until the practitioner "wakes up" or arises, which is done not suddenly but rather slowly, and then the practitioner leaves after a few seconds.

The price of admission to these places is twenty yuan.

If a truck breaks down or blows a tire, the monks fix it without any help. According to the Great Mongol, they are bad drivers and good mechanics, and they have been the cause of hundreds of accidents. They cause extremely dangerous situations on the highway. People still remember the day when one of these monks fell asleep at the wheel and killed fourteen children when he leveled a school in the region of Shi. The monk fled, leaving the statue of Buddha—smiling—which fell from the truck and remained in an upright position in the midst of the blood and the moaning. Since then, thousands of believers have made pilgrimages to this place; they call it "Buddha's dwelling in Shi."*

What is certain is that each time we see a monk repairing a truck or wiping grease off his fingers, we ask ourselves how this is possible and we smile. More than monks, they seem like little demons in a Buñuel movie.

The week before we left, we stopped at one of the intersections of a lowland highway with a freeway, and we tried to photograph the monks. They did not allow it. They behaved very timidly. After covering their faces, walking around, and shouting among themselves, they approached us with closed fists and threw stones. When we were relatively far away, we stopped and made faces. One of them laughed, pulled out his penis, and urinated. That attitude undermined everything we had thought about Buddhism until that moment.

The *Huangcheihuan Sun* has revealed that in all the republic there are more than one thousand trucks dedicated to Buddha.

---

* To be exact, it should be stated that of the types of Buddhas that circulate throughout the republic (the smiling one, the Buddha of harmony, the melancholy one, the wet one in the muddy rain), the Buddha of fertility is the most sought after. He is represented with a serious face with no sad expressions, and he is the only one who does not cross his arms or let them hang, but rather his arms are half extended in front of him with open hands. Couples dedicate themselves to him, and it is customary for the women to kiss the index finger of his right hand three times saying, "Buddha of fertility, show me the way" (*xicho padme kung no fa*). Upon retiring, they must bow their heads and not turn their backs until they have left the temple. For this wish to be fulfilled, one must drink the tea known as "spring stroll" for three consecutive days.

## B.

Beijing is an empire. It is the political city par excellence, and according to what people confessed to us, nothing moves without the state's knowing it. For this purpose the republic applies extreme measures, making sure that each citizen watches the others and denounces them before legal bodies charged with prosecuting the individual and fabricating a chain of guilt and pardon.

The case of the two carpenters is still famous. In the face of the accusation of illegally selling burnished wood, one by one they denounced fifty-two persons, including administrators and master workers in charge of controlling the market and regulating prices. This caused the wood to become unavailable, and wood-carvers and cabinetmakers had to work at other trades until the authorities forgot the case and the wood business became strong again.

This is not meant to horrify the reader. The citizens of Beijing are very phlegmatic, and they like to perceive their lives as though they were comedies of errors. These legal judgments awaken more a desire to persist than they do anxiety.

If there were one word to define B. it would be this one: model. The city is built along straight avenues with wide streets, and its architecture is both traditional and modern in style. From a tall building all other buildings can be seen, and such a view offers an impression similar to that offered by cities in northern Europe. The vision is confusing. Beijing is a caricature, and more than a city it seems like a deceptive machine. The buildings have been fitted with lights and covered windows, while the houses, in neoclassic style, have a pagoda roof or other element that makes the medley of styles more apparent.

The same thing is apparent with the churches: 30 percent of them are Catholic. They are built from a material derived from plastic, reinforced with rubber and gravel, and are painted red or magenta with windows all around and a cross on top. The Great Mongol, with a little smile, says that they are God's coffee shops.

Another of the attractions in B. is the machines that produce money (*gonsuwhoxig*). The young people gather around and for a few coins they win the equivalent of five dollars. It is terrible when these metal boxes become jammed. All Chinese temperance dissipates, and they kick the machine until it works or returns the money. Then the client goes off smiling to another machine.

One afternoon, walking toward the house of Lu Zhimou (a writer), we saw several adolescents dismantle one of these machines and beat the district watchman before running away.

Nevertheless, Beijing is a peaceful city. There are hardly any thieves, and the majority of deaths result not from assaults and robberies but rather from people going out after the 10:00 P.M. curfew. After this hour it is impossible to find public transportation, and sick or injured people must wait until six in the morning to reach the hospital.

Thus it was that, in Zhimou's house, some writers excused themselves, explaining that they had to leave early because people found on the street after curfew are incarcerated for violating the official provisions of the republic. Zhimou told how the writers watch one another and how they have to request "counsel" from the central government to meet with Westerners. If someone defied that rule, most likely he would disappear in a small provincial town.

When I tried to take a photo, they covered the lens and said no. The writers of the nation should not let the West see them. With that they stood up, acted haughty, and left. After a few minutes, Zhimou's wife—in traditional dress and bracelets—appeared with long pipes, little boxes of opium, and tea.

(She did not have to insist much. We accepted.)

## THE AIRPORT

Beijing's airport is like a fishbowl. It was built with thick glass that amplifies visibility and with rolling staircases that interlace the buildings and lead to various waiting areas. When an airplane takes off or lands, these stairs with transparent plastic railings and tan carpet turn the airport into an ant colony.

High up on the walls are stained-glass windows. They are neither small nor medium-size but large. They are more or less twelve feet long. They depict the Chinese via crucis through history, and in one of them a giant Mao appears cutting off the head of a dragon that bleeds from the mouth. This window, face-to-face with the runway, obliges arriving passengers to observe it.

As we approached it, we read, "Only a great leader together with his people is capable of severing the head of the dragon."

In other windows, Mao reaps crops with a sickle and teaches several children to read in a school.

These windows, of flashy colors and fine seams, are the most photographed of the three buildings.

To arrive at the airport one must take several freeways, first the one that leads to Shuking, then the one that passes the thermonuclear plant, and then the definitive one.

As is well known, the freeways have rest areas designed to relieve stress, and when we stopped at one, the unloading of boxes of fish at the docks and the peasants working the soil many miles away seemed more than isolated incidents, but rather they became connected naturally by a singular, unique space.

The same thing happened with the cemetery. From a distance, it looked like a rectangular diagram with signals and arrows; from close-up, it was a place of meditation and "encounter."

The interesting thing about Chinese customs is that, instead of taking flowers or food to the cemeteries (which is normal in various cultures), they take stones labeled with a phrase or image. For example, "your son who still loves you," or a depiction of a family seated at a table. There were tombs with mounds of stones on them and others with two or three stones to the side.

These cemeteries are very sober. Only a cross of wood and cement stuck in the ground and a small bronze plate with the name and dates of the deceased.

Trees surround the cemetery.

The Great Mongol, after kneeling for several minutes, told us how his father sunk a butcher's hook into his mother's neck and dragged her through Shuking "so that she might learn once and for all not to raise her voice at her husband." Afterward he hung her in the town's little shop and fled.

This man, it became known later, was shot trying to cross the border into Siberia.

The airport at Beijing is silent. People do not talk to one another, or they exchange brief words in quiet voices, leaning their heads and mouths quite close to the person whom they are addressing. The movement of the torso makes them seem like punching bags that roll over and rise by themselves.

When we presented our passports in the cabin for verification, the officials began to look at us and observe us slowly, trying to superimpose our faces on those in the passports. It took them several minutes to do so, and we took advantage of this time to bid farewell to the Great Mongol and to give him a hug.

Once inside, a customs officer approached us and by means of gestures let it be known that there were problems with our luggage. In the office, the Polaroid photos (750 in all) were scattered over the table, and two officials examined them carefully. Upon noticing our presence, the male official (in a suit with a short, loose red jacket and with darting eyes) approached me and punched my chest with his index finger and said, "You know nothing about China." To which I did not respond, trying to capture the details of the situation: an iron table, three medium-size photos of directors of the republic, gray walls, a male official, a female official, papers . . .

After placing the photos in uneven stacks, the male official (who went out constantly to consult with someone with a voice like the Great Mongol's) indicated, "These are the ones you can take," pushing forward a stack of about two hundred photos.

I took them and put them in a yellow envelope. When I asked for the others, he looked at us, and almost without opening his mouth, he said, "They distort the image of the republic" (making a gesture that said, "All dialogue finished").

And so we went out onto the runway and joined the line to go up the stairway to the plane. I looked again at Mao. The veins on his face were inflamed and the dragon no longer bled from the mouth, but rather it gyrated frantically upon itself and laughed . . . I tightened my grip on the little package with the photos again. We boarded.

*Translated by Douglas Edward LaPrade*

FRANCISCO GARCÍA GONZÁLEZ

# You Don't Have to Reach Heaven

The sun reflects off the asphalt. For the hundredth time, Ishmael shades his eyes with his hand to his visor, and he sees the truck.

"Five!" calls out the official dressed in yellow, who is allocating seats to people needing rides.

The couple climbs on, the old woman, the girl, and Ishmael, in that order. The old red Ford displays, thanks to its owner's inspiration, a faked coat of arms of the Transportation Ministry: a white-headed eagle lifted from the Harley-Davidson trademark emblem. Rather than hunting for himself, the eagle is snatching the prey caught by other hunters. In his talons the bird holds a gold shield with MITRANS spelled out on a diagonal stripe, and around the shield, in more or less Gothic lettering: FLEET OPERATOR. Fleet operator, a pretty mysterious business in itself, murky, could mean anything. When he was a child, Ishmael used to like coats of arms and medieval things and the knights and castles and banners and broadswords and the Crusades and honor and the Round Table. Under the emblem it says, I KEEP MY HANDS OFF MY FRIEND'S GIRL, and under that, I DON'T HAVE FRIENDS. The success of the joke depends on your attitude toward the girl, comments the yellow-uniformed man to the people who are still waiting for a ride. The truck used to transport cattle but no longer does.

As the girl climbs up the steps, Ishmael takes a good look at her, focusing on her feet first. Her feet are white; the tanner stripes of skin and veins indicate that she was wearing sandals at some earlier time. Unpainted toenails, carefully trimmed and smooth skin, hardly dusted with dirt from the road, suggest that she is a young woman of irreproachable hygienic habits, endowed with a certain degree of discernment.

Toes, heels, veins: it all looks good to him. Next, he takes in the rest of her. Tight jeans, green suitcase, breasts that test the elastic properties of the fabric. The girl wears her hair loose and colored red. Ishmael's experienced eye pulls down her zipper, slides off her jeans, underpants, tank top. Speedy Ishmael. Horny Ishmael. Poor Ishmael. The girl, naked amid the passengers, moves along holding on to the pipe that serves as guardrail, shoving her bag along with her feet. Ishmael moves along cautiously behind her. The space gets blocked and Ishmael's sack brushes against the girl's rump. Ishmael's body shivers and he's sure that she has sensed his riveted attention. Ishmael pulls back, the girl pushes her way forward. Again he unzips her and peels off the tank top. She shoves her suitcase forward. No space to move. Ishmael's got the rhythm of it now and pushes his way forward. This time an imperceptible movement forward presses his member against the delicious curve between her buttocks.

"Oops, sorry," says Ishmael.

The girl nods, her expression conveying, for now, that it can happen, in a truck, swaying from a railing pipe that's barely braced, and in the present scenario of shortages the country is living through, anybody could bump against her rear end, whether or not she or the involuntary aggressor likes it. Then she looks toward the road. They're going past one orange orchard after another, on both sides of the power line. She smooths her hair.

Ishmael can see her sweaty neck. His body hunger pushes him into inertia and its equations. Their speed and acceleration are interrupted in a new stretch of their journey. Ishmael's waist is at the height of the girl's hip as she stands facing the guardrail, her profile to Ishmael. For the first time he notices the hands holding on to the pipe. Her hands, just like her feet, are out of the ordinary. No polish on her fingernails either. Tiny islands of invisible blond down, delicate palms, lovely long fingers, hands curved around the pipe and Ishmael sliding closer, his hand now very close to hers. The girl gazes at the road, counting the rows of orange trees one after another, the posts, the clouds. The Iberia plane is a slow white line against the blue. Ishmael watches her gazing at the road. Women are terrible at geography. It's all set up for them by their hormonal maps: no innate sense of direction; a vague limbo with no spatial orientation; he remembers hearing this on some radio program. He slides his hand along the coolness of the metal pipe, the edge of his palm brushes the girl's fingers. Her fingernails are right next to Ishmael's dark hands. Her eyes are fixed on the landscape. Ishmael undresses her again. The suitcase is on the floor and he can't see her feet. Does this girl have any idea that Cirilo Villaverde used to travel along here on his way to Vuelta Abajo?* He can't tell from her expression whether she's aware of this at all. Ishmael moves his hand up; his knuckles are under her fingers. Ishmael squeezes his hand hard around the pipe; the girl barely manages to hang on.

---

* Cirilo Villaverde (1812–94): journalist, newspaper editor, and author of some twenty romantic novels, including the well-known *Cecilia Valdés o La Loma del Angel* (1839, 1882), in which the white son of a sugar plantation owner and his mulatto half sister are lovers; and *La excursión a Vuelta Abajo,* about the sugar-growing region where "You Don't Have to Reach Heaven" is set. Villaverde was very active in the movement for Cuban independence and was arrested for taking part in a conspiracy in Vuelta Abajo and in other uprisings. He was sentenced to death but escaped in 1849 and lived in exile in New York for most of the rest of his life.—Trans.

"Five!" calls out the ride allocator at the next stop.

In the shuffle of people getting on and off, her body gets pressed up against Ishmael's. Each one is aware of the other's heat.

Some people think that names make people who they are; it's an idea as old as it is naive, probably even fatuous or uncivilized, thinks Ishmael. But this woman could be named Blanca Felipe. That's pretty good, Blanca Felipe, the name suits her. Blanca Felipe evokes the protective rind that peels back dutifully when a fruit is ripe, the aroma of flowers at dusk after a rain shower. Blanca Felipe Blanca Felipe Blanca Felipe. Blanca Felipe's fingers on the knuckles of his clenched fist. Blanca Felipe walks nude from a room to the balcony, her swan's curve rump moves flexibly as Ishmael watches. Right when she crosses by the doorway, the breeze blows the transparent curtains and they cover Blanca Felipe's body. Her shoulders fall in distress. The girl moves her hand a long way from Ishmael's, closes her eyes and leans her head against her forearm. Ishmael reads this gesture as one of gentle fatigue rather than as one of rejection. Blanca Felipe open flower, juicy fruit offering itself, thick lips. Woman with half-closed eyes, head resting on her forearm. An old-fashioned title: *Image of Nude Woman Seen Through Transparent Curtain That Enfolds Her Body.* Ishmael sighs. He moves his hand along the pipe to the left. No one in his life has ever been named Blanca Felipe. It was the name he made up the night he made love on a stairway to a woman who trembled uncontrollably and wrote him letters she didn't mail from any post office or even put into stamped envelopes because she herself was the mail carrier and the message, and Ishmael's chest was the distant mailbox. It only happened once. Ishmael read the letter, while on the second step she watched him with her hands intertwined. Ishmael moved up to the second step; she went up to the third. When he pulled her to him, he realized that she was naked under her dress. "I wore it for you." The white-painted stairway reminded him of an eighteenth-century painting of a court scene. Beside a staircase, a group of idling courtiers wearing wigs was gathered around a woman playing a clavichord. The picture hung on a dining room wall at Ishmael's house. That day Ishmael decided to call the unnamed woman Blanca Felipe. Eventually, the woman went off with her husband to a distant kingdom. Ishmael stayed on this side of the world with the letters and a name that evoked the soft rind of ripe fruits, the aroma and freshness of orange trees in blossom.

The girl, not named Blanca Felipe at all, feels under her fingers the hand of the guy who got on behind her. The man's hand is hot and sweaty. She pulls away from it, but their arms press together. His arm is aggressive enough to make her react and realize that, as so many times before, she is the victim of a subtle pursuit. She looks at the man out of the corner of her eye. Disgusting, not her taste, she could never sleep with a guy like that. To be even more sure, she looks at his hands. Small, hairy, short, thick fingers. His fingernails aren't really filthy, but his hands are sweaty, his skin dark. His arm is sweating, too. She pulls hers away. Glancing at him, she can see how he's also peering sidelong at her. It's got to be the same guy who was pressing up against her bottom while she was hoisting the suitcase up. A guy like that— and here we have one of those bizarre coincidences unregistered by any form of memory—with dark skin, sweaty, short, low class, probably a real thug, insensitive, hateful, could only be named Ishmael. What an ordinary name, Ishmael. "Call me Ishmael," she'd never forget that book that began like that and was about whales, ships, crazy seamen. And as if that weren't enough, the main character was called nothing more and nothing less than Ishmael. That baffling book haunted her. The same ghoulish pleasure with which her boyfriend and some of his friends listened to the radio program *Point of View* had made her start reading that novel at least ten times in her life. Without ever getting beyond page twenty-five. The girl, not named anything like Blanca Felipe at all, hated the sea and the name Ishmael because hate for her father is the oldest and most deeply engrained feeling she has. She looks at this other Ishmael's hands. "Call me Ishmael," the guy seems to be saying to her. What else could a guy like this with such repulsive hands be called? He probably beats up on his girl. What could this Ishmael's girl be like? And she imagines the man hitting some guy who sobs in a corner like a little fag. "No, please no, honey, no, don't be like this with me." But it could just as easily be . . . a helpless woman in that same corner, sobbing her heart out after a beating. Her good taste and liking for the tiniest details made her imagine the victims stripped down to their underwear. In both cases, they've been slugged for being unfaithful to Ishmael. "No, honey, don't be like this, it's not what you think," sniveled each one in turn. She's witnessed this scene, the general layout of it, thousands of times. Ishmael, her drunk father beating up her mother. By the time she was thirteen, she'd known for a while that her father was an alcoholic. One day in school when she was leafing through the biology textbook, she came across a chapter about the effects of alcohol on the body. The text was written with the intent of impressing and convincing a thirteen-year-old that alcohol was something truly poisonous. And she was convinced. She thought about taking the book to her father and showing him the picture of the liver of an alcoholic compared to that of a nondrinker. The diseased liver—said the words under the picture—was the color and consistency of a charred rock. That day Ishmael, obscene and brutal, took off from home as he did from time to time.

"Five! As far as the compañera with the sack!"

Another group of people climbed into the truck. Ishmael in the midst of the brief jostle of humanity sticks as if casually to his place just behind *his* Blanca Felipe's rump. Blanca Felipe is sandwiched between the hunter and a passenger. Alert. In keeping with her role in the hunt, she feels Ishmael's prick against her bottom, and she thinks she can intuit the filth accumulated under there, between the glans and the foreskin. All calm, finally.

The closeness and the contact with the girl's body excite Ishmael. But Ishmael is timid, and any effort to approach Blanca Felipe with words seems almost impossible to him. Out of habit, he briefly considers the trite gambit of asking what time it is. Wondering about the time always opens or closes doors. He concentrates, and instead of seeming really strained, the four or five essential words flow out naturally. Blanca Felipe answers that it is four fifteen. Ishmael says something to her about the heat. To discuss the heat in these latitudes is to broach a subject about which everyone has opinions, often very definite opinions. They talk about the heat. The heat continues, but as a topic it is exhausted, drops running down Ishmael's forehead that he mops up with a handkerchief. Blanca Felipe answers his new questions solicitously. Ishmael smiles, sometimes it happens that people are not what they seem. He never thought he was so talkative. Never? asks Blanca Felipe, and she tells him that that word "never" sounds like they've known each other for a long time. Ishmael smiles again. Actually, it is seeming to him, too, that they have known each other for a while. How odd, right? Without quite realizing it, they are talking about themselves. Ishmael asks her what things she likes, and, in turn, she asks him. As often happens, Blanca Felipe is impressed with the young man's quick wits: Ishmael knows something about every topic. It's as though the girl were constantly playing at an infinite crossword puzzle. Blanca Felipe is a nurse and is coming from the hospital; she feels tired. Ishmael invites her to his room for a cup of jasmine tea. Blanca Felipe's lips tighten for a moment. Ishmael with the score in his favor stops being timid for once and answers for her.

"Five! Back as far as the lady with the child."

The room looks inviting enough. At this hour in the afternoon it's flooded with oblique sun that reminds him of the unreal light of a school of Italian painting. Ishmael has exalted ideas. From the dizzying heights of aesthetic contemplation, he checks to see whether Blanca Felipe is following him. Yes, she's taken the bait; he's reeling her in now, even though she may lose a few of her scales in the process. Ishmael, satisfied, holds out the tray with cups on it to her. Just as he guessed, she doesn't like it too sweet. Blanca Felipe, seated on the bed, sips with her eyes closed. The jasmine, the tea, the aroma, the smoke, and the rays of light braided into a wispy spiral. It had been a long time since he'd met someone with whom he has so much in common, says Ishmael. It had been a long time since she had met a man with whom she had so much in common, repeats Blanca Felipe. Ishmael looks at her. Blanca Felipe looks at Ishmael. Sparks fly, flames crackle. The ceiling is old, you don't find wood beams like that anymore, and you don't see lamps like that. Ishmael asks her if she is still tired. From the floor, Ishmael sees her feet, the cloth of her jeans pulled tight in the crotch, the fullness of her breasts, her armpits, her neck. He stands up, tells her that the way she's reclining there reminds him of an old painting. Italian Renaissance, naturally. He repeats the painter's name twice. Florentine? *Smiling Angel–Woman with Mirror Reclining on a Red Bedspread.* Ishmael changes the cassette. *Misa cubana a la Virgen de la Caridad del Cobre.* 1—Let me have a seat. Blanca Felipe moves over and Ishmael sits down beside her. Thanks, tea has been a godsend but she is still tired. She'd never turn down an offer like that, yes, she'd really like to have him give her a massage. Ishmael takes off her sandals. Just a foot massage? Ishmael caresses her instep, her graceful heel, the arch over the abyss, her exquisite toes. He puts on lotion and begins to rub them. Blanca Felipe doesn't feel the tickle, just the pleasure of giving herself over. 2—Kyrie Eleison. Ishmael brings them up to his mouth and kisses each of her toes, hardly opening his lips. The lotion and the dust from the road blend into one flavor. Ishmael runs his tongue the length of her soles. Blanca Felipe doesn't feel tickled, exactly speaking. Blanca Felipe half closes her eyes. The ceiling is a low and heavy cloud. His tongue plays with her toes and the cloud lowers to nest in her belly with the rhythm of a silent waterfall. Waterfall where the cloth of the jeans pulls tight and halves her dangerous pubic smile. A wave of vertigo shakes Blanca Felipe's belly. Oh, my feet! Lord have mercy on me. 3—Gloria. These are the feet that will offer salvation to men and to my name. Ishmael kneels on the bed. Blanca Felipe pulls her knees up and opens them. Ishmael is between them. His forehead rests on the zipper of her jeans, his lips skim over whatever her open legs allow him to reach. His mouth on her sex, up and down. Ishmael murmurs a fervent prayer that only the dangerous, vertical, mute smile can hear. Glory be to you. For you alone are the holy one. Warm rain, fountain and spring, where the seed is nurtured. 4—Mysterious transparency. Damp wound of the restlessness hidden behind the whiteness of the cloth. The sun between Blanca Felipe's thighs. The mysterious light piercing the spread body. Blanca Felipe is the ship that will be boarded by knights and the destiny of small gods. The cup will receive our blood and will be the grail sown by other grails. "Come board my ship." "Stamp your emblem on my skin." "Thrust your sword under my belly." Ishmael seeks the perfect angle offered by Blanca Felipe's restless legs. The spurs sink into the flanks. Ishmael soars over Blanca Felipe's ship's skin, over the white skin of his Barca Felipe. 7—Sanctus. 8—Agnus Dei. The lamb bleats, buries its nose in the sparse grass. The earth is warm and open. The damp grass of her pubis comes apart in his fangs. Blanca Felipe bites her lips. Ishmael gives a last mighty heave and feels that his boots and belt buckle are hurting Blanca Felipe's body. The sun bursts out: Oh, Hosanna! The blood of the lamb, the knight's sword, Ishmael's boots, the spurs in the flanks, the cup into which blood drips, ever the same, the only ending. Blanca Felipe twists around, hammers her weak fists on Ishmael's back: ecstasy that sounds like empty drum music . . . 10—Salve Regina, salve, salve, all one, all the prayers . . .

"Five! Just five!"

Ishmael, excited, presses against the girl, victim of an inevitable loss of control. It's a great erection, one of those that stiffens the rod accompanied by a tingling that takes over the scrotum and makes the glans swell up and the veins throb and then the excitement flows up out of the testicles and expands into the rest of the penis until the first drops spurt out.

What is Blanca Felipe thinking about?

Since today is a day full of little coincidences that come and go unremarked, the girl remembers a book, another book that her boyfriend has read out loud to her. It was about some interminable journeys the author made to some places quite a ways from Havana. Her boyfriend told her about how, over a century ago, people used to take this road out to an area or distant place they called Vuelta Abajo. She didn't even know which way was west, which her boyfriend always called—and who knows why— the Land of the Setting Sun. And somewhere there, Vuelta Abajo could be found, a place remote in time, full of sugar mills, slave barracks, sugarcane plantations. The book was enjoyable: it told about a series of pleasure trips that a man from Havana took to his distant properties. The man from Havana, besides writing about journeys, had gotten himself into a snarl of conspiracies and had written, either before or afterward, a very important novel about blacks and whites that everybody had to read in school, but for the life of her, she couldn't come up with the title or the heroine's name. It didn't matter if she couldn't remember stuff like that. The story was pretty gloomy, a complicated tangle of incests, passions, dances, knifings in alleyways. That story wasn't important; she liked the ones in TV soap operas better. Reading books was a bore, except when someone, preferably the man she was riding the races with in bed, read to her out loud. The road took an unexpected turn and merged around a bend with a railroad track. Now she had it! The guy from Havana who used to go to Vuelta Abajo was named Cirilo Villaverde; she remembered it now, seeing the railroad track. The guy also used to go by train . . .

The sound of the wheels and the continuous hammering of the machine's iron pistons made so much noise that even though it was a regular rhythm, it became more and more monotonous and deafening as they began to move faster and as they were beginning to ache from the lurching of the cars. All this, combined with the spellbinding view through the windows of the infinite variety of farmwork, trees, factories, and beautiful landscapes (more beautiful seen in a rush) lull her into a meditative mood. It's a while before she can pay attention to her travel companions. When she turns to face them, they are all conversing about various things, except for the gentleman seated at her side. She notices that he is gazing at her and she pretends indifference and distraction, then it suddenly occurs to her that she may have been impolite. She turns her head and their eyes meet. The delighted gentleman makes note of her little straw hat, adorned with a garland of white roses, its brim framing her face. She wears a dark dress, buttoned to the neck, with long sleeves and dark gloves. The gentleman also notices that she has blue eyes, filled with ineffable tenderness, very white skin, and that between the silk ribbons of her bonnet may be glimpsed some locks of auburn hair so soft and lustrous that they are indistinguishable from the silk. The gentleman between serious and playful whispers in her ear, "It is I, Don Cirilo Villaverde, indefatigable traveler." He says this to her and she feels herself fall into the vertigo of the gentleman's eyes, light as her own. Don Cirilo takes her hand and slips off her glove and admires the wisdom with which the Great Creator crafts his delicate creatures. She feels the impact of Don Cirilo's words down there below her navel. Her hand rests quietly between the gentleman's. Don Cirilo thanks her for coming to their appointment. Each time he sees her is a rediscovery of her divine attributes, and they will play at reenacting the circumstances of their first meeting. Today he has once again been surprised by her eyes and their tenderness, their blue mystery, he says, lifting her hand to his lips. Then a thread of saliva lingers after their first kiss until it runs into Don Cirilo's snowy beard. Just after they've crossed the bridge built over the river, they know they are approaching the cave, as the train goes past the steep rock walls. From a mile away, it looks like a black dot, the size of an orange, with two parallel railroad lines running into its center; as one gets closer, it widens, and finally one can see daylight on the other side. The locomotive enters it, carrying the furtive lovers in its wake, as it snorts and shoots off sparks, belching great clouds of smoke from its black smokestack. Don Cirilo whispers to her that before their very eyes looms the landscape that poets descend to hell to seek. The loud cry of "Get down!" echoed by all the passengers barely makes them turn around. Then there transpires the miracle of blackness, silence . . . there is no journey; she's alone with Don Cirilo in the midst of an eternal and distant night. She remains seated, while, standing, Don Cirilo removes first her straw bonnet, then her other glove. She pulls him to her, embracing his waist. Don Cirilo fondles her curls. Her arms tighten around him and she feels, pulsing against her breast, the stiff erection of the gentleman who writes about excursions, black women, and knife fights. Don Cirilo is lost in a forest of fastenings and ribbons and she feels the sweet certainty of what will happen in the next hour. Meanwhile, the gentleman's erection between her breasts and she letting herself be carried away. Meanwhile, this other erection here against her buttock persistent and real. How long has Ishmael been pressing up against her, erect against buttock and flank?

The girl takes a step away from *her* Ishmael, but she's already noticed her own reaction and that the erection is a good one, one of those that really stiffens up the cock. No doubt accompanied by that tingling that men swear takes over their scrotum and makes their glans swell up and their veins bulge out, and then it moves up from the testicles to the rest of the rod. The image crosses her mind of this Ishmael's dirty prick spurting out the first drops . . . She pushes two steps farther into the truck trying to put an end to it. A slight wave of nausea washes over her. Without her realizing it, while she was far from the truck, riding on an old train, this other Ishmael has taken advantage thinking of who knows what filthy act. No doubt Ishmael was thinking he could take her while she was immobilized after he'd beaten her so. She concentrates and now she's tied to the head of an iron bedstead, her body aching all over, injured by the metal and by Ishmael's leather belt. Where the leather strap hasn't raised welts, the marks of Ishmael's fists stand out. His fists have bashed her lips, her cheekbones, her back. Ishmael has also taken the wise precaution of tying her feet. In that position she can hardly move her body at all. Hands and feet tied, aching: this boy knows what he's doing. Bare-chested, Ishmael paces around the bed. He's still holding his doubled-over belt in one hand, slapping it against the other palm once in a while. Ishmael doesn't say a single word. The national coat of arms gleams carved in relief all over her body.

Shining beneath her breasts are the *gorro frigio,** the rays of the sun and the majestic palm in the middle of the sheet. On her navel, the central stanchion of the coat of arms, as immobile as she is. Mahogany and guava branches on her thighs. Three purple stripes repeatedly on her arms. Distant mountains on her back blur into a long mountain range. And between her buttocks and above her pubis: the single key that opens and closes doors, gulfs, mysteries, souls, secrets, and inner recesses of women. As a child, more than respect or veneration, the coat of arms managed to overwhelm her with its incomprehensible accumulation of capricious details. The national coat of arms on men's belt buckles—then absolutely anything could happen! Ishmael lashes her body furiously with his belt. Once again the *gorro frigio* is stamped on

---

* *Gorro frigio:* the Phrygian cap with one five-pointed star on it (as on the Cuban flag) that is atop the Cuban national coat of arms; a very prominent and important symbol of nationalism.—Trans.

her lower belly. The man lowers his pants. She knew it, she just knew it! Under and around the glans that filth is accumulating disgustingly that consists of a kind of strong-smelling white scum that people call smegma. Said straight out, Ishmael is a hell of a dirty scumbag. And since it's up to her to call this scene, she decides on a truce. She redoes the previous scene. This time Ishmael tosses the belt onto her body and says "It's your lucky day; today I want to share you with a friend: I'm sure you'll love him." Don Cirilo Villaverde, the gentleman and bearded traveler who writes about trains and black women infatuated with white plantation owners, is standing in front of the bed. Clad only in a top hat and holding a small coffer. His cock is boiling away like a locomotive at full steam. Don Cirilo stretches back his foreskin so his admirer can see the shaft's shine and splendid construction: the marvel of his turgid pillar. "You're a lucky girl." "Beside you, the muses would pale with envy." Then he gestures to Ishmael to prepare the desk. When all is ready, Don Cirilo opens the coffer. Inside it are the very white paper, the inkwell, and pens in perfect order. This time Don Cirilo will not be using ink, at least not the sort that poets usually use on these occasions. He tells the girl that between her legs she has the necessary fount of inspiration and ink. She feels the gentleman's fingers toying with her dampened clitoris, with its half-open labia, probing eagerly into her vagina. Her sex throbs flooded. Don Cirilo's member also spurts drops and the clear liquid runs over the gleaming glans. Then the storyteller gives himself over to his boring task. He moistens his pen in both fluids and the other, the serious story he's writing, spouts up in a feverish jet of spray. Now the black woman and the plantation owner are not going for an evening carriage ride through the palm groves. Now Don Cirilo describes in his ink, in her ink, how the white man and the black woman, siblings although they don't know it, grapple with each other in the darkness of a back street in the San Cristobal area of Havana. The plantation owner facing her, and his sister, her back to the wall, is astride him, flushed and innocent, in a repeat performance of their father's virile acts that endowed them both with their male and female juices. The black woman cries out shuddering and the girl touches the ceiling untroubled by the bindings and Ishmael's blows; she floats as if she were levitating from the pages that Don Cirilo has been extracting from his guts, "You're really a lucky girl." And she feels the hard bulk of the cock pressing against her side.

Ishmael has returned to the hunt and again Blanca Felipe lets herself be pursued for a few seconds. Her ears are still ringing with the cries of the black woman impaled in the alley. Ishmael presses against her aggressively. His swollen rod nestles against Blanca Felipe's hip. Ishmael doesn't understand Blanca Felipe's game: it's as though she's switching on and off, sometimes accepting his approach and sometimes not. Maybe the best thing to do would be to tackle her directly. But there are things about her he doesn't understand. It takes a lot of nerve to let a woman know you desire her with body language that's both discreet and clear. But it's even harder to put it in words, formulate a question that anticipates and evades rejection. Blanca Felipe's buttocks and hips, evasive, playful, were worth more than a hundred obvious or subtle words. Nah, he thinks, Blanca Felipe and he are creatures who act in an inexplicable way. And explicably or inexplicably Blanca Felipe slips away from him again, dragging her suitcase. Ishmael's hands can't resist pursuit. They slide along the pipe until they almost brush against his victim's fingers. The girl hopes that this time the distance will be definitive and the man will finally understand that her body, although at times it has remained passive, is spurning his persistence. She looks at the suitcase on the floor. Suitcases, made for journeys, also imply other tales and hers is very simple. Just about the first complete story we remember from childhood. Her mother has sent her off to visit her grandmother, who is ill. The contents of the suitcase reveal the changing times and the scarcity of medicines. Bayer aspirin, acetaminophen, oregano syrup, cotton, the prayer to Saint

Lázaro, some clothing, and, of course, a bottle of natural honey. Now remember, dear, her mother has warned her to take care and stay away from detours and don't hitch rides with strangers. At that point Ishmael addresses her and asks her where she's going. She tells him about her grandmother, a story that doesn't seem to bore wily Ishmael. Very unobtrusively, he gets off at the stop before hers, hardly saying good-bye. Ishmael runs and runs and gets to the grandmother's house first and peers through the window. It's true, the old lady is ill and lives alone. Ishmael looks around carefully to make sure that there are no neighbors around, or anyone from the police or the Committee for the Defense of the Revolution, and he slips into the house. Ishmael has small hands but he's strong. With one slug he silences the old woman and hides her in the wardrobe. The close timing spares the old woman from having the landscape fragments of the national coat of arms imprinted on her body. Pretty soon the granddaughter comes along and seated beside the bed, she begins the litany of escalating astonishment. "Granny, what big ears you have!" "Granny, what a big mouth you have!" "Granny, what big eyes!" "Granny, what big hands!" "Granny, what is that rising up under the sheet that smells so bad?" "Granny!" The girl wears an expression of terror, sure that her end has come. Ishmael has tied her up and lifts his doubled belt. The electric light glints on the star and the *gorro frigio*. He knows what will happen next. But the story doesn't end there. Don Cirilo Villaverde is in the doorway armed with a long musket. A shot and Ishmael's head blows apart like a grenade. The writer drops the musket and she feels his fingers play with her clitoris, her labia, circle the opening of her vagina. Soon she won't be tied up and . . . she knows that Don Cirilo's cock is swelling under his fly and is hard enough . . . as hard as the indefatigable battering ram wielded by Ishmael the inveterate hunter.

Blanca Felipe retreats again into the center of the truck, satisfied with her ability to relate words to things. Ishmael stays where he was. For the first time he becomes aware that various people are following the progress of the hunt, with interest or disgust. Ishmael looks at the suitcase. Blanca Felipe's feet are under it. Ishmael feels ashamed; rather, Ishmael feels a little bit ashamed. *Blanca Felipe Blanca Felipe Blanca Felipe,* he repeats. *Blanca Felipe,* open flower, ripe fruit, soft rind, fresh aroma of twilight flowers after the rain. Still ashamed, he thinks that "Blanca Felipe" is a good name. He overhears—by chance, really—two women who are discussing his erection in a tone of disapproval: "People will do anything right out on the street. It's going from bad to worse"; that or something like that must be what they are saying, he senses. Ishmael looks at the suitcase. How can he slow down his rising excitement? He usually finds it useful in these situations to think about the question of whether God exists or not. He plunges into profound reflection. Who is God? Where can he be found? Where does he come from? What made him? What has he done? What does he look like? Is he liquid or gaseous? Is he someone created by man? Is he a psychological phenomenon, a product of the mind, the imagination . . . ? His erection subsides a little. But it's got a ways to go, and, sure that the two women are still clucking about it, he gives up on the Creator and switches to platitudes: "the swallow is a bird that soars high and keeps an eye out for possibilities: we have to follow its example," "my best quality and my worst defect are being me," and something definitive, "no question about it, I like women who are the color of intelligence." The result is impressive: the spirit has triumphed over the body and shrunk it down. Blanca Felipe looks at the suitcase. What happens if this guy gets off right behind me and follows me along the embankment and grabs me by the hair and beats me and then he rapes me and when he's lying on me relaxed after the pleasure he's taken, then I tell him I have HIV and I'm just out of the sanitarium on a pass, then he'll hit me again and beg me to tell him it's a lie and I'll tell him it's the truth that he should look and find the sanitarium ID card and infuriated, he pulls away and looks through my stuff until he finds my IDs and he finds the certificate from the sanitarium which lists my treatment and he starts hitting me again this time more furiously, but even so he can't keep me from bursting out laughing, seeing how the devil and death are in cahoots, and Ishmael (because Ishmael and none other is really the right name for this guy) gets to his feet and starts to run without knowing where and an ambulance is coming along the highway with Don Cirilo Villaverde himself at the wheel. Ishmael looks at the green suitcase, the green of surgical scrubs. The surgical green reminds him of hospitals, the "romantic statistics and the cold tinsel of wedding cakes," and hospitals make him think of AIDS. *Romulus and the Sabine Women, The Rape of the Mulatto Women.* Ishmael transformed into a hero yells threats as he mounts Blanca Felipe in the middle of a field, after licking her sexual parts with the single-mindedness with which one dog licks another. Because that's what Blanca Felipe is, a bitch in heat who repeats the word "prick" over and over again on their wild ride as she feels the thrust of his rod, its aim and hardness the essentials of their adventure. Macho Ishmael shakes himself off, gets to his feet, enjoys the humiliation of the scene. But he hasn't finished enjoying himself when Blanca Felipe tells him it's AIDS she's got, not HIV but AIDS. Ishmael digs frantically through the suitcase until he finds the document, the certificate from the sanitarium, the treatment list on the pass. Enraged, he wants to kick her until he finishes her off and turns her into a bloody heap, but something stronger than him makes him abandon any resolve: it's not necessary to hit Blanca Felipe, it's too easy and useless to smash her diseased flesh. Something inside him has broken. In the distance the sound of an ambulance can be heard, announcing the Kyrie Eleison, the Agnus Dei, the Sanctus, the Benedictus.

Ishmael, a fan of heraldry, wiped out and shamed by another short, useless battle, gets down off the truck that was once used to transport cattle at the last stop. As the truck moves on, he sees before him the coat of arms with the Harley-Davidson white-headed eagle, the sign I KEEP MY HANDS OFF MY FRIEND'S GIRL, FLEET OPERATOR. Once he gets home he will write a poem about a sinuous continent that will burn, masking the primordial deed, like the narrator of stories who told his compañeros tales about the hunt they themselves had gone on just hours before,

The poem will say

I say:

> even knowing it, I had
> half of a city
> shadows in contraband of subtleties
> each one offered the beams of his own roof
> blood-drained lanterns, faint marker in the range of reds
> had the city
> that each morning vomited me out
> toward a beach where everything was in order
> I had your sex
> it was nothing other than the same taste
> of the only mollusk
> you had I had nothing
> when I could have been motor and sail in your pupils
> I stumbled across the bones on my way back to my beach.

At the moment when Blanca Felipe and Ishmael are face-to-face, one on top, the other underneath, Ishmael surprises himself by executing an involuntary salute that Blanca Felipe doesn't notice because she's rubbing her eyes with her hand in a gesture of fatigue. Blanca Felipe's real name, thanks to an act of folly on the part of Ishmael, her father, is Ladymary, or rather Leidimari. Leidimari exchanges a complicit look with the women who are seated: "There's crime everywhere you go these days, it's going from bad to worse . . ." Tonight she'll ask her boyfriend to come to her bed in a top hat and naked, and get him to talk to her first about the brother and sister, the black woman and the white man, who went at it in an alleyway, and about the streams running along the edge of the palm groves. Don Cirilo will yank on her mane, that fog at the end of their wild gallop is Vuelta Abajo, girl, do you understand me?

"Six!" said the official in yellow.

Ishmael's poem never had a final title. First he called it "M-C-M," for "merchandise-cash-merchandise." Then he thought that "Scrutiny" would be better, and more or less complacently he sent it to a contest organized by his town's cultural council every February fourteenth. Ishmael received the second prize and not the first because the judges decided that while the poem was salvageable, the title was a disaster. Second prize consisted of a dinner for two at El Gallo restaurant. Since Ishmael didn't have a guest, he went by himself. He spent the interval before he was waited on trying to think up a better title. When the waitress appeared, Ishmael asked her what her name was, and he explained why he was in the restaurant. She took an interest. He overcame his shyness and recited the poem from memory. The waitress liked it, but what did "Scrotiny" mean? That did it, women were wise about these things: the title was worse. They traded names and addresses. While he was eating, Ishmael imagined that the woman was named Blanca Felipe and that he fucked her on the stairs. When the image faded, he thought that the old man who was eating his soup making an infernal racket at the next table was Don Cirilo Villaverde himself, the novelist-adventurer, who was gesturing to him, go for it man, don't miss your chance, go after her: she's hooked. Ishmael was sure: nothing would happen this time either. As time went by, Ishmael forgot the poem.

*Translated by Mary G. Berg*

**AIDA BAHR**

# Aunt Enma

She was a black woman, big and old and fat, dressed in white from the kerchief over her kinky hair all the way down to her broken shoes. She held a stick in her right hand and gripped a sack in her left. Grandmother saw her stop in front of the window—watching in a silent and attentive way. Then she remembered that Aunt Enma, five years old at the time, was sitting right there with her dolls. A premonition set her running, distressed. The black woman didn't even say hello. She only said, "Take good care of that girl, señora, she's too pretty. So much beauty always brings harm." Then she walked off with slow, tired steps, dragging her heavy sack behind. Her words remained trapped inside Grandmother's head, becoming a thorn that she bore in silence for many years. She talked about it only after Aunt Enma left home.

The two of us were in the kitchen when thunder sounded, far off. Grandmother, startled, crossed herself.

"Look outside and see whether it's going to rain."

That order was my liberation. Not wanting to take a nap

after lunch had only gotten me stuck in the kitchen with her, unable to explore the nooks and crannies of the house where I was spending the day without my parents for the first time.

The sky stretched blue and innocent above the courtyard, but there was a ladder leaning against the wall. I took advantage of the implied permission in Grandmother's order and climbed up. Of course the first thing I looked at was the courtyards of the neighboring houses, whose disorder was so different from their facades. Then came a violent flash of light that didn't even require a glance. I dashed down the ladder, banging on every step, sure that a dark and furious mass was approaching from the west.

"A hurricane's coming!" I shouted in the kitchen on the run.

"Jesus, Mary, and Joseph." Grandmother crossed herself again.

Then she picked up the broom.

"We have to sweep the patio so the leaves don't clog up the drain."

I tried to follow her, but she shooed me inside. "Wake up Dionisio, and close the windows," she said.

You could say that Aunt Enma was raised as an only child, because Uncle Esteban and Papa were almost men by the time she was born. After Grandfather's death, she and Grandmother were alone in the house until Uncle Esteban brought Dionisio, four years before Aunt Enma would decide to take the road that she chose. Dionisio is Uncle Esteban's son from when he was studying in Havana. He acknowledged the boy and sent him money, but when the boy's mother abandoned him, Uncle Esteban couldn't have him because Aunt Matilde didn't even want to hear his name. So Dionisio came to live here. Although everybody said he was a difficult child, he didn't cause big problems for them. People remarked that he didn't show Grandmother much respect, but with Enma he was a perfect lamb. When she left home, it seemed Grandmother would most likely have trouble with him, yet now two months had passed and Dionisio's presence was hardly even felt. Grandmother was sad and dispirited, as if her life had ended the day her daughter had gone. That's why Papa sent me there to spend the day, so I could distract her. I was delighted, because until then I'd only been for short Sunday visits. Everything had seemed full of mystery. Aunt Enma too.

I ran into Dionisio's room and jumped on the bed. I must have given him a good scare, even if I was the loser because he gave me a shove that threw me to the floor. He was fourteen but had a man's strength. We both sat up at the same time, him in bed rubbing sleep out of his eyes and me on the floor rubbing the bruise on my leg.

"Are you crazy?" I got to my feet, offended, and left. In the hallway I turned around to yell at him again. "You better close the windows before Grandmother sees the furniture getting wet!"

I decided to take charge of the windows in the living room. I loved those barred, colonial bay windows that formed a semicircle big enough to serve me as a play space. Even then, at the age of ten, I liked to sit and read during the Sunday visits. Not for the book, but for the chance to show off my legs. The next-door neighbor had taken it on herself to point out that my legs were just like Aunt Enma's. That filled me with pride.

While I fastened the wooden shutters with their bolts, I heard the windows banging in the bedrooms and knew that Dionisio had decided to follow my advice. When I was done I ran into the kitchen in time to meet up with Grandmother coming back from the patio all sweaty, hair disheveled and dragging her broom. The first drops sounded like bullets hitting the zinc tiles of the roof. A bolt of lightning exploded over our heads and made Grandmother wince with her shoulders in what looked almost like pain. She tottered to her room, fell on the bed, and covered her head with a pillow. I had followed her in and didn't know what to do next. She lifted the pillow and said, without opening her eyes, "Go find Dionisio and cover the mirrors."

My grandfather built the house, and he made it with a high roof and enormous rooms, filled with furniture both heavy and big. When I was little girl I hardly ever went farther than the living room. I had the feeling I was in a castle with threats lurking on all sides. It could be that I caught this fear from Mama, who never felt at ease there and only accepted the Sunday visits in exchange for spending the important dates with her family, like Christmas and New Year's Eve. But I did like to go because of Aunt Enma, who used to sit with me in the window and invent tall tales. Whatever went on in the street meant something to us. She was so beautiful. On the other hand, everybody said, she had bad luck. She'd had three fiancés—one when she was just fifteen, when Grandfather was still alive—but for one reason or another they always broke off the engagement. Aunt Enma didn't seem to care. She was always smiling, always in a good mood. Sometimes she'd be self-absorbed, but little by little a smile would creep into her lips, an expression like she was tasting something, until she'd come out of herself and laugh and suddenly invent a new game, almost apologizing for having forgotten about me.

I found Dionisio in the hallway cleaning his nails.

"Grandmother says we should cover the mirrors."

"I know that," he said. His bad mood was still there in his voice.

I followed him to Aunt Enma's room. He opened a drawer and took a few towels out. He gave me some and suddenly smiled.

"We'll start with the living room."

I had never realized how many mirrors there were in the house. In the living room alone there were three, one of which needed two towels to cover it. In Dionisio's room there was one that took up the whole door of the wardrobe. Just as I wondered how we'd manage it, he threw the bedspread over it with the ease of someone who'd done this many times. In Grandmother's room we used the rest of the towels to cover the dressing table mirror and the night table one. In the bathroom, Dionisio covered the little mirror over the sink with the hand towel hanging there. I thought we were through until I saw that half smile that always meant he had some mischief planned.

"We haven't done Aunt Enma's room."

I realized then that this was true; we'd gone in to get towels, but we hadn't covered anything there. I followed him with curiosity and watched quietly while he took off the bedspread to throw it over the bureau. I was on my way out when his voice stopped me.

"There's one more."

I looked around, not seeing it, until he pushed the door closed. I almost screamed with surprise. A mirror even bigger than the one on Dionisio's wardrobe filled the entire bedroom door. What's more, with the door closed our images had suddenly appeared. It was like finding two people hidden there watching us. I was still hypnotized when Dionisio sat down on the bed, looking bored.

"It's so big," I said. "What are we going to cover it with?"

He shrugged.

"What have you covered it with before?"

"That one always stays like that."

He didn't seem to feel like talking—which made me want to ask.

"Why do we have to cover the mirrors?"

"So they don't attract lightning."

"Why is Grandmother so afraid of lightning?"

"Because that's how Grandfather died."

The revelation electrified me. I didn't react right away.

"Was he in front of a mirror?"

"No. He was crossing the street in front of the house."

The two of us were silent. Dionisio started to scrape dirt from under his nails again. I couldn't take my eyes off the mirror where for the first time I saw myself reflected with all of my surroundings. It was just as if I were watching myself perform in a film.

"If it's true that mirrors attract lightning, this must be the most dangerous one of all," I said at last.

Catlike, Dionisio looked at me.

"The lightning doesn't dare, because this mirror belongs to the devil," he said.

I was annoyed to have him take me for a silly girl.

"You're making that up."

He shook his head. All his attention seemed to center on his nails. He didn't even look at me when he said, "Aunt Enma was the one who discovered it."

"How?"

"One day she noticed that the back of the mirror is always black, and you can smell sulfur if you get close."

"Mercury," I said, mechanically, while a vague sensation of fear tiptoed quickly through my stomach. "That's what's in mirrors, mercury."

"This one smells like sulfur."

For sure I wasn't getting close to it to find out. I didn't want to be the butt of Dionisio's joke. I looked it over carefully and yes, with the window closed the room was dark, but it was true that way in the depths of the mirror there seemed to be a kind of black liquid shadow, moving behind what was reflected. Dionisio finished up his nails and got to his feet. He took two steps toward the mirror.

"At first Aunt Enma was scared, but then she got used to it. She saw that she didn't look as pretty in any other mirror as she did in this one."

All of a sudden he took off his pajama pants and looked at his reflection in his shorts. He posed like Tarzan and did several turns. His body was dark and skinny, and at the same time hard and strong. There was a splash of black hair on his chest.

"This is a mirror for looking your body over, for getting to know yourself. There's more to a beautiful body than a pretty face."

"My legs are prettier than my face," I blurted out.

"Let's see."

I stood up. He looked annoyed.

"You have to lift your dress up. The legs start higher than that."

I lifted my skirt to the edge of the elastic on my underwear. He looked at my legs appreciatively, making me turn around so he could see them from various angles. I looked at them too, in the mirror. They looked perfect to me.

"Yes," he said at last. "They're like hers. You know what she would do? She'd lie there on the bed and do poses, like somebody was taking pictures of her."

That sounded fun to me. I jumped onto the bed and started monkeying around. He corrected my positions and commented on how they seemed like this or like that. I was laughing so hard I forgot about the storm until a huge clap of thunder reminded me. I buried my head in the mattress and covered my ears.

"It's the lightning that kills you," Dionisio said. "If you hear the thunder, then the danger is gone."

I agreed and sat up. He gave me a persuasive look.

"Why don't you take off your dress?"

Something inside me said trouble was coming.

"You're still a girl. What's wrong with taking off your clothes? You haven't even got breasts."

"I do too," I said softly. "They're growing now."

He gave my chest a critical stare.

"Doesn't seem like it."

I didn't know what to say. The rain had gotten heavier and seemed to be drilling into the roof. The air felt damp, heavy, and hard to breathe.

"Aunt Enma had incredible breasts: white, very high, with

nipples that were big and pink. She'd touch them like this, pulling on them real softly, and the points would stand up like they were getting ready to jump off."

The memory seemed to hypnotize him.

"Why are you saying 'had'? Aunt Enma isn't dead."

He looked at me like he didn't understand what I'd said. He looked upset now. He'd even started to sweat, though that could have been from the heat. He moved away from the bed, close to the mirror.

"Take off your clothes," he begged. "I won't move from this spot. Aunt Enma let me see her naked and I never touched her. But if I put my hand on her body in the mirror she'd say she felt my fingers on her skin."

"You're lying," I said almost in a whisper.

"She said so. Try it yourself if you want to know."

I was afraid, though I couldn't explain why. At the same time I felt a violent desire to obey, to peek into that unknown world. I'd like to be able to say I hesitated, took my time making a decision, but in fact Dionisio didn't need to ask twice. Very slowly—this is true—I undid the buttons of my dress and then pulled it over my head. When I looked toward the mirror Dionisio had taken off his shorts and was standing there completely naked, displaying his sex surrounded by a strange dark fuzz that left on me the indelible impression of things seen for the first time.

"You have to take off everything," he said.

I shook my head in resistance.

"I won't move from this spot," he assured me. "Nothing's going to happen to you. Look, I'm naked too."

That last argument convinced me. It's stupid, but I felt it put us on an equal footing or something. To make things easier, he turned his back. He was watching me in the mirror, of course, though I only realized this later because at first he seemed to be looking at the floor. When I was lying naked on the bed, he moved his fingers to the glass and stroked the part that reflected my chest. I felt a tickle that probably came from inside, then a tremble, a strange sensation deep in my belly. He continued sliding his hands softly and smoothly, caressing the curve of my ribs, the shape of my navel, until his fingers closed over my pubis and I screamed, I screamed because I felt a tug, something half pain and half pleasure, a tug that stopped my breath and tried to penetrate me, and suddenly my whole sex stung and itched and burned. I curled up, desperately grabbing at my clothes to cover myself. Clumsily I tried to get dressed and got all twisted up, till at last I managed it and sat up in the bed. Only then did I see that Dionisio was still on his knees before the mirror, head resting against it, eyes closed, his hands . . .

I straightened my dress and stood on the floor. For I don't know how long, I stood there watching him without knowing what to do. Finally he collapsed to one side and leaned weakly against the wall. I seized the moment to open the door just wide enough to slide out, shut myself in the bathroom, and cried like never before, with fists pressed into my face, even banging my head into the wall. The storm had weakened, and when I managed to calm down it was barely raining. I washed my face and went to my grandmother's room. She was still in bed but now she'd uncovered her face and silently watched the ceiling. I sat down next to her, seizing onto her hand.

"Why did Aunt Enma go be a nun?"

She sighed before answering.

"She heard God's call."

We didn't say any more. She held my hand tightly. Finally I found the courage to speak.

"I think she was running from the devil."

She gave me a shocked look, and I thought she'd say something, but she only sighed and shook her head.

"Grandma, isn't it true that I'm not as pretty as Aunt Enma?"

She seemed about to break into tears.

"She's prettier," she said. "But beauty doesn't always bring happiness."

I never spent the day at Grandmother's house again. When we went to visit I'd sit in the living room and barely say hello to Dionisio. I thought staying away from him and from the mirror would be enough.

*Translated by Dick Cluster*

ABILIO ESTÉVEZ

# The Horizon

## THE CATASTROPHE

My grandmother is turning eighty. We haven't seen her because she hasn't come out of her room for days. My mother told Ana, the maid, to clean well and to pay special attention to the chandelier in the living room that has thousands of tears giving off sparkles and musical notes. The piano looks like new, it shines like a milliner's mirror and seems distinguished with its open lid uncovering the mystery of its bronze cords. The furniture and porcelain gleam like pieces of the best china on the dining room table where a tablecloth has been placed. They say my grandmother brought it from Valenciennes on her honeymoon. Also, in the dining room on top of the hutch is a sign with the well-painted letters (we're sure Violeta will be a great painter), HAPPY BIRTHDAY. And flowers, lots of flowers, gladiolus, gardenias, pansies . . . My grandmother has always liked flowers. On her chair, at the head of the table, is her gift, a big box wrapped in golden paper with golden ribbon too. No one knows what it is except for Mom.

Right when the grandfather clock strikes nine, Grandma comes down the stairs. She likes to be punctual. Her punctilious need to be punctual always seemed funny to us. My mother says she gets ready ahead of time and puts her ear up to the door and opens it at the precise moment she hears the clock's first strike. We don't know if she has on an outfit so blue it seems black or so black it seems blue. It is an old, ripped dress with a lace collar that must have been white at one time. Her so-white hair, usually well combed, is down and falls messily over her shoulders. What is most surprising, though, is she's not wearing shoes. I see my mother blink nervously, frown, open her mouth. My father coughs. The rest of us stay quiet, waiting for the order to sing "Happy Birthday." The order doesn't come and Grandma silently comes down the stairs and looks at us, even though it's obvious she doesn't see us. She doesn't say anything, doesn't smile, we don't kiss her, we let her go by and follow her, respecting her silence. We see her sit down in her chair, at the head of the table, as if we were victims of a hoax, as if we were in the presence of an imposter. My mother hands her the gift. Grandma looks at her own hands. I'm unaware if the others notice she's not wearing her sapphire ring and that those hands, with their short and dirty nails, trembling a bit and not taking the time to untie the box, don't seem to be my grandmother's. I tell myself her eyes are sad, but to use the word "sadness" is a way of classifying something that escapes my comprehension with a feeling I know. Grandma's eyes look irritated, fixed, and the only thing I can say is they are not my grandmother's eyes. I also realize the most shocking thing about her face tonight, what has made her older and more unrecognizable, is the absence of her dentures. A smell of urine mixed with sweat overpowers the scent of flowers, the scent of sandalwood my mother uses. A bit recovered from her initial perplexity, my mother exclaims "Happy Birthday, Mom," but her tone isn't happy no matter how hard she tries. She unties the ribbon herself, rips the golden paper, and opens the lid of the box. My mother screams and in the scream there is authenticity. In the box is the Princess of Lamballe, the dog that for eleven years has been my grandmother's faithful companion. Its eyes and mouth are open and you can tell, from the stiffness, it's been dead for several hours. My mother quickly closes the box hoping my grandmother doesn't notice. My father coughs again. Violeta signals Ana to serve the meal. My mother looks around her as if trying to see where the real gift is. Andrés kisses the guest of honor's forehead. She keeps looking at (or pretending to look at) her dirty hands.

The pork is wonderful, Silo says. He's the only one who's eating. The rest of us pick at our food. My father drinks beer and I'd swear he's smiling. My mother has tried several times to tell a confusing story about a birthday in Tampa, during the War of Ninety-five, even though there's no doubt she'd rather not tell anything. And so she calls Ana for any reason at all and gives silly orders like asking for sauce or bread. Later she's quiet, looks at Grandma and asks if the pork is well roasted, and the anxiousness in her question reveals the real question she doesn't ask. The only moment of relief we have is when we go to the living room to have coffee and Violeta plays some dances by Ignacio Cervantes on the piano.

I'm not sleepy. I look out the window at the dark sea, or what should be the sea, because it's difficult to know where the earth ends and the sea begins in this darkness that extends below my window. Andrés is sleeping. I know, though, Andrés isn't sleeping; his closed eyes and heavy breathing try to deceive me. I pretend to be deceived, look out the window, the sea can't be seen at night, only a language filled with promises is heard, a sweet voice, it's easy to understand why Ulysses had to tie himself to the mast of his ship. Violeta says The Waves groan. She, romantic, nostalgic, a little affected, sees a cry of anguish in everything. I say The Waves sing and in each wave a siren hides, and Andrés and Silo laugh at me. The house is beautiful and surrounded by sea, on a hill so enclosed by water that it seems like we live on an island. If it's low tide, we can go down to the road with no problem; if it's high, you need to cross a little wooden bridge (like the ones you see in Japanese prints). Then yes we are on an island. One day something will happen and no one will hear us, my mother says, who is always afraid. My grandfather wanted to build a house here not only because he loved the sea but because he was *mambí*, he was in the war. He got so fed up with people that afterward, from exile in Tampa, and with the honor of having achieved colonel, he looked for the most distant place, the island within the island, to cure injuries, to forget. He bought this land that didn't interest anyone and had a house built with excellent wood, to his capricious liking. With two stories and a figurehead in the front, the house looks like a sailing ship. At night, lit up, enclosed by the sirens' grave song, it appears to be a sailing ship held in a dead calm.

Storm. Night forebodes storm. Night forebodes. Night. Storm. Friend, I write you these lines and I cannot hide my fear.

I am listening, I know they are not voices from the sea, even though it's evident it has become angrier. I do not see it, but in the blackness I discover the threat. Only with his eyes Andrés lifts his head. I go to the door, I open it very carefully, I realize the voices are coming from the dining room. I go out to the hallway and up against the wall, I come closer to the stairs. My parents are fighting. Their shadows are projected onto the wall. My mother's shadow is small and has a short head and is like her whining voice; my father's doesn't stay still for one moment and becomes bigger. His voice is strong, surer than his shadow. I hear some of the words he says: locking up, craziness, order. I have the impression my mother is sobbing. The shadows disappear and silence follows (I mean the only silence possible in this house-island surrounded by the sea). I go back to my room. Andrés is in front of the window. I call him, I'm going to tell him my mother . . . He puts his finger to his lips, he moves toward the darkness that extends beyond the window and remains still for a long time, silent, unmoving. There is going to be a storm, he says with his beautiful, strangely hoarse voice. The world is going to end raining.

It will never clear, friend. This rain will be here forever. The wind will pull the house from its weak foundations, will throw it in pieces to the sea, no, it won't clear.

It's as if the whole house had come down. I jump out of bed and see Andrés open the door and go out running. I hear screams. Silo jumps down the stairs. Violeta is in her white robe, hair uncombed, like she never would have let us see her. What was that? she asks with her hands covering her face. We don't know where Ana's voice asking us to go back to our rooms comes from. Andrés turns on the lights. My father appears with his pajamas muddied, he doesn't notice us. It's Grandma's room, Andrés tells me, we go there in spite of Ana's threatening voice. When we get there, we discover my mother sitting on the floor, unmoving, looking at the tips of her toes.

Covered in clouds of dust, wood and roof still reverberating, my grandmother's room, the last one, built over the terrace in the right wing of the house, has fallen. It was a lot of work to pull the lifeless body of my grandmother out of the rubbish, which furthermore didn't look like my grandmother's body but a mannequin in whose obstinate eyes I thought I saw fierceness, irritation, what had escaped my understanding at dinnertime and that, for lack of a better word, I wanted to call "sadness."

Against all predictions, the morning of the collapse is a splendid summer's morning: tranquil sea, blue almost green, unreal. Luminous, brilliant, it makes the dark curtains that have been hung in the living room look out of place, mocks the lit candles, takes the solemnity away from the box that has been placed where the piano had been, at the foot of a silver crucifix covered in happy sparkles. Even my grandmother's face beneath the glass where there is a nice play of light seems smiling and satisfied. Why wouldn't she be, on this beautiful morning of the collapse. Dressed in black, using a mantilla, wearing dark glasses, my mother is moving back and forth in the rocking chair. She holds a white handkerchief that she doesn't need. I'd swear even she's cheered up by looking out the window at the sea and the providential day. Ana first brings her a cup of linden tea that she refuses, then the rosary with large, black beads (they say Grandma brought it from Rome, blessed by Pius XII), and the album filled with stamps from around the world, a collection sponsored by a celebrated brand of cigars. Of the important relics kept in Grandma's room, this old, unimportant album was the only thing they could salvage. Seated on the piano bench, Violeta cries. Silo says my sister cries because of the Sevres vase my grandmother had promised her and that shattered to pieces. I don't believe him. Grandma and Violeta got along well. Her predictions for her cultured, elegant granddaughter didn't escape any of us. Violeta embodied for her all the good that a young lady from our family could offer, whose ancestors go back (she said it with skepticism) to Boso, brother-in-law of Charles the Bald, founder of the kingdom of Arles. My father wears an elegant suit and looks over the accounts. Sometimes my mother watches him; I think she is going to say something, but then she goes back to looking at the window. Andrés walks along the beach, sad as well. Silo goes repeatedly to the box and looks at Grandma curiously. I don't dare say he's anguished, I don't dare say anything about Silo, it's hard to say anything about him that's convincing, he's a mystery, he knows it and enjoys it. As for myself, I should recognize it, I'm not suffering like I ought to. It even bothers me that in my head I'm humming *Mariposita de primavera, alma con alas que errante vas* . . . I always thought my grandmother was important to me, and right now I don't realize she's dead or it doesn't matter.

Death? Did I say "death"? It's the first time I associate this word with others like "storm," "omen." I also associate it with "sea." Death? I am crying and they look at me. They think I'm crying because of Grandma.

You're the only one who comes to the funeral. We don't know anyone else. As you can see, the house is on a hill and I already told you when the tide rises it looks like it's completely surrounded by the sea. Yes, friend, those who live on an island should never aspire to have company, much less sympathy visits. The worst isn't the solitude; what's so hard is, besides us, and you, of course, there is not one human being who sympathizes with the collapse, with us having lost our grandmother, and with her, the valuable relics that gave faith to our lineage.

## THERE WERE NEVER DAYS LIKE THESE

Is it August, December? This detail that would not change the course of things doesn't matter to us. The days are the same, magnificently the same. The sun rises earlier, at five, and dawn is a delight. Not even the most capable poet could describe the tints the sky and sea take on before this color that no beryl could imitate. There are never clouds. At most a tiny cloud that quickly passes by and disappears just as quickly. It's as if the landscape were reflected in a mirror and we are always bewildered, the sun in our eyes, because light also blinds. My sister Violeta sits in the wicker chair, sad, facing the easel and canvas that she doesn't paint, looking off into the distance. Silo, Andrés, and I spend our days at the beach. I'm going to be sincere with you, our joy has its origin in the idleness that has followed my grandmother's death. I hardly see my mother, and she and Grandma were the ones who concerned themselves with our education. So it's been days since we've taken out a grammar or geometry book, they don't torture us with the lesson . . . *Mio Cid movió de Bivar pora Burgos adeliñado* . . . we don't see ourselves obligated to bothersome translations of *Athalie,* which never ended; oh, Racine, how we ended up hating you, you were the most hated man (along with Mio Cid) on this wretched planet. Wretched planet? My mother would say you are abusing adjectives. Yes, and what of it? It is necessary, nonetheless, to recognize that no one who wakes up early in this house and watches the sky and sea could associate the adjective "wretched" with the noun "planet." Laugh at Eden. The Garden of Earthly Delights is this hill, this limpid house and sky and sea (I say "limpid" and I almost feel my mother's ruler hitting me, her disapproval, Son, one must be simple in his expression, affectation says lack of elegance, it leads to ridiculousness). Mom, I feel like being ridiculous, I lack elegance. I'm free. Do you remember when you talked to us about Rousseau and the "natural man"? Finally, I'm living naturally. Look at these luminous days! It's not worth it to think, read, let boredom take you away, sigh like Violeta does every three seconds. On days like these we just need skin, eyes, hands, ears, mouth . . . Humans are the sum of their senses.

"Natural man," "splendid days," "senses" . . . Do you know these words, friend? Nonetheless, let me tell you, sometimes when we lie down on the shore and the waves come toward us, we are attacked by fear. A second of fear, which doesn't make it any less of a fear.

Night comes and we're dead tired. Now the three of us (Silo, Andrés, and I) sleep in the same room. Silo falls asleep immediately, with a sleepiness that makes him akin to a hard rock. Andrés looks at the maps and takes out the old compass, he cleans it, he spends a lot of time staring at the nervous needle. Sometimes he talks about Manila, San Juan, New York, Venice. And most of all about the horizon. He's obsessed with the horizon. He says it's not an imaginary line, that there the sky and the sea truly come together and only separate when some brave soul tries to conquer it. The sky and sea open their door for those who are courageous, he says. I admire Andrés. I like his big hands that row the oars so well, just like I admire his rough beauty, the darkness of his skin, his eyes so dark, deep. I like to see him tall, agile, different from us, the blonds, the weak, the languid, results of such an old cast that is, for this very reason, sick.

Andrés lies down next to me. His body gives off energy, heat, which instead of provoking contagiousness, just hurts me. He takes one of my hands as if ignoring how much it scares me. He stays silent and I think he's going to sleep when I hear his voice, beautiful and hard like his hands. I'm not scared even though a bad omen turns me around, no ocean in the world can be still for so long. I turn this bad omen I don't understand around in my head and besides realizing omens were made to not be understood, to not be worth anything, I think I know why a feeling of fear merges with the happiness we are living now, the terror of these beautiful days, of the still sea. What happened to Grandma isn't the only thing; something else will happen. I don't know if it's for better or worse, it occurs to me that it's for both, that in the end "good" and "bad" are two words that are united more than we are capable of understanding. We are living extraordinary days, yes, but what's extraordinary can also appear with a face of tragedy. He lets go of my hand and doesn't talk anymore even though I keep asking him questions. To tell you the truth, I'm worse than before, with the same ignorance and a little more fear.

In the beginning, I don't recognize whose waltz it is that floods the house like on the days we have parties. Silo and Andrés are sleeping. I secretly get up, go out to the hallway, and go down the stairs. It's my mother who is seated at the piano. Violeta is also in the living room with her white silk robe and irritated eyes. My mother plays the piano with her head low, her eyes closed. Chopin, her favorite. I'd never heard her play so well. I'm going to come closer when my father enters. Violeta and I look at each other. My father comes dressed in the clothes of my *mambí* grandfather, the rough, yellowed shirt covered in medals, and on his head a *yarey* palm hat with a little Cuban flag. He doesn't notice us. He goes to the piano and slams it closed, trapping my mother's hands. She makes no gesture of pain. Later he makes her get up, he takes her away. I can't tell what time it is because the clock has stopped.

Naked on the sand, Andrés tells me how on a certain occasion a ship crashed against the wall the sky and sea make there, and it smashed into pieces that are still adrift. Only the chosen ones are able to pierce the wall, he explains, we owe to them the myth that the horizon is an imaginary line. I don't ask him chosen by whom; truthfully, Andrés isn't talking to me. I listen, pretending his conversation doesn't interest me, seemingly absorbed in building a sand castle. Silo doesn't come with us anymore. Andrés and I swim the whole day, and when we're not swimming, we run on the beach, we climb the sea grapes with the binoculars, to make out the arrival of some ship, of the brave, of those who are capable of piercing the horizon. Andrés tells long sea stories about Sinbad the sailor, about Nostromo, he tells me the tragic story of the White Whale and Captain Ahab. No one calls us, no one looks for us, we return home when we want, when we're hungry, to stay later on the beach and finally end up on the shore until night begins to fall.

## I FORBID YOU TO COME BACK HERE, MY FATHER SAYS

Violeta doesn't paint anymore. The easel stays in the corner, the canvas lightly colored in blue. My sister forgot her magnificent seascapes; she hasn't returned to her desolate beaches where there is no coconut tree, no boat, no net, just the sea that startles, the well-shaped line, the world that ends, the stormy sky, gray from so many clouds. My romantic, languid, affected sister walks around now with an old book lined in leather and with golden edges. She wears one of Grandma's old dresses that she looks ridiculous in. Silo makes fun of her. Fortunately, she's never taken Silo seriously and limits herself to looking at him with a look that doesn't stay on him, that goes through him, like she looks at all of us. We have reason to suspect my sister isn't here. Sometimes I see her writing and I know she's writing to Michel the Moroccan.

I'd never seen a man so tall and strapping. They said his boat had sunk due to a storm. I didn't believe the story, couldn't accept that a man with his whiteness had been a sailor at one time. I remember his eyes, so blue that from far away he didn't have pupils. I remember him seated in front of Violeta, in the vis-à-vis in the living room, tense and voluminous voice like his chest, gigantic hands over his thighs as if he wanted to hold back the impetuous movements his body was accustomed to. It was the time that Violeta quickly became more beautiful and painted the loveliest seascapes, those that are in the closed terrace, the one that doesn't face the sea. Afterward, Michel the Moroccan stopped coming. According to what was said, he had met up with a Greek ship with the hopes of getting together enough money to ask Violeta to marry him.

First, Michel the Moroccan's leaving. Then, my grandmother's. Violeta spends the day sitting in the chair, her eyes fixed on remoteness, dressed in an outdated suit that makes her look ridiculous. Sometimes she writes. Days ago I saw her slip a piece of paper into a Bacardi bottle and throw it into the sea. She watched how the bottle laboriously moved away from the shore.

Lots of days Andrés and I go on a trip. We've gone to the foot of famous volcanoes, traversed an entire city of palaces and streets that are canals of dark waters. We cross large deserts, unending meadows, in enchanted forests we breathe in the scent of frankincense and sandalwood, we disembark in ports of pestilent waters, we climb mountains, we enter caves that go practically to the center of the earth. We'd traveled so much and so far, we hadn't noticed my mother had disappeared.

Not only her but everything that had to do with her. We furtively searched in vain for her throughout the house. Today I asked Ana and she said I had dark circles under my eyes. Surely you're not eating enough. Violeta is hiding. She's still wearing her fin de siècle dress, still carrying that old book, and she's hiding, and when it becomes inevitable that we find each other, she smiles so it's pitiful. Friend, believe me, Silo spits every time I talk about Mom.

This is the darkest night. I ignore the reason why. Silo doesn't sleep with us. Andrés has *A Captain at Fifteen* open over his chest and his eyes closed, satisfied breathing. I, who went the whole day without traveling, worried about my mother's destiny, cannot sleep. Besides being dark, the night is hot. Apparently, the wind can't pierce the wall-horizon either. There is nothing beyond it except an immense emptiness that scares me. I know he's sleeping but I tell Andrés I want to go downstairs and I kiss him on the forehead. I am barefoot to make the least amount of noise and go down the stairs as if on each one a snake lies in wait. In the little room decorated in the Louis XV style where my mother and grandmother taught us, I discover that the secretaire where we kept folders and pencils is missing. I try to open the glass window; useless, it's locked. The glass looks steamed up. A light moves there, outside, a ring shows the yellowed sand that is in no way the same sand during the day. I'm late in noticing, the light comes from a flashlight, it looks like Silo, my brother, or whoever it is, he walks slowly, his head lifted. Sometimes he stops. When the light gets closer to the window, I move away. With a big step I'm hidden in the shadows that are projected by the boards that have been put up where the clock was before. From here, without anyone seeing me, I have a good view of the living room. My father comes in and stands in front of the mirror. He's wearing Grandpa's dirty, yellowed *mambí* suit. He's taking medals out of their boxes and putting them on his chest. Afterward, a tricolor ribbon, a saber. He looks at himself for a long time in the mirror, satisfied, he moves his mouth with an exaggerated expression, gestures with his hands, raises his arms, the veins on his neck stick out and his face reddens because of the effort. Later, evidently tired, he lets himself fall into the armchair. Ana comes in with a glass of juice on my mother's silver tray and kneels in front of him. My father pays no attention to Ana's presence. He rests his forehead on his folded hands, like an exhausted man filled with worries. Ana lowers her head as a sign of respect. I take advantage of the moment to come out of the shadows. I go as fast as I can through the hallway to my mother's room. The door isn't closed; it easily gives under the push of my hand. The room is empty. Along with my mother, the great pillar bed, the enormous wardrobe with three doors and oval mirrors, the prie-dieu where she prayed with her rosary every night, the armchair where she sat to embroider and tell us stories about the War of Ninety-five have all disappeared. I don't know what to do in the empty room. I say "Mom" and the echo repeats the syllable roughly. Then a hand falls on my shoulder. Yes, friend, it's my father, the tired voice of my father says no one ever lived in this place, this room was always empty, go to bed.

## FIRE

I have Andrés's binoculars. It must be dawn and the sea and sky become the same reddish or blue tone, I don't know which. Despite the breeze, the sea is unmoving. I insistently look at the line, which, according to Andrés, is not imaginary. Long, severe, it seems to curve as if its ends wanted to converge in us. I feel like the line encloses me, iron band around us. Suddenly, there, far away, three white dots appear. I pay attention, focus the binoculars, yes, three white dots that little by little become three caravels with their sails unfurled. I run to where Andrés is. Let's go, wake up, there are three ships on the horizon. My cousin opens his eyes, looks at me, first eyes of incomprehension, then of incredulity. This doesn't stop him from seizing the binoculars and running to the window. He swears. The caravels don't exist. Don't you know this sea of ours provokes hallucinations?

The horizon is getting nearer. I'm serious even though I

know you won't believe me. It's getting nearer. Like a rope that tightens around us. The rope of a hanged man. To flee, I don't see another solution. What do you think?

There's a great fire, Andrés, by the sea grapes. Don't say any more stupid things; yesterday there were three caravels. Today it's true, I swear, by the sea grapes. If you say another lie I'll throw you in the sea with a rope around your neck.

A few yards from the blaze, sitting on the sgabello from the sixteenth century (my mother cherished it as the most valuable piece of her collection), is my father. He's still wearing the *mambí* suit, the medals, the tricolor ribbon, but not the hat. His hair has grown and moves messily with the morning air. The smoke from the blaze changes him to a blurry figure and it's hard to uncover the expression on his face, even though I have my reasons to suppose his face doesn't express anything at all. From time to time, moving away, Ana pours alcohol on and the flames come alive, their fiery tongues grow, the powerful dark column rises even more, filled with minuscule pieces of wood. Silo takes care of putting more on the fire, offering it, reverently, as if he were addressing an ancient and severe God, the collection of Louis XV furniture, the pieces of the secretaire and of the grandfather clock that had been destroyed previously, the two paintings by Chartrand that were near the entrance, Violeta's seascapes, the Gallé vases, *Las horas felices* by Guillermo Collazo, friend of the family and my grandmother's favorite. Later go the books, the collection of Bibles from so many eras, original editions by Mercedes Matamoros and Nieves Xenes signed by the authors, poems by Alma Rubens written in Poveda's beautiful writing, my *mambí* grandfather's memoirs. The fire changes from red to white and the lovely column of smoke has a pleasant smell. My father gets up. He is suffering, obsessed with carrying out a duty that a higher force demands of him. He throws to the fire Violeta's book, the collection of poems by Julián del Casal, afterward the sgabello that my mother would never let us sit on. Then he moves away with his head low.

Violeta appears naked. Ana runs to her and hugs her. Andrés says to hide her nudity; I say to stop a suicide.

The house is empty. Instead of furniture Ana has put boxes and to decorate, in old beer bottles, she places wildflowers that soon die. I don't know what happened to the curtains and the rugs. They most likely met the same fate, the fire. To walk through the parquet is now risky, our steps echo in the house and there are places that are off-limits to us. Our steps denounce our presence right when we would like to be invisible. Even though there is a fun side to the parquet and our steps. Andrés and I specialize in recognizing steps. Violeta isn't part of the game because she doesn't walk in the house. Since the incident with her nudity and the blaze we don't know where she is. Silo is a soldier, sure of himself, powerful, he deserves the world's respect; his steps sound as if the heel hits first and then the tip of his boot falls strongly as well. He stands at attention, clicks his heels, goes through the house like an owner visiting his properties, something that belongs to him and that no one can take away. Sometimes he makes long stops, pauses in which we imagine him observing the house's every detail. Ana's steps are those of someone who knows she's in a place that is in no way hers. Unlike Silo, she walks with her whole foot hitting the floor, and in a weak way, the same as if she were foreseeing danger, like waiting for someone to tell her, Go back to your place in the kitchen, your role is over. It's not like she walks that much in the house either; she limits herself to a few places, and even though no one has prohibited her, she imposes these boundaries on herself. My father strolls around with a step as weak as it is strong, incurably tired. I say "strolls" because it doesn't seem like he's going anywhere; it's obvious he, as opposed to Silo, doesn't feel like the owner of anything except his own desperation. You can easily tell it's him because of the time it takes for one foot hitting the floor to follow the other. I can't explain why, yet, Andrés and I are sure he first hits the outside border of his shoe before completing his step. We can't explain how we know, because of his steps, my father's solitude. When his insecure and anguished shoes are heard, Silo's strong boots quiet and Ana's defenseless sandals run to a corner.

They are desolate steps, friend, sad steps of a man who does not know what his destiny will be.

We woke up to find the house surrounded by barbed wire fences. In the corner four potent searchlights. A sign on the door declares off-limits going down to the beach, much less looking at the horizon. They destroyed the little wooden bridge, the one that looked like the cute little wooden bridges in Japanese prints.

## ARCADIA

A giant man leans over me, one of his big hands on my mouth and an index finger on his. He asks me to be quiet (an unnecessary indication; terror has me paralyzed). It doesn't take long to recognize him. In the darkness his eyes shine like false blue, and his forehead, his cheeks, illuminated by light coming from I don't know where, shape Michel the Moroccan's mythic face. He must have come from far away, his all-powerful body smells of other lands, of distant sweats, of algae, of different seas. Andrés is standing, cleaning with his shirtsleeve the compass that we found one time in the sand. In two strides Michel the Moroccan crosses the room. He looks out the window various times, makes sure the gun is loaded, stops to listen behind the door, and, shaking his head, takes the compass from Andrés and throws it on the bed. He goes to the door, opens it a little. Incredible, this giant moves without provoking a single creak in the parquet. Light doesn't enter through the small crack in the door, not a sound. He carefully closes the door. The house seems dead. Michel throws me some clothes. I begin to get dressed. He spreads a piece of paper with writing over the bed. He doesn't speak. With a pencil he limits himself to drawing a circle and writes "house"; the pencil follows an almost straight line that then breaks upon bordering what I suppose is the cliff entrance toward the right of the house; it continues moving farther away, now in a discontinuous way. When the line stops, Michel the Moroccan sketches a cross, writes "cove," draws a boat. "Here." Later he goes to the window and gestures for us to come closer. Silo goes by with the flashlight and the rifle hanging from his shoulder, he moves farther away to the other side of the house. Michel the Moroccan points to a part of the fence where a suspicious mound of grass can be seen. He returns to the paper. He writes: "First, Violeta and I will leave. Fifteen minutes. One of you. Fifteen minutes. The other one. Crawl. The boat." He takes Andrés's compass for a moment and smiles. He returns to the door, he turns around for a second to look at us, giving with his closed right hand the thumbs-up. No matter how much we pay attention, it's impossible to hear giant Michel the Moroccan's steps. Andrés and I go to the window, on opposite sides, up against the wall, scared. An enormous amount of time goes by. If Andrés weren't here, I wouldn't believe this is happening, I would think, It's just a dream, it could be, both of our dreams brought on by desperation. Silo goes by various times with the flashlight and rifle. My brother is the only living thing in the night. Beyond the circle that the searchlights form, darkness extends. The silence is complete, like the darkness. The sea can't even be heard tonight. Sometimes, I can't be sure of it, I can hear the flapping of birds on the roof, but I must be making it up. There's a moment when Silo disappears and Michel the Moroccan's shadow shifts toward the fence, picks up the grass that hides a hole that goes from one side of the fence to the other, and gestures. My sister goes cautiously to him. Michel makes her crawl. Without great difficulty, Violeta makes it to the other side. Michel follows her with even less difficulty. They run holding hands. Before arriving at the border where light becomes impotent facing night, we hear many shots and Michel the Moroccan's body falls on the sand.

The collapses don't surprise us anymore. They form a part of our daily lives. The day before yesterday the kitchen came tumbling down (Ana was lucky that in that instant my father had called her to polish the medals on his chest). Yesterday it was the dining room. Today, at dawn, part of the living room. Even though if you really thought about it, what importance does the living room being destroyed have? It's only a warehouse with bags of sand my father wants to defend himself from an attack by who knows whom. After the collapse, my father gathered us together in what was at one time my grandfather's office. I had been there a few times, and always with reverence. The furniture of black and austere wood startled me, the dark curtains (ever since the war my grandfather was afraid of the light), the portrait of my mother painted by Romañach, the sketch of Havana seen from Casablanca by Mialhe, the tiny Cuban flag next to the portrait of Martí. Nothing remains except the desk chair where my father sits with such an air of fatigue that I'm afraid he'll fall asleep at any moment. Children, he says, I want to talk to you about death. And his voice sounds like it comes from far away, from the remoteness of exhaustion. Death is more important than life . . . and he nods, his eyes close, a trickle of drool runs from the corners of his mouth. Ana hurries to wipe it. My father opens his eyes, raises a hand, his forehead shines with the ray of sun that enters through the window, a worthy death makes us heroes, and these days . . . he stares at a point that does not exist. These days only heroes . . . he lowers his hand, closes his eyes again, does not sleep, and if he sleeps, he exclaims anyway, Only heroes have the right to live, that is to say, to die with dignity. An imperious, prolonged silence drives Ana to move closer and wipe away another trickle of drool.

Andrés puts the binoculars, some books about the sea, the compass, a threadbare quilt he stole from Ana, and some pieces of old bread in a bag. It's nap time, the changing of the guard. Silo must be with my father in my grandfather's old office, and it's Ana who walks around the house with the rifle. Ana is fat, old, slow, which is why she keeps watch during the day. It's the least dangerous one. We go down the stairs slowly, which contradicts our anxiety. We take advantage of one of the balconies on the right wing of the house having fallen to slide rapidly through the rubble and get to the old terrace in the back. There we stay beneath the stairway that leads to the sand. It seems Silo and my father continue on in the office. Ana, who tires quickly, is seated on the trunk of one of the ironwood trees that my father had cut. Andrés takes advantage of this, goes slowly to the fence, as if he were not risking his life in doing it. One of the wires is cut and he smiles to show me he has been prudent, he knows what he's doing. The opening is big enough for us to escape. Andrés goes through with the agility that characterizes him. I, behind him, trying to contain my nervousness. I'm next to the fence. Ana, who seems to have heard my footsteps, turns around, looks at me with her eyes enormously open, as if she were experiencing my terror, and raises the rifle. I am paralyzed, waiting for the shot. My cousin comes running, he pulls me by my arm and Ana lowers the rifle, sits down again. I go through the hole in the fence and run toward Andrés, who has disappeared into the sea grapes.

Do you want to know why Ana didn't shoot? My grandmother and I are the only ones who know the secret. And my father, of course. Andrés is Ana's son with my father. So really my cousin is my brother, and so, because of Ana, he is different, beautiful, strong.

This is Arcadia, Andrés yells, look at it. Scarce strip of sand enclosed by two cliff tops. The purest and bluest water you could imagine. He looks at the sky. There is only one cloud; it looks like a dove that changes into a girl, that changes into a gazelle that changes into an angel and then breaks up and disappears. The horizon, the not-imaginary line. Only the most audacious may cross it. I know the story of a man who succeeded in crossing the horizon. The bow of the ship hit against the invisible wall. It was necessary to show all force, to head toward the place the devil closes with a powerful fist, and the boat broke into pieces. He, nevertheless, was able to pass to the other side, miraculously.

The days are beautiful here. We eat raw fish, silver fish that come close to the shore and let themselves be fished, gently, by hand. We drink coconut water. We bathe ourselves in the warm water anytime. We sleep in a cavern with sand for a floor. And we built a raft. It wasn't easy. We didn't know where to find wood that could make it across the ocean, so beautiful and for this reason dangerous. In the end, not far from here, we found various coconut trees with blackened plumes whose trunks we could use. Also, three tires and a piece of a mast. The raft is built. The only thing I can say is that it is beautiful tied to a rock on the shore, swaying to the soft movement of the waves. Andrés looks at it as if it were a woman. I am scared of it. And even more when I look to the sea and there far away, the impenetrable line or wall, the horizon. Andrés came up with a departure date, he wrote it in his diary, but he doesn't want to reveal it to me. He knows my fear. So, in silence, as if I were the enemy, he's filled various bottles with coconut water and gathered enough grapes. He's arranged the compass, the binoculars.

A vessel appears. I say "vessel" because that's what Andrés called it, jumping for joy. In reality it is a large white sail, the wings of a gigantic seagull that flies level with the sea. Sometimes it gives off glimmers and it seems like the sun reflecting a mirror. We must set sail today, Andrés says. I try to make him see the danger that leaving this clear, cloudless morning would represent. Silo would find us, would sound the alarm, would shoot, the efforts of these days would be lost for two seconds of imprudence. He doesn't listen. He looks at the horizon with the binoculars, smiling, Let's go, he orders me, and taking me by the arm, he makes me put all we'll need for the trip on the raft. It's time, he exclaims, and I see in his eyes, in the tension of his arms, that it would be useless to dissuade him. He climbs onto the raft and calls me urgently. I stay at the shore not looking at him, my eyes fixed on the unmoving sea. I'm not going, Andrés, it's crazy. My cousin, my brother, looks at me with eyes like my father's and his voice is now hard and authoritative. Being free doesn't matter to you? Yes, I replied, being free matters to me, but this place also matters to me because it's mine, I don't have any other place to go where I would feel happier, there must be some reason why I'm here and not somewhere else. He doesn't say anything. He unties the raft and guides it with a long stick of bamboo. Good-bye, Andrés, have a good trip, may you be happy wherever you land, I want to be happy too in this place I believe to be mine; most likely though, you can't be happy remembering our place, and I cannot either dreaming of the place you will go.

## ENVOY

Yes, friend, you can believe me or not, but years passed, twenty, thirty, many years. Numerous events (or perhaps only one with the appearance of many) took place. My house was completely destroyed. My father disappeared into the rubble with his *mambí* suit now threadbare, colorless, without medals, repeating terrible words while he cried, inconsolable, like a hopeless lover. Violeta, languid and pale, jumped to the sea from a cliff, but didn't fall into the sea (she wasn't even that lucky) but hit the rocks, blood-less, like a porcelain doll. One clear morning the body of my brother Andrés, which the sea had the delicacy to respect, washed up on the shore intact, so beautiful and happy I could not believe in its death. It has been a perfect and silent companion to my soli-tude. In a little mound of dust that went around making whirl-winds over the reefs, I recognized my mother's ashes. Believe me, friend, I'm tired of seeing boats, canoes, triremes, coming closer. They are nothing more than mirages in these waters. Look, here you have the collected messages from faraway bottles, the most desperate, sullen, indifferent messages, full of complaints. I've seen and imagined so many things! I don't know where life ends and delirium begins. Who can assure me the caravels that appear on the horizon are real? Can you perhaps give me faith in the certainty of what I see? Think what you like, truth and lie are no longer different, or at most there's only an unimportant distinction. Right now, I have no other choice but to throw myself to the sea, swim without desperation, like other times, and even though other times I have been deceived, here you have me swimming with the same innocence toward those caravels I see coming with their sails unfurled.

*Translated by Víctor Rodríguez Núñez and Katherine Hedeen*

**ERNESTO RENÉ RODRÍGUEZ**

# The House, Serrat, Cinema, and . . . Do Narrators Still Dream About Prose Poets?

*All revelation is ambiguous,*
*especially poetic revelation.*

—María Zambrano

I was just walking along as always, entertained; I passed by a house on the corner, and I suddenly heard a song by Joan Manuel Serrat coming in all directions. *Son aquellas pequeñas cosas que nos dejó un tiempo de rosas . . .* The equipment that broadcast it had to be an Aiwa, a Philips, or something like that because it sounded so damn good it made you want to lick your lips. And there I was in pure ecstasy, standing on the opposite corner where I went to buy cigarettes at the local dive. Me, someone who has never had a drink or even showed up in a place like that, I walked in to buy some cigarettes solely to justify my briefly lingering. There are times when such places are ideal for channeling certain necessary pauses.

More than by that particular song that put me into an unexpected trance, it was the next ones from which I construed a whole repertoire. The volume of the sound, the surprise, whatever it was—the crux of the matter revolved around another set of factors that rested on that resonating residence. Like so many others, this house for me, which in spite of everything had always been there for years and years as if it were never on the corner, as if its doors were inside. Meanwhile, it immediately occurred to me that these might be new tenants celebrating the simple occasion of a *permuta,* a grueling apartment swap. However, if that's what it was, there was no trace of any move. I mean the simple act of viewing its facade gave me the impression of having seen the owners before and forever after. I don't know. Some things are like this and that's that. If I were to continue on this path of families and houses, I would never even finish putting the icing on the cake of the first part of the story. What's astonishing about all of this is very simple but, at the same time, very entangled.

It turns out that days later, I went to the Journalism Department at the university to hear a lecture, given by the art critic R., about Cuban audiovisual as well as about some recent global trends in cinema. During R.'s talk, in a sublime, particularly lively moment in which he was really getting carried away—I mean truly excited, pointing furiously from clip to clip—I heard him say something like, "One should not search for poetry, because it comes forth by itself." This left my neurons out of commission, and at the same time it sent me light-years away from the rest of his words, just like I'd been with Serrat's songs. R. stamped his mark on the act of artistic creation. He inspired me to broaden the meaning of that phrase, take it out of that context and introduce it into the everyday, while still considering the properties of the big leagues.

No more or less, from that lecture on, I tried to apply the little phrase "to wait for poetry to come forth," a somewhat sensitive situation, since I saw it circularly, but commentaries aside, there was something that did not fit and made me momentarily ambivalent. It was difficult to get out from the quagmire. Then I saw that I needed to get some distance and to treat it as if it were a mathematical formula—adding, subtracting, dividing, multiplying: the verb "to search" is a synonym for "to investigate," "to find out," "to scrutinize." And, the verb "to come forth" is a synonym of "to be born," "to spring up," "to germinate." Therefore, the sum of these terms is equal to, in the first case, "to go to the gathering of," and in the second, "to leave for the gathering of" . . . Ignoring the fact that appearances deceive, both results, at first glance, can be viewed as one and the same. They are not the same nor are they written in the same way. Just looking at this dilemma from a bird's-eye view was enough for a realization to dawn on me in addition to a "do not bite off more than I can chew," while I tried to relate the phenomenon onto itself, as if it were the unfolding of elements and I were a scientist, a philosopher, and even a dilettante. And as someone once said—it must have been a cosmonaut—who can be anything more than a dilettante?

Nevertheless, I ought to dispel the core of this matter or, I should say, deduce the synonyms, in order to simplify this text until the end because otherwise there is no way to explain its narrative structure (even though these days, a destructured design is totally in fashion, and in spite of the fact that neither the Real Academia Española nor the *Oxford English Dictionary* has yet to catch on and actually include the auditory image in their pages, the vendors can count on me for supplying their inventory).

Let's say that, as it is logical, I will begin at the beginning with Serrat's song, the house, and me . . . R.'s words and, above all, my resistance to them guide me on the route to follow.

I live in a marginal neighborhood overrun with dilapidated houses, potholes in the street, trashy people, gossip and backstabbing, black-market deals, street fights, bad taste, bad words, and delinquents. It's really total chaos—and if you go in, you will never find your way out. Nevertheless, for the residents of this neighborhood, to live without all that suffocation seems to be more problematic than being deprived of oxygen. As for me, if I could, I would jump ship without a second thought. I say this without any embarrassment or sense of triumph.

Well then, Serrat, at the house on the corner, without back-tracking a step, is an anachronism. At the same time, it is something sublime, even at full blast. In thirtysome years, I had never heard in that context anything but salsa, romantic songs, drenched in kitsch and repeated ad nauseam, like what happens these days with *reguetón,* rap, groups of adolescents like those in Harlem or in the *banlieues* of Paris. From a stereo, that we might as well refer to as $160.59, placed on whatever container in the neighborhood, all hanging out to lyrics that sound like: . . . *quién tiró la tiza, el negro ese)\** . . . I mean it's a song that I like just fine— let's be clear here. But a Serrat? No, only at my house, at a volume that you can hardly hear unless you plaster your ear to the stereo. And as if that were not enough, accompanied by an exquisite fruit tea that you can't even find in spiritual centers, and since cinema is already a leitmotif throughout this story, imagine the tea in Sevres china cups like those of San Diego Perrugoría in *Fresa y chocolate.* In other words, in this neighborhood, I clandestinely enter into the scenery or just look at what I happen upon: poetry in itself. Whatever, say it as you like, this "in itself" is at the core of R.'s statement. Let's remember his words: "You ought not search for poetry, because it comes forth by itself." Before such a pronouncement uttered by a prestigious art critic who, every so often and especially in adverse situations, lets that *little macho from Cayo Hueso* slip out, you can feel as if you don't have any say in the matter. If R. says it, it is because he already pondered over it or because it just came out like that, of its own accord. Like everything, this is an attempt at a story and not an essay, not a story-essay in the style of my contemporaries— E.P.C or E.P.C. And certainly not in the style of the author of this

---

\* "Who threw the chalk, this black guy" is the refrain of a rap song by the Cuban group Clan 537, a group that was popular among youth and controversial for the manner in which it addresses issues of race and class.—Trans.

story, E.R.R. So, I will locate a story as soon as possible in order to draw in the Aristotelian reader.

*Beginning with the flavor of a lump in your throat:* And if I feel like approaching poetry from behind, even if it's going to erupt by itself like one of Venus's nipples, if you'll pardon my vulgarity. Well, if we're pursuing this line of thought, sure—who wouldn't give it his all or let he who is without sin cast the first piece of chalk? In that case, we would be before a catalyst, an indicator according to S.A., a professor at the Creative Writing Center where I study. However, according to another professor named R., from the moment it begins, every story carries within it the instability of desire, which indicates to me that in the story about the house, Serrat, and . . . me, at least according to R.'s postulate, there's a desire, a hidden piece of information in . . . a Chinese box? No, I really can't stand them. Well, not quite, I can take the Chinese part and I'd even provide the boxes. However, I am more taken by the challenge of not waiting for poetry to come forth. To try to search for it is not only to discover or to bump right into it, that's to say, to see if it is possible to obtain as if it were an advance payment. Afterward we shall see if approaching poetry from behind is also conceiving it without this suspicious ostentation that seems artificial to us, in other words, with hardly any spontaneity.

To search for poetry or not, that is the dilemma. But if it is a desire that comes forth from me without speculating, I've already earned a few points in my favor. And if I were to make an analogy with R., well, to search for poetry or not is the same because in the end, it just appears suddenly, maybe, where it is least expected, at the house on the corner. But if it does not hit you in the face or does not even just emerge, and life without poetry, you already know . . . don't even bother because it's a sham. In such a case, you just have to go to find it in some ivory tower? Does someone have the address? Sure, for such a task one hardly needs anything: a soul, sentiment, and a heart; and a few more little things to write a story. Or to develop what they call the climax. Come on, it's about time to loosen the knot on my tie.

*Climax charged with synonyms and antonyms that don't have anything to do with each other:* If the master writer-poets like Jorge Luis Borges say that the most important part of the story is the beginning and the end, why even worry about the climactic tying together? I am getting a knot in my throat just thinking about it. Certainly, certain tongues, theoretical ones, say that the conflict ought to be considered from all different angles—when you're talking about a bond, some made-up story, and a knot on one's tie. So, the reader needs to be a TV viewer of tear-jerking soap operas. There is a reason they exist from Monday to Friday on channel six. The other day when I was arriving at her house, I surprised my *new girlfriend turned into love before the soap opera,* and she didn't even say hi. If, on the contrary, it had been my other girlfriend, the penultimate one, who sells iced guava cubes and is a fan of Colorama, Enrique I, and of the chick that sings—what is it that she sings?—then nothing would have been out of whack. But this one who's studying in her fifth year of philology and is a raving fan of the exquisite Rolling Stones tune "Fool to Cry," of "La Internacional" by PPR (according to the Lucas national video awards or the television), or P Para Ricardo (according to the radio or J.C. on his morning program), or Porno para Ricardo (according to . . . according to their identity, according to their job)* as well as of so much classical music that she gets lost in the Basílica Menor de San Francisco de Asís, no, no, it couldn't be . . . at this point in time with the Cuban soap opera, it's without poetry and scenery and has cardboard for walls . . . But no one realizes? Incredible! No, not only does it lack the means to produce,

---

* Porno para Ricardo is a controversial Cuban punk band. Given that the word "porno" forms part of the controversy, it is referred to by all of these varied names.—Trans.

but the artistic direction is terrible, and we're not talking about money, that episode after episode, the bagasse comes out through the pores of the screen, if it were a Brazilian one, well then, my Dulcinea from Arts and Letters would escape without a sound. After all, a minute of silence, one has to acknowledge that Brazilian soaps are made with a budget, a staying-up-all-night carefulness, at least an outline, an attempt at poetry that one is grateful for even if one is a partisan of the genre made in Santiago de Cuba. OK, returning to my girlfriend from this story, as a consequence, I found myself before the first conflict, or as if this were not enough, upon asking her, if she really liked these *culebrones,* she said to me very sincerely, without a touch of irony, that she didn't know the significance of that synonym for "soap operas," literarily meaning "big snakes." I let this go, but I could not take it when she criticized me for being a male chauvinist when I explained to her Cortázar's notion of a female reader. If it is in this state that the rest of the Philology Department finds itself, what will the future hold for us embryos in literary workshops? Dear God, Raymond Carver, would you like to do us a favor and help us out? Or, tell me, what did we talk about when we were talking about love, or should we say, about poetry . . . ?

> I have dreamed of you so much that you are no longer real . . . I have walked so much, talked so much, slept so much, with your phantom, that perhaps the only thing left for me is to become a phantom among phantoms, a shadow a hundred times more shadow than the shadow that moves and goes on moving, brightly, over the sundial of your life.
>
> —Robert Desnos

R.D., thank you for giving to Carpentier your passport to the City of Lights, even if it was merely for the Festival of French Cinema at the Film Archive from the twelfth to the thirteenth of this month.

Since I am at the climax posing as the denouement, you ought to recognize, dear reader, that this narrator is still in a crisis, in a jam, I'll tell you, perhaps like the prose poets who still dream of being narrators, *quizás, quizás, quizás, thinking, thinking,* and, without losing perspective on my desire, my evidence, and my motives. Remember that, in spite of the out-of-placeness of *my new girlfriend turned into love before the soap opera,* this image is in itself poetic, perhaps because poetry, in fact, is contrasting and, damn it, let there be poetry, but if I had not gone in search of it, or rather, of my girlfriend, and if I didn't have my antennae tuned in on account of R.'s words, in the precise instant in which poiesis is the seed that sprouts, I would never even have found Little Red Riding Hood's wolf because you can never go back . . . This all leads me to you, Benetton. On the one hand, things seem to appear when you are least searching for them, but if you ignore your sixth sense, then forget it—whether it be written in Sanskrit, recited by Buddhist monks and even by rabbis who study the Torah and scrutinize the Talmud. It is preferable to continue trapped in the TV spiderweb of the everyday, perhaps like this story that doesn't seem to have either a head of a master shot or a foot of a denouement.

*Denouement starting with grace notes like catalysts and informants:* A short while ago, a group of companions from our Creative Writing Center, along with two or three guests (two or three of them turned out to be poets from that romp of a workshop reminiscent of Lezama Lima's Farraluque in the Alamar neighborhood of Havana), all met at N.'s house for a little get-together with the pretext of reading one or two of our pretexts—come on—the redundancy or cacophony is worth it. In my case, I was after my top secret of those days: that was to find out if one could or could not find poetry when one searches for it, whether it be in a colander or a pair of yellow tennis shoes on the corner of Forty-second and Fifth, just like in Fernández's story "Procesión lejos de Bretaña," only that a colander and a pair of tennis shoes could stand in for poetry, as the dollar is plainly convertible into pounds sterling. Before all, let me be clear that N. (that is her literary pseudonym) lives, commentaries aside, in Cocosolo. It was past twelve at night when, with a few glasses of Corsario rum already in us, we gave ourselves over to the task of reading. Yes, there was tremendous desire to read, a damned desire to read. We objected to the month of vacation that the highest in command gave us, although we know without anyone pointing an index finger at us what it means to count on this type of center on the corner of Twentieth and Fifth, except . . . Coleridge's flower and Martí's slippers. For such a reading, with a degree of tact and strategy (a poetic touch), we took advantage of the presence of one of our most worthy guests: the professor S.A., who I must profess, was quite a character, and as we read, he just passed out on the bed. First it was N.'s turn to read, the host of the party. All the stories were genius except for mine. Nevertheless, it turned out that mine was the most polemical—poetry in itself—and, all modesty aside, when there's smoke, there's fire. In contrast, as a post-testimonial, "poetry in itself," the word "genius" was in the mouth of M., who didn't bring anything to read, but to compensate, when minutes before we were singing *voulez vous coucher avec moi ce soir* to the base of some guitar strums, he really let it go on the mikes, if you were to see it: genius. There were also other guests who weren't writers but conveyed the best public and unpublishable opinions. In this case, Lorenzón, a housepainter, stood out. He asserted, in utter controversy with Professor S., that Corín Tellado, a paradigm of the popular romance, was as worthy as García Marquéz because she got her own way—a real businesslady, all-time—and that surely in Cuba, even a master like Carpentier, in one of his *lost steps,* at some point or another, devoured her, although our professor, a resident of Jesús María, another neighborhood that won't even make it into the annals of this story, altered the direction of the events (or rather, of the slaps between him and Lorenzón) upon arriving at the magic words that left everyone with their mouths wide open, "there is no perfect story, period," and so on, of course. Anyway, this is not the point, as you know, a shift to allow for poetry: *step aside, the original is coming . . .*

*Epilogue a):* more bored than in discord, it occurred to my workshop companions to play the movie game. I hadn't said to you that film is an intrinsic part of this knickknack of a story. The little game consisted of guessing the names of such and such a film that the other team specifies. We were two teams, the ridiculous ones and the stupid ones. The ridiculous ones were narrators, and the stupid ones were poets, on whose side I found myself. I don't know if it happened clandestinely, obviously, or by chance. Be careful, one moment please: chance. Here is the key to the substance with which you evaluate your dreams. After all, I also write poetry. Upon confessing this, it is inevitable not to feel like an infiltrator, swimming among narrators, from the point of view of the poets, I'd become *Our Man in Havana* . . . Agent 007, maybe because of the seventh art and its offshoots. Yes, it was an honor belonging to the losing team. Although the difference that I am mentioning would not be the only one between the teams. For example, in the game, there are rules that join literature to the visual language of deaf people, and if you want: take it or leave it. The narrators assumed it as if they were Cortázar's *Famas,* and the poets, of course, as *Cronopios* and Quixotes from part 1 and Sanchos from part 2, that *always were walking in flowers,* we put up with a lot to get to this healthy way of passing time. Exactly as I desired, I wanted the narrators to win the laurel. We could call it the R., but it was inevitable, film is one of my poetic passions. We triumphed as the cock first crowed out the "worst" of the titles in the history of cinema that appeared like the letter of triumph that poetry and chance had reserved for us and that the team of the ridiculous, with all its indicators and informants, could not guess. Yes, in spite of having in their favor a half-Brazilian girl who looked like she was on our side more than on theirs—

another Agent 007. I would have liked to give this story the same name, this title that I am not about to say, so that I may save it for the next game. Of course, hard and ephemeral cash.

Hardly in any time, if you wait long enough, we started up the literary gathering again, this time in Lennon Park. There, beside the image converted into a *loyal statue with its back toward the future.* How was it possible? I could not stop remembering that Professor R. had his scholarship revoked, only for carrying a magazine that contained the Beatles from Liverpool. And I and I and I should have known better, like a chameleon and the force of Nostalgia; in that instant, I became a song, daydream, and nothing.

*Epilogue b):* Up until now, the art critic R.—despite considering him my ol' pal from the times of *Nostalgia* and the days of *Sacrifice,* although my favorite, it's difficult, may be *Stalker,* and his, perhaps I shouldn't ask him—should recognize that after Tarkovsky, the classes with all that you wanted to know about poetry and were afraid to ask, what didn't get under your skin even though it was shoved down your throat . . . Moreover, it confirms to me—makes me recognize that, even like this, such as in life as in art, mother of invention, son of a stiff, the punch cards for a player piano, where things acquire another veneer, this other poetic dimension, I give thanks to his phrase "you should not search for" . . . or, a curious thing, as if R. and this other voice, D.H.L.—authorized and in his own right—had formed an agreement. Please let's bow our heads. I listened to him at the Creative Writing Center the other day, as he said, in reference to a story that suffered from severe adjectivitis:

> Poetry ought to spring up from the text without needing to add anything.

Well, I hope that this farce, that is about to finish, at least connects the unbreathable essence to the square nose of the hypotenuse man, but also, by pure contingency, it gives me the goddamned impression that searching for is leaving in pursuit of . . . and coming forth is also going out in pursuit of . . . and that in itself, poetry, however you put it, whoever said it already said it, *is an act of faith.*

*Translated by Jacqueline Loss*

**SOLEIDA RÍOS**

# Gerona

With Mario in Gerona: throngs of people amid vacancy and desolation. You sense you are suspended, not planted on your own two feet, and you can't see, are unconscious of, what's coming. Mario appears from one moment to the next, and as usual comes from far away. He knows the place you call Gerona. You are confused, aching with desire. Spinning in idle speculation, you selfishly crave him, but with a bland, dull ache.

Mario goes into the bedroom of your apartment—yes, it's still yours, though you left long ago. Blithely, you surrendered it, but either through blind luck or a finely calibrated mix-up, it's still your apartment.

You'll leave him in the dilapidated apartment, with its unresolved ownership, where the walls shift against each other and the corners aren't plumb. There must be a tilt to the ceiling or floor that creates the graceless, unstable lines. As though the wear and tear had been conceived, a deliberate aging. Depressions in the gray walls. Signs of a negligent hand, maybe just lazy, haphazard slaps by elbow or foot on the unfinished cement walls, mottled and untroweled—a surface the texture of crushed paper.

Yes, you leave him there and go directly (for you, another re-turn?) to the offices (a spectral simulacrum, like the apartment). You need to arrange everything: permit, documentation, every last item. Endless, unendurable details.

The office rooms are sordid, their doors aren't true and only half close with the help of a piece of knotted fishing wire or ny-lon rope attached to a bent nail. Pairs of tables and chairs—grade school castoffs—along with broken desks that stand upright only because their legs are tied with barbed wire. This is the real-ity, like it or not. And there sits the son of a bitch that *you* inter-rogate, insolent bitch that you are.

"Is it yes or no?"

Even when it's "no" it will always be "yes." You feel the cor-rosive "no" eating at you until what supports you, your frame, cracks. The heart issues orders to curse, to shriek, but your mouth silences you. Mario should be able to stay with you in the apart-ment. That's why you're here, why you travel from room to room, introducing yourself and speaking little, hearing nothing. Running with words, your ears refuse to listen anymore. You search for the "yes" to your well-mannered conformity, but you know you won't hear it in the voice of the One Who Speaks. The One reclines in a chair that must have once been a high school desk. You watch for a sign, or signs.

This will take time. Walking down the narrow halls, open-ing the doors of the first to the last room . . . (The One removes the bent nail, grabs the twisted fishing wire or nylon rope, pushes on the door, and finally it screeches loose of the floor.) You enter nervously, obsequiously, announce your presence through a rep-etition of pseudogestures and meaningless queries. You're out of sync, as usual, with the precise order required by the code. Doc-uments are rapidly unstapled, verified, and so on . . . Leaning back in his chair, the One Who Speaks reviews each document one by one, in a simulation of scrupulous care, or, wetting his index finger with his tongue, merely shuffles them as he taps a pen on the uneven desktop . . .

"Something is missing!" the One Who Speaks, Official, Other, exclaims. You think you hear glee in his voice.

Surrounded by a clot of hot, stagnant air, inside I've turned to ice. I can't tell which documents are missing in the exhaustive list. He's already reviewed them once:

"First, a photocopy of your identity card, a notarized document that verifies your co-ha-bi-ta-tion (lacking legal status), and the original of the deed or the right to reside in said property. Do you understand? Barring that, the agreement . . . *X* duly and legally signed by an authorized ministry signatory at *your earliest opportunity*. Got that? Nobody else will do. In addition, ration card, official census of building, and a document that attests to the property's size in square meters, or current number of residents." You peer at all the dusty knickknacks in the room—it will always be "yes"—then at a series of photographs (small, medium, large) that have either bleached out or were originally shot in black and white. They hang from twisted red and blue ribbons tied to nails scattered on the peeling, whitewashed walls—it will always be "yes"—along with numerous awards, diplomas, and distinctions with date, stamp, signature. In Gerona, La Victoria, or La Fe on a day and month, 1982.

Now Pretty Boy emerges from this welter as though ungluing himself from a spiderweb of impossible complexity.

"I've worked in La Quinta and I know," says Pretty Boy González Castañer, the ecologist and poet, "I'll get you out of this mess."

So this is the way I leave, liberated (?) from the web. I walk toward the apartment, head erect, pace slow, steady and careful, like the broken, though undefeated, stallion that Mario once sketched at the beach. One step forward, two, three . . .

"Do you recognize *him* as one of the pursuers?"

"One of the pursuers from La Garza?" Pretty Boy is taken aback: " I don't personally know him, but yes I do recognize him and I'll bet you he's one of them. He may not be one of the top guys, but he's involved, all right."

It's said that they used to say, "*La Garza,* heaven of dummies . . . dummies on the horizon . . . ," only to later inquire, "What could that mean? Who was responsible? (We'll assume it was someone chosen from a list . . . ?)"

They read it out loud actually, grinning, or maybe they bribed him with a smile then proceeded with the interrogation:

"Him?" They mentioned a name, another name . . . "*Más Mir,* Mr. Insight Full? Sure? But . . . just him?"

He was a resident of La Victoria. It was only natural. "The Poet, Mr. Insight Full, Francisco José . . . ? He was the one who wrote *it* up? And, what's more, added those *details?*"

(Read, lies.)

Night and day. Here, also farther away, crossing the waters. In new suites of offices, toward new meaningful endeavors, "*Más Mir?* Mr. Insight Full? How can that be . . . ?" Impossible, or maybe not. In turn, I respond convincingly with, "details, precise details?" Then I say, if I remember correctly, "Do you realize . . ."

"*La Garza,* the Heron? What more were you going to say? A delicate, pearl white bird belonging to the swan family . . ." and dryly, at least until it makes you either nervous or furious, and, you can't deny it, with a certain desire to confound, . . . "herons, either they're in the air or picking at cattle."

Pick *what?* Fly *where?* Mr. Insight Full's *dumb* heron? Right, we knew that all along . . .

The Interrogator writes, *They're going to their homes to vent their rage.* Words they must have mistakenly picked up from Pretty Boy Castañer himself.

Always game, Pretty Boy accompanies me while I shop then I go on alone.

Everything you select is for Mario, to share with Mario in the apartment. Why so mean, so penurious, then? I don't know. I calculate, select, purchase. It's not his fault, or mine. It's that "no" that's been written on my skin. The Metabolism of No.

So you go. I go. Full of misgivings, I find that Mario is absent and a skinny, graceless intruder is lying on our makeshift bed with a bundle of her belongings. She's virtually taken possession of the place. My apartment, this shadow.

Mario enters, leaves. Outside they clamor for him (man, woman, child). They call him by name, "Mario Hogoblin . . ." requesting who knows what. Mario responds in all seriousness, applying himself to the task at hand with the care and precision of a doctor. On one of his trips in or out, Mario explains to me that it wasn't he who had decided where to house the intruder. The intruder rocks herself in the apartment's only chair and gazes at me indifferently, a phony indifference nonetheless. Skinny, graceless, and phony. Where will this lead . . . ?

I smell a rat. This is what I think. I feel it, too. Mario sympathizes. After all, the endless traipsing in and out, his humble dedication to the ones outside, and, what's more, an intruder who has taken over . . . Finally, to know (because he just thought it, and in a moment, he'll say it) that he is forced to curtail his visit to a mere four days . . . it's too much. He'll leave and we won't have had the time or opportunity to become intimate. I shouldn't say anything to him—nothing at all—about these awkward circumstances.

Even though Mario is physically different from what I imagined—he's taller and more muscular, with faraway, dull eyes in a melancholy face—still, this Mario knows me, reads me! He beckons, and we sit down together on a gray, withered, peeling tree trunk (you watch a line of poisonous ants diligently truck chunks of green leaf, then disappear into their refuge in the earth to finish the job, to fulfill their destiny). Sweetly, solicitously, Mario cradles my head, gazes at me, he who isn't he, leans in until we are locked in an embrace. Then, afterward, when he lets you go, you feel something soft and supple in your mouth. You spit bits of flesh, but no blood or lymph, into your hands. The skin of his tongue.

*Translated by Barbara Jamison*

## ANNA LIDIA VEGA SEROVA

# The Girl Who Doesn't Smoke on Saturdays

*for Lourdes*\*

---

\* According to Manín, it's a great offense to dedicate this story to such a beautiful friend as Lourdes. But I don't dedicate it because Lourdes is like the protagonist, deformed, but rather because she, like this character, mysteriously does not smoke on Saturdays.

With each day that passes, it becomes harder and harder to think of going out. I get up and pace the apartment: from the bedroom to the bathroom, from the bathroom to the kitchen, from the kitchen maybe to the dining room, when I'm not eating standing up in the kitchen, then I return to the bedroom, to the bed. With each day that passes, fewer people come to visit me. This doesn't bother me; when someone comes, telling me their stories from out there, I feel I'm not missing anything extraordinary. I have my music and my books and goldfish and someone to run my errands to the corner store and a Saturday lover named Jorge Luis, but I call him Doc because he's a doctor. He comes early in the afternoon and we pass the day together making love and arguing and making love again and arguing again until night falls and he leaves. Then I return to bed wanting to sleep because that's what I like the most.

*Just to sleep. Sleep-sleep-sleep. Mother was giving a hug and rocking, sleep, she was singing, sleep, my love. Look, Mom, look what I have here and here and here . . . That's nothing, sleep, sleep-sleep-sleep; I will give you a little kiss and it will go away . . . Please, Mom,*

*do something quickly! Already there's more here, here, and here ...*
*Mother hugs and gives kisses, one, two, three, then begins to tear at the*
*skin with her teeth, biting, chewing, swallowing, and again biting.*

*The blood ran from the corners of her mouth and stained the blue*
*dress. Look, Mom, look what you've done to me. It's nothing, she re-*
*sponds with a bloody mouth, sleep my love, it's nothing.*

You've got to do something, repeats Doc, Saturday after Saturday. You can't continue this way, you're sinking. Don't come
telling me what I have to do, I say, Saturday after Saturday. He
brings me magazines where there are all kinds of materials about
disfigured people who have been able to carry on and move
through their lives, he talks to me about willpower, about the ne-
cessity to have willpower. In these moments I hate him. You can
leave me whenever you want, I tell him, I'm ready for you to leave
me anytime. We both know this is a lie, he answers, and holds me
and kisses me, moves his hands across my body, across my magnificent body covered in hair, across my proud body covered in
thick black hair.*

*The hair sprouts from my pores and expands around me and en-*
*velops me. Hair sprouts from my eyes and my mouth, becomes tangled*
*with my tongue, obstructs my breathing, creates ridges in my throat.*
*Someone with my voice says: look at that beast, that vermin, tie it up,*
*destroy it. I feel a giant foot coming down on my body, crushing me,*
*my bones break, my tissues burst; the thick mass of hair with blood*
*and flesh is all that remains of me. Someone with my voice says: sleep,*
*love, sleep-sleep-sleep, and Mom sweeps away what was left of me*
*with a reed broom.*

Once a month my mother comes. Before, everyone came:

---

* A few years ago an acquaintance, a radio announcer, said she received a letter
from a girl who wanted to kill herself because her body was becoming covered
in hair. I don't know what happened in reality, but I made my own story. And
if she, the real girl, reads this, she will know that there are people who think of
her without knowing who she is.

Mom, Dad, Dante, Loretta, and Alfredo. They sat silently in a circle and watched me, not daring to say a thing. One day I told them: I'm not a monkey, go to the zoo. They were offended and never came back. Only Mom comes with her thin fingers that seem like paper and the blue dress that smells of childhood. She brings food, cigarettes, and money. She leaves the packages on the tabletop and secretly dries her tears. Do you need anything? You shouldn't smoke so much, you're so thin. I'm fine, I reply, I don't need anything. Are you sure you don't need anything? I'm sure, don't worry. You don't want me to sweep here for you or wash some clothes? No, thanks, I'm not an invalid. She passes the handkerchief across her eyes, sighing. And if you shave? she asked one day, would you like me to shave you? That's worse, Mom. Fine, she gets up disappointed, I'm going. Her paper fingers twist the handkerchief and squeeze tears onto the floor. Take care of yourself, daughter. You too. The inevitable torture of hug and kiss. The smell of childhood that remains long after she leaves.

*The park custodian was the guardian of the swings and the river of leaves beneath the swings. All of us children feared him and that fear made us shout cruel things. He only smiled and continued to sweep the leaves with a reed broom. We thought he ate raw children; he was horrible, seemed like an animal, he did not have teeth and was covered in hair. We thought he ate children raw, we cried at night, until our parents got rid of him. The park went into ruin, drowning beneath the leaves. Look, Mom, there's no park, there are no swings, just the river of leaves that rises and rises. It's nothing, sleep, my love, sleep-sleep-sleep. Mom lies down and begins covering her with leaves, burying her beneath the leaves. Her skin is covered by black bristles, her teeth fall out, and now it's not Mom but the guardian of the park who has returned to eat her raw.*

Saturdays are special days and not only because Doc comes. Really, Doc comes precisely because Saturdays are special days. I get up early, put on the reggae cassette, the only reggae cassette I have, I change the water in the fish tank and begin to organize, wash the mountain of plates accumulated during the week, clean the clothes. When my house is impeccable, I take care of myself. I undress and carefully go over my body. Patches of virgin skin still remain, on my knees and belly, although they slowly disappear beneath the stains of hair. I prepare the bathtub with bubble bath and dried rose petals, I submerge myself, I wash myself, slowly, for a long time. I brush the hair with a hairbrush, with a sponge I clean the parts still intact. Then, wrapped in a towel, I rub myself with perfumes, creams, powder. So, standing over a newspaper, I carefully trim the projecting hairs, parting them. Finally impeccable, like my house, I put in the second Saturday cassette, Celtic music, and dance naked until Doc arrives and we start to argue and make love. Saturdays are special, I don't spend them sleeping or trying to sleep, like the other days, and I don't smoke a single cigarette.

*Sleeping interminably. Sleeping in search of a dream, among so many nightmares, a sole dream, that dream. Sleep-sleep-sleep to return to the dream of the girl of white and smooth skin, of the girl who walks naked among the multitudes showing off her white and smooth skin, of the girl I am. My mother runs toward me in her dress of sunflowers, my father pushes through the crowd; with him are my siblings and friends. She is so beautiful, says someone with my voice. She is so beautiful, the girl that I am in the dream that I search for.*

I don't think I can come next Saturday, says Doc. I knew this could happen at any moment. I thought I was prepared so that this could happen at any moment. Nevertheless, he catches me off guard, like a slap. Fine, my voice trembles, if you can't come, don't. Look, he says, don't be like this. I simply have a commitment, a friend's wedding . . . You don't have to invent excuses, I interrupt. I'm not inventing, it's not what you think, you know very well that you can come with me, if you want to. You know I won't come, and that's why you say it.* I don't say it because of that, completely the opposite, though you're in a tantrum, let's see if you'll decide to leave this hole you've created for yourself. That's none of your business! I scream. Yes it is, he hugs me, I want you to be happy because I love you. Do you think I can be happy exposing myself to ridicule? What ridicule? Still he hugs me, but I feel that this time we won't end up in the bed as usual; that fills me with panic, but I'm uncontrollable, completely uncontrollable. Do you know what will happen if I leave here? Yes, I know: nothing will happen, absolutely nothing! I will stop traffic, little old ladies will faint, children will cry terrified, and women will throw rocks at me! I explain screaming. You think you're too important! He screams at me, nobody cares about you, that's the reality, nobody cares if you leave or not! He screams, nobody cares about anyone, not about you, not about anyone! He screams. Now he's let me go, now he's not holding me anymore and that fills me with panic. That's what you think? I say filled with panic. That's what I think, he responds. In any case, I'm not going to leave, I say. Never, not anywhere? Never, not anywhere. Definitely not? Definitely not. Well, then there's nothing to talk about, he gets up and walks to the door. Let me know if you change your mind, you have my number, he begins to open the lock. If you leave now, don't ever come back, I declare filled with panic. Is that what you want? That's what I want, I'm sick of you. Rot away, then! He shouts. He leaves and closes the door. Go to hell, I shout at the closed door. Imbecile, asshole, fucker! I shout at the door. I hate you! I shout filled with panic.

*The night of the monster-women, the great carnival of the*

---

* Once in the Coppelia ice-cream parlor I saw a girl like this. I don't know if it was the same girl from the letter to the radio announcer. She wore a short and very open dress and had enormous moles of hair on all parts of her body. People stared at her, it's true, but she handled it with so much ease that she only inspired respect.

*monster-women. Bird-women and bull-women, spider-women, cockroach-women, rat-women, and among them, at the very center, me, the wolf-woman. Long live the queen! They howl and place the crown on my head. Long live the queen of monstrosity! They howl and place the crown on my monstrous wolf head. That's not me, I try to explain to them, I'm the girl with white and smooth skin, this is a mistake; but only bellows come from my throat and get lost in the sounds of the jubilation and someone laughs and laughs with my voice.*

Lisette came to visit me. She is a very amusing dwarf who works at the funeral home making wreaths for the dead and comes once in a while to bring me dried rose petals. I was about to leave, as you took so long to open the door, I thought that you had gone out. I was sleeping, I explain, you know that I never go anywhere. She tells me the latest jokes about the dead, working in a funeral home develops one's sense of humor. In your dreams, I ask flatly, have you never seen yourself normal? I mean, have you ever dreamed you were tall and beautiful? No, she responds, I am what I am, that's all there is. We talk for a while longer, about other things, but now there is something that doesn't work, something wrong. You seem different, she mentions when leaving, you should smoke less, sleep less, dream less. Thanks for the advice, I respond, close the door, and return to bed.

*What a strange little spot, Doc caresses the stain of hair on my shoulder. I have another one here, I show him my thigh and he kisses it. So good, it's like plush. Look at this one, it's bigger. Uhmmm, Doc licks it, so good, so good. You're a cat, a tasty cat, my cat. Meow, I say, meow. A large cat, covered in hair. Meow. Fat cat, move, sweet cat, continue, don't stop, shameless cat, pig, wag your tail, disgusting cat. Stop, I say, please stop. Go on, beast, move your bearded ass, keep going, stinking beast. Stop, I scream, stop right now, but I don't hear my voice. Only cat sounds. Meow. Meow.\**

---

\* Sometimes, in my dreams, I look different than I am. Mostly in erotic dreams. It startles me and I spend the day upset, like someone lost.

When it's time to boil milk, I feel my pubic hair graze against the handle of the oven. I know that I will masturbate right here, in the middle of the dirty plates with bits of food, beneath the lamp of scant, cloudy light. A kind of competition: to make myself come before the milk boils. Or better yet, at the same time, like a symbolic act. The skirt between my finger and clitoris, an exotic detail. Evocations of scenes, fantasies, and the milk foaming at the edges. Low moans, searching for Doc's exact pitch, varying the sounds and the finger's movements (now moving in gentle circles a little to the left), eyes watching the steaming milk, visions grow bolder (a mouth around my clitoris, your mouth on my clitoris, my mouth on my clitoris). The milk gets bigger, like a penis that grows inside a mouth (my mouth around a penis, a penis in my mouth, your mouth on my mouth on your penis, your mouth on your penis). The milk is rising, the milk is a foaming penis, my finger licks the wet skirt, the milk is a volcano of penises about to overflow, my clitoris holds milk about to erupt, my left hand blindly turns the handle, the milk rests suspended at the edge of the pot, the right hand—the five fingers—appeasing with uneven beats that threaten to rip the skirt.

*I rise into the air seated on the broom and little by little my hair begins to fall out burying the city. A tiny Doc runs below, shouting something and making gestures with his hands. I wave to him. See how beautiful I am? I ask, showing off my skin that shines in the sun. I do somersaults on the broom, laughing. See me, Doc, see how beautiful I am? I look down and I can't see him, he's stuck in the middle of all the hair I've rained down on him. Doc, I cry, I'm worth nothing, Doc, without you nothing matters . . . Sleep, says Mom, sleep, love.*

Without opening the blinds all the way, I look outside. The piece of street illuminated by the sun delights me. The unkempt grass in front of the house grows higher, the flamboyan tree burns with flowers and also there are flowers in the grass. Some people walk by; I perceive their silhouettes against the light, and the murmur of their voices reaches me. A group of children runs in the opposite direction; I feel their laughter. There on the corner is the public telephone. I can't see it but I know it's there, about fifty feet away. I go back to bed but I don't sleep, I can't sleep. I just smoke and masturbate. But insomnia also has its own nightmares.

*Come, baby, Mom extends her hand to me, come, don't be afraid. I am in the middle of the living room, gripping tightly to the arms of the armchair. Walk, says Mom, she is so big compared to my one-and-a-half-year-old height, walk, just one little step. I feel a strong vertigo as I release the grip of the armchair and terror blinds me, but Mom's voice transmits confidence and security. Come, my pretty doll, come my treasure, she extends her hand. And I take a step. It's horrible and exciting, this first step in life. And she lifts me up, laughing, holds me above her head, laughing, spinning with me up top, laughing, and the room spins around me.*

It's Saturday. I get up, look out the window. Doc won't come and I want to smoke. My goldfish have died, they all awoke belly-up. It's Saturday, my house is dirty, I'm dirty, hairier than usual, I want to smoke, and I look out the window. Flowers from the flamboyan fall onto the grass and there is no one with a broom of reeds to sweep them. The mailman passes on his bicycle, whistling. Someone receives letters, visits, someone certainly receives their lovers on Saturdays. I put on the reggae cassette, the only reggae cassette I have, but I don't wash dishes or organize. I watch from the window how flowers from the flamboyan fall on the grass. Out there, not fifty feet away, is the telephone. But I'm not going to leave. No one will make me leave ever again. I put on the Celtic music cassette but I don't dance, I look out the window at people passing in the splendor of midday. I will never leave, *I open the door to see the stretch of street in front of my house better, I look out from the crack,* I will never leave here again, never, *I open it a little more, dazzled by so much green and gold and fire. I take a few steps.* I will not leave. *My feet sink into the grass, into the flowers.* I have nothing to go out for. *The smell of hay, of the park, and the swings, of wind. A few more steps.* I will never, never leave my house. *Flowers from the flamboyan fall on my head and my shoulders and Doc appears suddenly and lifts me up and spins me around in his arms and some human figures stop in front of my house to watch us.*

*Translated by Alexandra Blair*

# About the Authors

ALEJANDRO AGUILAR (b. Camagüey, Cuba, 1958) is the author of several collections of prose and poetry and, most recently, of the novels *La desobediencia* and *Casa de cambio*. Aguilar currently resides in Philadelphia, Pennsylvania.

C. A. AGUILERA (b. Havana, 1970) cofounded the journal *Diáspora(s)* and is the author of several volumes of poetry and prose including *Tipologías, Retrato de A. Hooper y su esposa,* and *Das kapital*.

AIDA BAHR (b. Holguín, Cuba, 1958) has authored, among other titles, *Fuera de límite, Hay un gato en la ventana,* and *Las voces y los ecos*. In addition, she is the director of Cuba's Editorial de Oriente.

EDUARDO DEL LLANO (b. Moscow, 1962) is a scriptwriter, poet, and prose writer. *El elefantico verde, Criminales,* and *Los viajes de Nicanor* are among his many titles. He has also cowritten several critically acclaimed films, including *Alicia en el pueblo de maravillas* and *La vida es silbar*. By himself he scripted the short film *Monte Rouge*.

ABILIO ESTÉVEZ (b. Havana, 1954), a novelist and playwright, has achieved acclaim with his neomagical realist novel, *Tuyo es el reino,* translated into English as *Thine Is the Kingdom*. His novel *Los palacios distantes* was translated as *Distant Palaces*.

FRANCISCO GARCÍA GONZÁLEZ (b. Havana, 1965) is a writer, editor, and screenwriter. His short story collections include *Juegos permitidos, Color local,* and *¿Qué quieren las mujeres?*

ALBERTO GUERRA NARANJO (b. Havana, 1963) has published, among other titles, *Disparos en el aula* and *Aporías de la feria.*

LEONARDO PADURA FUENTES (b. Havana, 1955) is a journalist, a critic, and one of the most internationally known writers from Cuba today. He is most acclaimed for a series of detective novels, featuring the adventures of Lieutenant Mario Conde, published in Cuba and in Spain.

ENA LUCÍA PORTELA (b. Havana, 1972) has published numerous short stories and novels, including *El pájaro: pincel y tinta china, La sombra del caminante,* and *Cien botellas en una pared.*

SOLEIDA RÍOS (b. Santiago, Cuba, 1950) is the author of several books of poetry and prose including *De la sierra, Entre mundo y juguete, El libro roto, Libro cero,* and *El libro de los sueños.* An English translation of *El texto sucio* entitled *Incantations* is forthcoming.

ERNESTO RENÉ RODRÍGUEZ (b. Havana, 1968) is a prose writer, poet, videographer, and documentarian. He has directed the videos of musical artists including Porno para Ricardo, Amaury Trineo, Sociedad Habana Blues, Kinde, and Combat Noise.

ANNA LIDIA VEGA SEROVA (b. 1968, Leningrad) spent her early childhood in Cuba before returning to the Soviet Union at age nine. At twenty-one, she returned to Cuba. She is the author of several books of short stories, most recently *Legión de sombras miserables* and *Imperio doméstico.*